"We need to talk about our relationship."

"*Allrecht.*" He looked at her warily.

"I think we should get married," she blurted out.

"You—" he began, then cleared his throat. "You do?"

She nodded. "I love you, and if you don't know it, then there, I've said it." Emboldened, she went on. "I don't think you realize how soon harvest will be over—"

"I know when harvest is," he interrupted her.

"Well, you seemed surprised at what time of year it was when you picked me up in town to have pizza."

"I just haven't been in town to notice how busy it is now," he said defensively.

She shook her head. "We're getting off track. If you don't love me—if I'm completely wrong about the way you feel—then say so."

The AMISH FARMER'S PROPOSAL

BY BARBARA CAMERON

The Amish Midwife's Hope

The Amish Baby Finds a Home

The Amish Farmer's Proposal

The AMISH FARMER'S PROPOSAL

BARBARA CAMERON

A Hearts of Lancaster County Novel

FOREVER

NEW YORK BOSTON

Forever
Hachette Book Group
1290 Avenue of the Americas, New York, NY 10104
read-forever.com
twitter.com/readforeverpub

First Edition: April 2022

Forever is an imprint of Grand Central Publishing. The Forever name and logo are trademarks of Hachette Book Group, Inc.

ISBN: 9781538751688 (mass market max), 9781538751664 (ebook)

Printed in the United States of America

OPM

10 9 8 7 6 5 4 3 2 1

*For my maternal grandparents,
who came here from Sweden,
started a farm, and raised nine
children.*

The AMISH FARMER'S PROPOSAL

Chapter One

Abe took off his straw hat, wiped the sweat from his forehead with a bandanna, and settled the hat back on his head. Summer wasn't the best time to be walking around on the roof of his house—especially midafternoon—but it had rained last night and a leak had sprung in it, so he had to take care of it now.

Nothing like being woken up by a cold stream of water falling on your face in the middle of the night, he thought irritably. This on top of a bad day when two of his cows had gotten sick and needed the vet. Then his buggy had broken down on the way into town and needed a wheel replaced.

It had been one thing after another lately, until he'd begun to feel like Job. He'd stayed up late last night going over his books, trying to figure out how he was going to pay his taxes and other expenses with milk prices continuing to fall. Well, he supposed it was better to be up here doing a roof repair in summer than in the middle of a Lancaster County, Pennsylvania, winter.

Movement caught his eye. He watched as Bessie, one of his older dairy cows, walked slowly through the pasture, her tail twitching at flies. His gaze swept over the land spreading out around the farmhouse and barn. The dairy farm had been in the *familye* for generations, and like other successful Amish farms here in Lancaster County, the farmhouse had been added on to as the *familye* grew larger.

The *familye*. It wasn't going to get bigger if things kept going on as they were. Abe knew his *eldres* wondered when he'd get married and start a *familye*. But he was just twenty-four, and Amish couples were waiting to get married at a later age, just as he'd heard *Englisch* couples were these days.

But he had recently begun dating a *maedel*—Lavinia Fisher, with her lovely hazel eyes and the way she had of listening to him and making him feel everything was going to work out *allrecht* when he spoke to her about his worries.

Abe sighed. Later sections of the house had newer roofing, but sadly the original part of the house had a patchwork of shingles done through the years. He bent and studied the place where he figured the leaking was happening and nodded. He'd do more patching up and hope he could replace this section of roof soon.

With a sigh, he forced himself to look away from the

depressing reality of a roof long past its prime—and the expense it would be to repair it—and focused on a positive. His herd of dairy cows was healthy, except for the two yesterday. That was what he needed to remember. When it came time to replace the roof, *schur*, he'd have to pay for the supplies, and they didn't come cheap. But many of the men in his community would spend the day helping him, and the women would serve them all a meal, and it would be a time to come together.

But a frown creased his brow as he watched his herd in the pasture. What was he going to do if milk prices continued to fall?

Who'd have ever thought people would stop drinking cow milk as much as they had? Why would anyone call something milk when it was made of almonds or rice or whatever? Milk came from cows like those in the pasture, not from nuts or grain. Why, he'd been drinking milk since he was a *boppli*, and look how strong and healthy he was. Drinking milk made your bones strong, helped you grow. What could be better than cow's milk?

He shook his head and bent to examine a shingle he figured was located right about where the leak had sprung inside the house. *Schur* enough, it had worked loose through all the years of bad Pennsylvania weather. He pried it off and tossed it down, then did the same with a few around it. Leaks never came from just one bad shingle.

Working steadily, he replaced a good-sized section of shingles, then told himself he needed to stop and take a break. He straightened and pulled out the bottle of water he had in his tool belt, but it slipped from his fingers and rolled down the roof to fall to the ground below.

He sighed and pulled off his hat to wipe away the sweat from his face again. Maybe he'd climb down the ladder and drench himself with water from the hose before he started the afternoon milking chores with Wayne, his part-time helper.

A rumble of thunder made him look up. He realized he'd been so absorbed in his worries and his work that he hadn't seen a storm approaching. He turned and started down toward the ladder leaning against the roof, when his foot caught on a loose shingle he hadn't seen when he'd climbed up.

His arms flailed as he felt himself slipping and sliding down the roof. He fell off the side and watched as the ground rushed up at him.

* * *

Lavinia saw Abe working on his roof as she drove her buggy toward his house. She frowned. She knew he'd patched it several times this past year. It had rained last night, so the fact that he was up there meant that the roof had leaked again.

Poor Abe. Things *schur* seemed hard for him right now. They'd talked so often lately about how worried he was about the farm he'd taken over when his *dat* developed health problems.

She pulled up in the driveway and sat there for a moment. The house looked a little sad. It needed a fresh coat of paint and some new shutters. But it wasn't likely Abe would be painting it anytime soon. A *gut* roof would take precedence over things like a paint job.

A clap of thunder startled her as she got out of the buggy and walked up the lawn. She stopped and looked up to see the clouds swarming gray and menacing above.

A water bottle came sailing down from the roof and hit the ground with a splat.

And then she watched in horror as Abe fell off the roof and landed in a heap just feet away from her on the front lawn.

Lavinia screamed and rushed up to him. He lay so still, twisted on his side, one arm bent at a terrible angle. She knelt and touched shaking fingers to his throat. There, she felt it—a pulse. Weak, but it was there. She let out the breath she'd been holding. He was still alive.

Help. She had to get help. But she didn't own a cell phone, and even if Abe had one in his tool belt, as she knew he always did, it was underneath him now, and she didn't dare move him to get it.

Frantic, she jumped up and ran to the road to wave down a car. The *Englisch* driver slammed on the brakes, pulled over to the side of the road, and got out.

"Are you crazy?" he yelled. "I almost hit you!"

"Call nine-one-one!" she cried. "Abe fell off the roof!"

Once she saw him pull out his cell phone and make

the call, she ran back to Abe and knelt again beside him. He hadn't moved and appeared to be barely breathing. Tears sprang into her eyes. His face was turned to the side and bone white.

"They're on their way," the driver told her when he rushed up to her. "The dispatcher said don't move him."

She nodded as she used her hands to wipe tears from her cheeks. "I haven't moved him. I knew not to."

"We need to keep him warm, keep him from going into shock. I have a blanket in the car. I'll be right back."

"Thank you," she said when he returned with it. She tucked the blanket around Abe and prayed he wouldn't leave her. This man had become too important to her these past few months.

"He's going to be all right," the *Englisch* man said, giving her a reassuring smile.

She shook her head and fought back panic. "He fell so far. And he hasn't moved, hasn't made a sound."

"I'll pray for him," he told her.

She dragged her gaze from Abe and stared at the man. This stranger who looked to be barely in his twenties had stopped to offer not only help but also hope.

It seemed like hours before she heard the wail of a siren.

"Help's here," she told Abe. "Hold on. Don't leave me, Abe."

Paramedics raced up, carrying equipment bags. Lavinia rose and backed away to give them room to work.

"I need to get some information from you," one told her.

She nodded and mechanically gave him Abe's full name, but when he asked if Abe had any medical issues she shook her head. "I don't think he has any. He's healthy. He's never sick."

Another paramedic brought a gurney, a long plastic board, and a neck brace. They worked carefully to put the brace around Abe's neck and a splint around the arm that was bent at such a contorted angle, then inserted the board under him.

The process seemed to take forever, but the paramedic who'd taken the information from her explained quietly why they moved so slowly. A broken bone could tear tissue and cause internal bleeding. Moving his spine could cause permanent damage. They didn't want to injure Abe more, he said. Numb, she nodded and tried to listen but could only hear her heart beating loudly in her ears.

The *Englisch* stranger approached her and held out a business card. "I wrote my cell phone number on the back. I want you to call me if there's any way I can help."

She stared at the card, then at him. He had such kind eyes. "You helped so much calling them. I don't know what I'd have done if you hadn't come along."

"Someone else would have come and helped. You take care. Your man is going to be fine."

"Thank you."

Then she was distracted as the board Abe had been

placed on was laid on the gurney and then wheeled to the ambulance. When she looked up, the stranger's car was gone.

"Ma'am? You want to ride along with us."

It was a statement, not a question. She started to say she wasn't Abe's *fraa*, was just a friend who'd begun to hope she was more...but his *eldres* were off visiting their other *sohn* in Ohio, and there was no one else.

Surely it wasn't wrong to walk alongside the gurney and climb into the ambulance when they got Abe safely inside. She told herself that as she took a seat on the bench inside and watched as they hooked him up to all sorts of things she didn't understand and called the hospital and said even more things she didn't understand.

All she knew was she had to pray harder than she'd ever done in her life.

* * *

The staff at the emergency room had more questions about Abe that she tried her best to answer. One nurse showed her to the waiting room, and when she walked inside and saw the phone, she made a beeline for it and called her *mudder* at her Amish arts-and-crafts shop in town.

To her relief, her *mudder* picked up on the second ring. "*Mamm*, Abe fell off the roof! I'm at the hospital with him."

"Slow down. Is he going to be *allrecht*?"

"I don't know. They have him in the emergency room and they had me go to a waiting room. I'm calling you from there. Do you know how to get in touch with his *eldres*?"

"I don't have my address book here at the shop, but I can call the bishop and see if he can help."

"Address book?" Lavinia thought for a moment. "No, wait on that, *Mamm*. I'll ask the nurses if Abe had his cell phone. He always puts it in his tool belt whenever he climbs up on the roof. If he still has it and it isn't broken, maybe the number for his *eldres* would be on it."

"*Gut* thinking."

"It's about time. I haven't been able to think. He fell just as I got to his house."

"I'm *schur* it was horrible to see him fall like that."

"I don't think I'll ever forget seeing it." She closed her eyes, shook her head. "Oh, *Mamm*, the buggy. Our buggy is still in front of Abe's house. I just got in the ambulance when the paramedic said I could come with."

"I'll see if I can get your *dat* to take care of it. I can join you at the hospital as soon as I close the shop."

"That would be *wunderbaar*. I don't feel right leaving Abe here all by himself."

"I'm *schur* the bishop will go there as soon as I call him."

"Let me see if I can find a number for his *eldres* first and I'll call you back."

"*Allrecht*. You call me if you need me."

"I will."

"Try to stay calm, *lieb*."

"I will. *Danki, Mamm.*"

"It'll be *allrecht*, Lavinia."

Her *mudder*'s words reassured her as the stranger's had. She hung up and found herself pulling the card from her pocket. **Jason Halliday. Web Developer. Innovative Computer Solutions.** There was a business address and phone number on the front, and he'd written another phone number on the back.

She wouldn't call him for anything, but she'd write him a thank-you note later. It was the least she could do in return for him not only stopping to help but also calming her. Offering to pray for Abe.

A man dressed in scrubs appeared in the door. "Mrs. Stoltzfus?"

Lavinia knew it was wrong to act like Abe's *fraa*, but she had to know how Abe was. If the bishop came, she'd talk to him, tell him what she'd done, and let him handle things. But for now she had to know how Abe was doing. Be of any help to him that she could.

"Yes." She stood, but he waved her to her seat and sat opposite her.

"I'm Dr. Patterson, the ER doctor. I thought I'd give you a quick run-down of your husband's condition. I understand he fell off a two-story house?"

She nodded.

"He's got some serious injuries. We've done a CAT scan, and he's got some severe spinal bruising, but he didn't break his back, so that's good news. He's got a concussion, and his left arm is broken. We're doing tests to determine if he has any other injuries."

Her heart sank. "That sounds horrible. How can he survive all that?"

"He's young and healthy, and that'll count for a lot. They're taking him up to surgery to deal with the arm injury now. Don't expect to hear anything for a couple hours." He rose. "A nurse will come in as often as she can to give you an update, but this isn't going to be quick. He may be in surgery for at least a couple of hours."

She gulped and nodded. "Thank you for coming to tell me. Oh, do you know if Abe had his cell phone on him? He always puts it in his tool belt when he goes up on the roof."

"He did have it. I'll have a nurse bring it to you."

"Thank you. Thank you so much for everything."

"The next few hours are going to be critical, but I can assure you he's in the best of hands."

He left her, and she thought, Ya, *he is. Abe's in His hands.*

A few minutes later, a nurse came in with Abe's phone. "The doctor said you were asking about this. It was in your husband's tool belt, just like you said. It's cracked, but it might still work."

Lavinia thanked her, said a quick prayer, and then began fiddling with the phone. She didn't own a cell phone, so she didn't have much experience with them, but she must have done something right because it turned on. She looked in the address book. *Schur* enough, she found a number for Abe's *eldres*.

She took a deep breath. Time to call Waneta and Faron and tell them what happened.

Chapter Two

"Lavinia, there you are."

She jumped up and hugged her *mudder*. "*Mamm*! You came!"

"I remembered Emma was helping at Hannah's today. I called Hannah to see if she could spare her, and she said of course. Emma rushed right over. Said I should be here with you."

Lavinia nodded. Emma would feel that way. Her *dat* had had a heart attack last year and she'd sat with her *mudder* at the hospital.

"How is Abe?"

"He's in surgery to fix the arm he broke in the fall. The doctor warned me it could take at least two, maybe three hours," Lavinia told her, and she looked at the clock on the wall. "I don't expect to hear anything for at least another hour. The doctor seems to think he has a *gut* chance of having a full recovery since he said Abe is young and healthy. But *Mamm*, I saw him fall off the roof. It was horrible. And he never woke up in the ambulance."

"We'll pray," Rachel said, and she clasped Lavinia's hand as they bowed their heads.

A nurse walked in. "Mrs. Stoltzfus? Abe is still doing well. I'll be back when we have another update."

She was gone before Lavinia could ask when that would be.

Then she realized that her *mudder* was staring at her thoughtfully.

"They assumed Abe was my husband when we came in," she explained, feeling guilty. "I didn't stop them because I knew they wouldn't tell me anything if I wasn't married or related to him. He doesn't have anyone else here."

She looked at the cell phone she clutched in her hands. "I called his *eldres*, and his *dat* said they'd start back as soon as they could. He and Waneta were visiting their older *sohn* in Ohio."

Rachel nodded. "*Gut.* I'm not going to lecture you about not telling the truth under the circumstances. And I have eyes. I can tell when two young people are more than friends."

Lavinia blushed.

"I sent your *dat* over to help Wayne with the afternoon milking and chores," she said. "I'll call the bishop, and he'll arrange for other men in the church to take care of things while Abe is in the hospital."

"He'll be grateful to hear that when he wakes up." She refused to believe he wouldn't wake up. She had to believe he would be *allrecht*.

An hour passed. Her *mudder* told her a funny story about John, Emma's little *bu* she'd brought to work at the quilt shop that day. John was a regular fixture there and popular with the customers. After Emma had rushed over to take charge of the shop, John had entertained her while Rachel waited for a ride to the hospital.

Lavinia knew her *mudder* was trying to cheer her up, and she tried to smile.

Her *mudder* fixed them a cup of tea. "Did you have lunch?"

Lavinia shook her head. "I was taking lunch over to eat with Abe since I had the afternoon off from the shop. The picnic basket is sitting in the buggy."

"Amos has probably discovered it and eaten everything in it."

She managed to smile. "Knowing *Daed*, I'm *schur* he has."

"Mrs. Stoltzfus?" A doctor appeared in the doorway. He was dressed in scrubs like the other doctor but pulled off a mask as he entered the room.

"Yes?"

He sat in the chair opposite her, looking very tired. "I'm Dr. Hamilton, head of surgery."

"Hello. This is my mother, Rachel Fisher."

The doctor nodded at her. "Your husband came through the surgery and he's in recovery now. We had three main areas of concern when he was admitted: a concussion, some spinal injury, and a broken arm. The orthopedic surgeon has set the arm. His back isn't broken, but there's some bruising and severe swelling we're going to be watching for the next few days." He took a breath and met Lavinia's gaze. "I don't want to alarm you, but we're concerned about the head injury and—"

"Are you saying he's in a coma?"

His tired face took on an expression of compassion. "No. Right now he's in recovery and hasn't woken up from the anesthesia. We won't know the full effects of the head injury until the anesthesia has worn off. But in layman's terms, a coma means a patient is unresponsive, not reacting to voices and activity around him. It's often a way for the brain to sort of take a rest when it's been severely injured or shocked." He waited a moment, then continued. "I also need to talk to you about his spinal injury. He may experience some paralysis."

"Paralysis?" Her blood ran cold. "Abe is paralyzed?"

"We don't know if he is or if it'd be permanent," he said quickly. "But I need to warn you that when Abe wakes, he'll be concerned if he can't move his legs."

It was all too much to absorb. Her heart felt like it was going to beat out of her chest and she felt cold. So cold. She heard her *mudder* asking questions and tried to calm herself. How would Abe feel when he woke and couldn't move? How would he take care of his dairy farm if he couldn't walk?

"It's important to stay positive and wait for his body to recover from the shock of the fall," the doctor said. "And the surgery. He'll be in our intensive care unit for a time, and we'll monitor him carefully."

"When can I see him?"

"A nurse will come for you soon. You can see him for a few minutes. Then I suggest you go home." He rubbed a hand over his face. "This is going to be a long journey, and you'll need your rest. I don't expect your husband to wake until morning. Do you have any questions?"

She shook her head.

"I know it's a lot to take in and it's scary. But in most cases the paralysis is temporary. His body needs time to recover from the shock of the fall and the surgery. If you have any questions or concerns, call the hospital and they'll put you in touch with me."

"Thank you, Doctor."

He nodded and left them.

"Well, as he said, it's a lot to take in," Rachel said quietly. "But God has His hand on Abe and knows what He's doing."

Lavinia didn't feel *schur* of that at the moment, but she stayed silent. Abe was still here and she had to focus on that.

* * *

The nurse who led her to the room in the intensive care unit tried to prepare her, but it was still a shock to see

Abe. His face was as white as a sheet, with one arm in a bulky cast and suspended by a pulley above the bed. Machines beeped and flashed on each side of the bed. A line blipped on one, showing his heartbeat, but even when she stepped closer, she could barely see his chest rise and fall.

"Talk to him. Let him know you're here," the nurse encouraged her as they stepped closer to the bed. "We know that patients can hear us, and sometimes a familiar voice can help them wake from unconsciousness. Stay positive in what you say. He needs your encouragement."

She turned to a rolling cart that held a laptop and typed something into it, then left the room.

Lavinia picked up Abe's hand—the one that didn't have a cast on it—and held it. She leaned down. "Abe, it's Lavinia. Do you hear me? The doctors tell me you're going to be *allrecht*. Will you wake up and talk to me?"

But he didn't open his eyes, and if he heard her, the blipping on the heart monitor didn't show any sign of reaction.

"Abe? They won't let me stay but a few minutes. Please wake up for me." She glanced over at the doorway to make *schur* they were alone. "They might not let me stay if they find out we're not married."

She sighed. It was probably unrealistic to think he'd wake to the sound of her voice. Not after all he'd been through. The surgeon had told her he'd probably not wake until morning. Still, she squeezed his hand hard and willed him to wake, to let her know he was in there working hard to come back.

There. Was it her imagination? Did she feel something? She stared at their hands. It wasn't her imagination that she felt a faint pressure, was it?

The nurse came back into the room, glanced at the machines, then gave her a sympathetic look. "I know it looks scary. But he's doing well."

"I was hoping he would wake up. The doctor said he wouldn't until morning, but..." She trailed off.

The nurse smiled and nodded. "But you still hoped. You should go home, get some rest, and come back tomorrow."

Lavinia gave Abe's hand a last squeeze. "I'll be back bright and early in the morning," she told him. "So you have a nice sleep, and I'll see you then."

She walked back to the waiting room and sank into a seat next to her *mudder*. "Abe didn't wake up while I was there."

Tears welled up, and she threw herself into her *mudder*'s arms. "Oh, *Mamm*, he looks so awful. I'm so scared."

Her *mudder* held her and patted her back. "Shh, don't cry, *lieb*. He'll be *allrecht*. You'll see."

Lavinia felt limp when the storm of weeping stopped. But she refused to leave when her *mudder* urged her to do as the doctor said and go home to rest. She just couldn't leave Abe. She couldn't.

* * *

Abe heard Lavinia talking to him as if she was at the other end of a very long tunnel. She kept urging him to open his eyes and talk to her, but it felt like he was being held someplace strange. He felt light, floating.

Her voice drifted away and he slept.

He heard her again, louder, more insistent, but a weight held his eyes shut. Couldn't she see it? He tried to move, and his body screamed as if it was broken in a million pieces. He gasped and tried to speak, but the pain was too huge.

"Help me! I hurt!" he yelled. Then he heard a weak wail no louder than a *boppli*'s.

But he felt someone pat his arm, and then he felt a blessed numbness. He fell into it and slept.

He woke to the sound of machines beeping and an antiseptic smell he recognized. The smell was familiar. He'd been a boisterous *bu* and been to the ER with his *mudder* often enough to know it. He was in the hospital.

That meant he was alive. He opened his eyes, and the bright light made him shut them quickly before trying again.

"Look who's awake," a woman said.

Abe turned his head and winced at the shaft of pain the movement sent through it. The woman was dressed in scrubs and had a stethoscope around her neck. He watched her fingers fly across the keyboard of a laptop.

She stopped typing and looked at him. "How are you feeling?"

"Like I fell off a roof." His voice sounded rusty, as if he hadn't used it in a long time.

She chuckled. "Nice to see you have a sense of humor." She studied the machine next to his bed. "BP's good. How's your pain? On a measure of one to ten."

"Twenty."

She adjusted something on a plastic tube that ran into one hand, and the numbness swept over him again.

The next time he woke, the light was dimmer. He wondered what time it was and turned his head, looking for a clock. This time it didn't hurt so bad. One o'clock. But was that a.m. or p.m.? One wall of the room was all glass with a sliding door. He knew that meant he was in the intensive care unit because he'd visited a friend there once. If only a nurse or doctor would walk past, he could wave to them and get them to come in....

His gaze swept back, and as it did, he saw one of his arms suspended above the bed by a pulley. It was encased in plaster with just the tips of his fingers sticking out. *Allrecht*, a broken arm. That wasn't such a bad price to pay for falling off a roof. And the whopper of a headache.

He frowned. But there was something else that didn't feel right. He felt weighed down by more than the cast on his arm. When he shifted, he couldn't feel his legs. He tried again, figuring the blanket covering him might be weighing his legs down...but he couldn't move them at all.

Terrified, he felt around for the call button for the nurse, but couldn't find it. Panicked, he raised his head to look for it and was on the verge of calling out when someone walked into the room.

"Lavinia!"

"*Ya.* Abe, it's *gut* to see you awake!" She moved closer to stand beside the bed.

"I can't feel my legs! Lavinia, I can't feel my legs!"

She picked up his hand and stroked it. "The doctor said you might have some paralysis, but he thinks it's temporary."

"The doctor. Where's the call button?" He twisted his head on the pillow. "Help me get the nurse in here, have her call the doctor. I need to talk to him."

"I will. But you need to calm down," she said, and he saw her glance toward one of the machines next to the bed.

She found the call button, but before she could press it, a nurse hurried into the room.

"I need to talk to the doctor!" he blurted out. "I can't feel my legs!"

"I told him the doctor thinks it's temporary, but I don't think he believes me," Lavinia told the nurse.

"I'll have him paged," the nurse told him. "He's doing rounds right now so it shouldn't take long. Try to calm down. Your BP is going up."

Lavinia pulled a chair up beside the bed and took a seat. "Abe, look at me. I wouldn't lie to you."

"But what if it isn't temporary?" His free hand clutched the sheets. "What if...?"

"Abe, please, try not to worry."

The nurse returned. "The doctor's been paged and

should be here soon. Is there anything I can get you for now?"

"No. Thanks," he added when he realized he sounded curt.

She turned to Lavinia. "Can I get you some coffee?"

"No, thanks."

Abe looked at Lavinia. "Thank you for coming. Just before you walked in, I was wondering if it was one in the morning or afternoon. I guess it must be afternoon."

She nodded. "Abe, I called your *eldres* last night. One of the ER nurses found your cell phone in your tool belt. It was cracked but it worked." She pulled it out of her purse and handed it to him. "Anyway, your *dat* said they would start home this morning."

"Seems like the phone fared better than me," he muttered as he stared at it. The display was a spiderweb of splintery cracks, but when he hit the last number she'd called, he found she was right about it working. He set it aside as a doctor walked into the room.

"Mr. Stoltzfus. I'm Dr. Hamilton, head of surgery. I was one of the surgeons who operated on you last night."

"It took more than one?"

He nodded. "Dr. Morrison set your arm. How are you feeling?"

Abe glanced at Lavinia.

"I can step out," she said quickly.

"No, it's all right." He looked at the doctor. "I'm scared. I can't move my legs."

"I think it's temporary," the doctor said. "We'll be running some tests. I want you to try to relax and let your body heal. It's been through a lot."

He pulled some little tool from his pocket, pushed the sheet back from Abe's legs, then ran it across one of Abe's feet. Abe frowned when he didn't feel anything. Then the doctor performed the same test on his legs. Abe still didn't feel anything. He barely noticed when Lavinia slipped out of the room as the doctor moved the tool up his legs and asked questions.

She slipped back in again behind the nurse pushing her rolling cart with a laptop. The nurse stood beside the doctor and waited for him to finish his examination. When the doctor turned to her, she typed the instructions the doctor fired at her rapidly, nodding and asking him questions.

Abe frowned as he studied Lavinia while the two talked. He thought it looked like she'd been crying, but when she realized he was staring at her, she wouldn't meet his eyes.

"You'll be poked and prodded plenty starting tomorrow, so get some rest," the doctor advised. "I have to go finish my rounds now. See you tomorrow then, Mr. and Mrs. Stoltzfus."

Abe nodded. "Thanks, Doctor." He watched the doctor leave the room, and then he turned to Lavinia, looking puzzled. "Did I land on my head? I don't remember us getting married."

Chapter Three

Lavinia stared at him. She was relieved he was awake and obviously not suffering from all the things she had imagined a head injury could cause.

And she could tell that even despite all he'd gone through, that humor she loved about him seemed to still be there. There might be a look of puzzlement on that handsome face of his, but she heard the teasing tone in his voice.

So she called on the drama skills she'd perfected in *schul* plays and worked up tears and made her lips tremble. "You don't?"

That threw him off balance. He stared at her, looking uncertain. "I—*nee*."

She laughed and then sobered and felt her lips tremble for real. "We're not. I lied yesterday. The paramedics assumed I was your *fraa*, and it was the only way I could come with you in the ambulance and be here until I could call your *eldres*."

"Then I owe you my thanks."

"I don't want your thanks. We're friends. You'd have done the same for me if I'd been hurt and my *familye* was out of town."

She stood and paced the room, then turned to look at him. "I didn't know what else to do. Now I'm going to have to confess to what I've done."

"Perhaps you could wait to do that."

"Wait?"

He nodded, then winced as the movement brought pain. "I want you to be able to visit. If your not being a member of my *familye* means you can't visit, maybe you could wait on that confession."

She stared at him for a long moment. "Do you want me to come see you?"

"I do." He yawned and looked like he was having trouble staying awake.

A nurse came to the door and tapped the watch on her wrist. Lavinia nodded. She turned to tell Abe that she had to leave for a while, but he'd already fallen asleep.

She walked over and picked up her purse, which she'd set beside the chair, but she couldn't resist going back to the bed and stroking the thick mahogany-colored hair back from Abe's strong, handsome face. It was something she'd always wanted to do.

With a sigh, she drew her hand back, walked out

of the room, and made her way to the waiting room. She'd have time for one more visit before she had to go to work.

"Lavinia! There you are!" Waneta Stoltzfus rushed in, followed by her *mann*, Faron, who was moving slower and leaning heavily on a cane. "We got here as quickly as we could!"

She stood. "Abe will be happy to see you. He woke up this morning and he's talking normally. The doctor seemed very encouraged."

Waneta's round face was drawn and pale. She took a deep breath. "We stopped in here before we went to the nurse's station, since you said you'd be here."

"Abe's still in the ICU, and they're only allowing short visits right now. Just fifteen minutes." She paused, bit her lip. "Abe was feeling very discouraged about not being able to feel his legs when he woke up."

Waneta swayed, but when Faron wrapped his arm around her waist, she insisted he sit down before she would take a seat.

"We talked about this on the way here," he murmured to his *fraa* as Lavinia rushed to get her a cup of water from the cooler in the corner of the room.

"I wanted it to be a bad dream," Waneta said, taking the cup from Lavinia and sipping.

"He's doing so much better than I expected," Lavinia assured her.

She didn't tell the woman she'd been afraid Abe wouldn't wake. Waneta didn't need to hear it. Abe's *eldres* were older than her own, in their sixties, and

Faron had become frail the last couple years after being diagnosed with multiple sclerosis.

"Give yourself a few minutes to catch your breath, and then I'll take you to the nurse's station. When you see Abe, I think you'll feel better."

"*Danki*, Lavinia." Waneta patted her hand. "Abe was so lucky you were there to get him help. Who knows how long he might have lain there until someone came by." She glanced at her *mann*. "Just like his *dat* did before his MS, climbing up on the roof without having someone near. Always thinking he can do everything by himself."

"Now, Waneta, I never fell off the roof, did I?" he asked with a grin.

"*Nee*, or who knows how bad your MS would be now?" she said with a shake of her head. She took a deep breath and tossed the paper cup in the wastepaper basket. "Let's go see our *sohn*."

Lavinia sat on the chair next to her and took her hand. "Waneta, I don't want you to be alarmed when you see Abe. He got banged up quite a bit, and it was a bit of a shock for me to see him the first time. And when he woke, he was so scared when he couldn't feel his legs. But we have to hold out hope for him. We need to remind him the doctor feels it's temporary."

Waneta met her gaze levelly. "I understand, dear one. But I think as a *mudder*, this is kind of what I expected for years while raising a rambunctious *bu*." She gave Faron a tremulous smile. "He'd tell you that. It's just a lot later than I thought it would happen."

She got to her feet. "And I *do* believe the paralysis is

temporary. I've been praying hard since you called us, and I do believe God listens."

Lavinia stood and hugged her. "I do as well."

She walked with them to the nurse's station, watching the way Waneta matched Faron's slower pace. She saw them exchange a loving look as they approached the station and thought how *wunderbaar* it must be to have a partner to face life with.

"These are Abe's parents, Waneta and Faron Stoltzfus," she told the nurse.

She beamed at them. "Nice to meet you. Abe's woken up several times this morning, and the doctor's very encouraged. Let me take you in to see him. I'm afraid we have to limit visits to fifteen minutes, and no more than two of you at a time."

"I'll wait for you," Lavinia told them.

She returned to the waiting room and called her *mudder* to tell her she was going to be a little late. "Abe's *eldres* just got here. I'd like to stay a little while longer to talk to them."

"No problem," her *mudder* told her. "It's a little slow at the shop. I'm glad they got there safely. You stay with them and take care of anything they need. I know Faron's not in the best of shape with his MS. The stress of hearing about Abe and the bus ride can't have been easy on him. Let me know if you feel you need to stay at the hospital the rest of the day."

"*Danki, Mamm.*"

After she hung up, Lavinia fixed herself a cup of hot tea and sat waiting for Abe's *eldres* to return.

When they came back into the room, Lavinia's heart sank. They looked older somehow. Waneta's lips were trembling, and she barely made it into the room before she burst into tears.

Lavinia snatched up the box of tissues from a nearby table and rushed over to her.

"I didn't cry when I saw him," Waneta sobbed. She took a handful of tissues and mopped at the tears streaming from her eyes. "I was afraid I would upset him. But I didn't cry."

"You did *gut*," Faron told her as he patted her hand.

When she saw him begin to weave on his feet, Lavinia quickly urged him to sit down.

"Can I get you some coffee?" she asked.

They nodded, so Lavinia went to the machine on the beverage table and poured it.

"Waneta? Sugar? Cream?"

"Two sugars, just a little cream."

"Black, *danki*," Faron told her.

The coffee seemed to revive them a little.

"When's the last time you two ate?" she asked them.

Waneta shrugged. "Our *schwardochder* packed us some sandwiches and coffee for the trip," she said vaguely.

Her *mudder* had told her to take care of them. She knew what she needed to do. But before she could, a nurse stuck her head in the door and looked at Lavinia.

"Mrs. Stoltzfus? I wanted you to know that we're taking your husband for some tests. He'll be gone from his room for a while."

"Thank you."

She watched the woman hurry away, then looked at Waneta and Faron. Their gazes were avid on her. "It's a long story. Well, maybe not that long," she amended. "Let's go get something to eat in the cafeteria."

* * *

"We won't be gone long," Susan, his nurse, assured him as she pushed his bed down the hall. "Then you can see your family again."

He frowned. While he'd been glad to see them, it had been so hard to watch them try to hide how scared they were when they walked into his hospital room.

"So, your mother said she and your father have been out of town visiting relatives," Susan went on cheerfully, nodding at other staff as she passed them. "It's nice to get away this time of year when it's so hot."

He remembered how hot it had been fixing the roof before he fell off. And summer was far from over.

But he wouldn't be climbing up on that roof anytime soon. He knew Wayne and other men in the community would be taking care of his farm while he was in the hospital. But what about after he got out? The doctor said he thought that the paralysis was probably temporary, but feeling hadn't come back yet. And even when it did, how long would it take for his broken arm to heal? Just how long could others take over his responsibilities, especially when it was the busiest time of year for farmers as harvest neared?

The nurse stopped at an elevator and they waited. "Sorry it's taking so long," she said. "It's always slower in the daytime when more staff and visitors are using them."

"It's not like I have anywhere to go."

She nodded sympathetically. "It's hard being down when you're active. You're a dairy farmer, right? Bet that's a lot of work."

"It is."

The elevator doors slid open with a pinging noise. "Here we go."

They went down several floors, and when they exited the elevator, she took him into a section labeled **MRI Diagnostic**. There, two male technicians helped transfer him to a machine that reminded him of a tunnel. He was strapped in and told he had to lie still. He wanted to ask them if they were joking, but he could see they weren't.

"What kind of music do you like?" one asked, and then he frowned. "Sorry, are you allowed music?"

"We sing hymns."

"Hmm. How about I put on some Christian music? It'll help you relax."

"Sure."

The music wasn't familiar, and it didn't really help him relax, but it did seem to tune out the weird sound the machine made.

The test seemed to take forever. He wondered what Lavinia and his *eldres* were doing. He felt guilty for the time everyone was spending on him. If he got back to being himself, he was going to find some way to repay Lavinia, his *eldres*, his helper Wayne, and the church members for all the time and the worry.

At last, the music and the machine noises stopped, and the technicians transferred him back to his hospital bed. Then he had to wait for the nurse to come for him.

"So sorry, we had an emergency on the floor," she said when she rushed in. "I bet you can't wait to get back in your room and have some lunch."

"It's no problem."

She pushed the bed toward the elevator. "I know the food's probably not as good as what you're used to, but we try. And maybe I can stretch your visit with your family a little longer to make it up to you."

"Thanks." He yawned.

"So how'd you do?"

"Okay. Fell asleep for the last part of it."

"I couldn't do it the time I had to have one. Too claustrophobic."

The elevator opened and she pushed the bed inside. The doors closed and the elevator began moving.

"You keep doing as well as you are, and we'll lose you to a regular unit in no time."

He wanted to ask her how long he'd be here, but the nurses always answered his questions with, "Ask the doctor." He hoped that was because it was hospital policy for them not to answer such questions and not because they didn't want to discourage him by telling him he'd be with them a long time.

Susan chatted easily as she pushed the bed from the

elevator toward his room. He didn't know where she got her boundless energy and optimism. It didn't seem to flag, even through twelve-hour shifts of caring for seriously ill or injured people like him.

"Now, let's get you all hooked up again, and then you choose: quick visit with your family or lunch first?"

"Family."

She beamed. "I knew you'd say that." She worked quickly to attach the monitors to the machines that blinked and beeped, then hurried out of the room.

A few minutes later, his *eldres* walked in. Abe thought they looked a little better than they had earlier. He wanted to ask where Lavinia was but figured it would sound rude—as if he wasn't happy to see them.

"So how was your test?" his *mudder* wanted to know. "I hope they didn't stick a bunch of needles in you."

"*Nee*, just put me in this big machine that made strange noises. I still managed to fall asleep for part of it."

"Rest is what you need so your body can heal," she told him.

"*Bu* used to spend too much time sleeping," his *dat* said with a snort as he sat down on a chair by the bed.

Abe thought his *dat* looked thinner and frailer than he had when he and his *mudder* left for their trip. He felt a stab of guilt thinking how hard the bus trip must have been on him.

"That was years ago when he was a teenager, Faron," Waneta responded as she brushed Abe's hair back from his forehead. "Can I get you anything?"

"Just hand me that cup of water, please?"

"*Schur.*"

She insisted on holding the cup while he sipped from the straw. He wanted to tell her that his hands worked fine—or at least one of them did. It was his legs that weren't cooperating.

He glanced at the doorway when he heard a cart being pushed past the room. It was loaded with lunch trays.

Waneta noticed his gaze shift from the cup. "Lavinia insisted on taking us down to the cafeteria and buying us lunch."

"That was nice."

"*Ya.* That was right after the nurse came in and called her Mrs. Stoltzfus," Faron said.

Abe choked on a mouthful of water and reddened. His *mudder* moved the cup away from him and frowned in concern. "You *allrecht*?"

He took a deep breath. "*Ya.* About that."

"Don't tease the *bu*, Faron," Waneta admonished as she used a tissue to dab at the water on Abe's chin.

"But it's fun," he muttered as he met Abe's gaze.

"Don't mind your *dat*. Lavinia explained everything." Waneta glanced at the clock, then walked over to Faron and held out her hand. "We need to go."

"We just got here."

"Nurse said fifteen minutes, and it's been fifteen minutes. We can come back in a little while."

Faron got to his feet and patted Abe's hand before walking out of the room.

A few minutes later, Lavinia stuck her head in the door. “I thought I’d just come say hi before I go to work.”

She had to go to work. Of course she couldn’t sit around all day just so she could come in for the short visits the hospital was allowing. He felt his spirits plummet. “Come in.”

“I got you something to keep you company,” she said as she walked up to his bed and handed him a small bag from the hospital gift shop.

He reached into it and pulled out a black-and-white-spotted stuffed cow with a silly grin on its face. The tag on her collar proclaimed she was Molly Moo Cow.

A laugh escaped him as he stared at it. “Looks a little like Bessie.”

“I thought so, too.”

“Can you stay a few minutes? Molly’s great, but she’s not as *gut* as a visit with a *fraa*.”

Lavinia blushed as she sat down in the chair beside the bed. “About that.”

Chapter Four

Lavinia sat down in the chair beside the bed. "Talk about embarrassing. One of the nurses called me Mrs. Stoltzfus in front of your *eldres*. I had to explain things to them." She sighed. "They were nice to me about it. Said they understood."

"They've always liked you," Abe said. "It was nice of you to take them to lunch."

"I've always liked them, too. Your *mudder* has always made me feel *wilkumm* at your house. It was a pleasure sharing a meal with them. I was concerned that they might not have eaten on their trip back."

She glanced over as a nurse carried in a tray and set it on the table beside the bed.

"We have an extra tray if you'd like to eat lunch together," the woman told her.

"Thanks, but I had lunch with Abe's parents while he was having his test."

"That's nice."

The nurse started to lift the dome from the plate, then placed it back down as her name was called over the intercom.

"I'll be right back," she assured them, and hurried out of the room.

"I can help you if you like," Lavinia told him.

Abe lifted the arm that was encased in a cast. "That would be great. It's a little awkward with this."

Lavinia rose and lifted the dome, and the scents poured out. "Roast beef. Your favorite. And mashed potatoes and gravy. Your *dat* had the same meal in the cafeteria and said it was *gut*."

She cut the beef and forced away the memory of how Waneta had helped her *mann* when his hands shook too badly to feed himself. Either his MS had gotten a little worse since the last time she'd seen him or the trip had tired him greatly.

She pulled the paper from a straw, stuck it into the glass of iced tea, and watched him eat. "Has the food been *allrecht* so far?"

"*Gut*, but nothing like *Mamm*'s."

"Give her a day or two to rest up from the trip and I bet she'll be bringing your favorites to you."

He poked a spoon at the bowl of Jell-O. "Haven't had this since I was a kid." He glanced up at her. "Maybe you could see your way to bringing me some of your brownies."

She smiled. "I could do that."

The nurse returned. "Sorry I got called away. You folks doing okay?"

"Just fine, thanks."

She noticed Abe didn't eat as much as usual, but she supposed he didn't have as much of an appetite lying there as he did working his dairy farm all day. She decided that when she visited tomorrow, she'd make *schur* she brought him the brownies he'd requested. Maybe see if she could make one of his favorite foods.

With that thought, Lavinia stood. "I have to go."

"I—" He stopped.

"What?"

He shook his head. "Nothing."

But she saw something in his eyes...a look of such pain. And something else. Something that spoke of such sadness and naked longing it broke her heart. She moved closer. "What is it, Abe? Are you in pain? What can I do?"

"Stay," he whispered. And then he shook his head again. "I'm sorry. I'm not being fair. I know you have to go. You've been here so much."

Unbearably touched, she moved closer and touched his hand. "I wanted to be here. Listen, I'll go call *Mamm*, see if she needs me at the shop. Otherwise I'll stay a while longer with you and your *eldres*."

He nodded, looking so relieved she was glad she'd suggested it.

"Get some rest. I'll see you later."

His eyes were already closing as she stepped back from the bed.

When she returned to the waiting room, she saw Faron was dozing, his head back, as he sat on the plastic sofa.

Waneta looked up from the magazine she was reading and smiled. "That big lunch put him right to sleep," she whispered.

"Same thing with Abe. He was falling asleep when I left him."

"*Gut.* It'll help him heal."

She sat down on a chair beside Waneta. "He asked me to bring him some brownies tomorrow."

"My Abe's always had a sweet tooth." Her blue eyes twinkled. "And he's always loved your brownies."

Lavinia blushed. "I'm *schur* he's going to ask you to make some of his favorite food once you've rested up." She glanced at Faron. "I'm going to step out of the room and call my *mudder*, see if she needs me to come in."

Waneta patted her hand. "You can stay right here unless you want privacy. Won't wake Faron. He's going to be out for a while. The bus trip was hard on him." She frowned. "Don't repeat that to Abe."

"I won't." She had suspected the trip had been difficult for both Abe's *eldres*. She pulled Abe's cell phone from her purse and called her *mudder*.

"Amish Treasures, Rachel speaking."

"*Mamm*, it's Lavinia. I'm calling to see if you need me to come in. If not, I'd like to stay here."

"*Nee*, it's slow. How is Abe?"

"Better. But I'd like to stay and visit with him a little more."

"Do that. How are Waneta and Faron?"

She glanced at Waneta. "Why don't you ask her yourself?" She handed Waneta the phone. "*Mamm*'s asking about you."

The two women chatted for several minutes, and then Waneta handed the phone back to Lavinia and she finished talking to her *mudder*.

"You should take the phone home with you today," she told Waneta. "It's Abe's. He probably has the charger for it at his house."

"*Allrecht.*"

They spent the next hour chatting. Waneta wanted to know everything that had been going on in the two months she and Faron had been away visiting their oldest *sohn*.

Faron woke and glanced around, looking a little disoriented. "Must have dozed off for a few minutes."

Waneta laughed and shook her head. "Nearly two hours."

He grinned at Lavinia. "She exaggerates."

Waneta nodded soberly. "It was only an hour and fifty-five minutes."

Faron laughed and slapped his knee. "She's got a sense of humor." Then his smile faded. "How's Abe doing? You went in there after us."

"He's concerned," she said carefully. "But I keep reminding him the doctor's hopeful. I'm *schur* the doctor will know more after the test Abe had today."

Several people walked in, talking about a family member who was in surgery.

"I need to stretch my legs," Waneta said. She looked at Lavinia. "Walk with me?"

"*Schur.*"

"Maybe you could walk past the cafeteria, see if they have another piece of that pie we had for lunch," Faron suggested.

"Now who's got a sense of humor?" Waneta asked. "Never stops at one slice," she told Lavinia as they walked out of the room.

"My *dat*'s the same. Abe, too. Especially if it's your pie."

"That's the first thing I'll make Abe. Maybe his favorite fruit pie."

"Apple," they said at the same time.

When Waneta teared up, Lavinia hugged her. "He'll be feeling better in no time," she told the older woman. "You wait and see if I'm not right."

* * *

Abe smiled as he dreamed of walking among the rows of cows being milked.

His *dat* had started him working with the cows when he was barely toddling, introducing him to them, letting him watch him hook up the automatic milking equipment. Sitting Abe on a little wooden stool, his *dat* had showed him how to squeeze the cow's teats and aim the milk into a pail the old-fashioned way. Abe had fun aiming a stream of milk at a barn cat that lapped at it eagerly until his *dat* chided him for playing. Soon he was walking alongside his *dat* and hooking the cows up to the equipment that milked them now—a process that wasn't as much fun as doing it by hand but was a lot more efficient.

The work was long and hard. Cows had to be milked twice a day, and the cow barn had to be scrubbed immaculate. It was a big responsibility and one he didn't take lightly. This was a product that people consumed, and the Stoltzfus farm would exceed all the standards for as long as he lived.

His older *bruder* had married and now helped run a farm his *fraa*'s *familye* owned in Ohio. So it fell to Abe to take over when their *dat* was diagnosed with MS and needed to retire.

Now, in his dream, Abe walked through the cow barn and felt pride that he was carrying on the tradition that had been in the *familye* for generations. Something was wrong, though. He heard a cow mooing in distress. She sounded like she was in pain. But though he walked and walked and checked each one, the sound grew louder, more painful for him to hear. He couldn't stand to hear an animal in distress. He called out their names, telling them he was coming to help.

And then he woke, panting, sweaty, and found he was the one in pain, lying in a sterile white hospital bed, unable to move his legs.

A nurse rushed in and looked at the machine that recorded his blood pressure. "Your BP's a little high. What's wrong?"

He took a deep breath, tried to calm himself. "Bad dream."

She frowned as she took his temperature. "How's your pain level on a scale of one to ten?"

"About an eight."

"Hmm. Let me put in a call to your doctor, see what we can do, okay?"

He nodded and winced as his head reminded him it didn't appreciate the movement. "Thanks."

"Do you feel up to seeing your family for a few minutes, or do you want to wait until I get you something for your pain?"

"Maybe I should see them. I'd like to persuade my mother to take my father home. He has MS, and I can tell the bus ride here was hard on him."

"I think that's a good idea." She pulled a moist towelette from a box beside the bed and wiped his face. "There. Anything else I can do before I call the doctor?"

"No, that felt good. Thanks."

"Hang in there. It's going to get better." She smiled at him and left the room.

He hoped she was right. He didn't think things could get worse.

When his *eldres* walked in, he was glad he said he wanted to see them. His *dat* looked even more tired than he had earlier, and he could tell his *mudder*'s energy was flagging, even if she did her best to look bright and cheerful.

She placed a paper bag on the bedside table before she sat down on a chair. "A little snack Lavinia and I picked up for you in the cafeteria. Your favorite. Apple pie and a carton of milk."

"Sounds *gut*. Sounds better than the Jell-O at lunch."

"I'll bring you something from home when we visit tomorrow."

"The pie isn't bad," his *dat* said as he sat. "Not as *gut* as your *mudder*'s, but it'll do you until you get hers."

"I don't want you to fuss," Abe told her. "You both look tired. I'd like you to go home and get some rest."

"We're fine. Your *dat* took a nap in the waiting room."

"*Mamm.* Please?" He glanced at his *dat*, then back at her. "Besides, you'd be doing me a favor checking that Wayne has taken care of things."

"Now you know he has. That young man works as hard as you do."

Abe looked at his *dat*. "I'd really feel better with someone there after he does the chores."

"*Bu*'s right," Faron said. "It's hard to relax leaving things in someone else's care. And Wayne doesn't live on the property, even if he is just two farms down the road. Abe, we've been talking to your *bruder* and he wants to come down to help, but we've told him Wayne and I will manage."

"Thank him, but he's got enough on his hands with his own farm in Ohio." Abe really was concerned about how tired they looked. "Please, go home and get some rest."

Waneta sighed. "*Allrecht*, we'll go home in a few minutes." She grinned mischievously. "Maybe you just want more time with Lavinia instead of your old *eldres*."

He felt his face heat. "That's not true. She's a friend."

"*Schur.*"

"I think I'd like that pie now," he said, hoping to distract her. "Maybe you could help me with it, *Mamm*?" He held up his arm with the cast as he'd done with Lavinia. "This makes it a little hard to manage."

It worked. Waneta took a plastic container and a carton of milk from the bag. She set them on the table and moved it over the bed. After opening the pie box, she handed him a plastic fork. Then she opened the milk carton and stuck a straw in it.

"Like *Daed* said, not bad," he said, after he'd chewed a bite and swallowed.

"This is from the Abbott dairy," she noted as she studied the carton. "*Gut* to see the hospital buys local."

Abe sipped the milk and found himself remembering how he'd been worrying about milk prices before he slipped and fell off the roof. But he wasn't going to say anything to his *eldres*. He didn't want them worrying. Besides, his *dat* was retired, but Abe knew he kept up with the news, and they'd talked a week or so before his accident.

"So what shall I bring you tomorrow?"

"Meatloaf," he said immediately. "I've missed it since you've been gone."

"And apple pie?"

He grinned as he forked up more pie.

They chatted a few more minutes before they got up to leave. He was nearly undone when he saw the tears in his *mudder*'s eyes as she bent to hug him. His *dat* swallowed hard before patting him on the shoulder.

"I'm going to be *allrecht*," he assured them with more conviction than he felt.

"Of course you are," his *mudder* said in a voice that sounded husky. "See you tomorrow."

Lavinia came in a few minutes later.

"You *schur* you're not too tired?" he asked.

"*Nee*. I'm fine."

But as she took a seat, he saw the faint lavender shadows under her eyes and wondered how much rest she was getting while visiting him as much as she had been doing.

The nurse came in. "Doctor got back to me, upped your pain meds." She injected the syringe in her hand into the IV. "That should work very soon. Just use the call button if you need anything," she said before she left the room.

"I told my *eldres* to go home," he told Lavinia. "They looked so tired. Especially *Daed*. Maybe you should go home, too. You've been here all day."

She smiled. "Trying to get rid of me?"

"It's not fair of me to expect you to sit around here all day just to visit with me a few minutes whenever they let you in." He looked away for a moment, then met her gaze. "I was feeling sorry for myself earlier, and I think I put pressure on you."

She reached for his hand. "Friends are there for each other."

He stared at her and wondered if the sudden lift of spirits came from emotion or from the pain leaving him as the medication took effect.

"I—" he began, but then he stopped. How could he say he wanted to be more than friends at a time like this? He didn't know what was going to happen to him. Best to keep his thoughts to himself for now.

"What?"

He shook his head and was grateful it didn't hurt when he did. "Nothing. I think the pain meds are kicking in."

"Why don't you take a nap, and I'll see you in a bit." It was a statement not a question, because she rose and patted his hand lying on top of the blanket.

"Then you'll go home after?"

"We'll see," she said. "We'll see."

He wanted to be firm with her, but he felt himself drifting, and then he knew no more.

Chapter Five

Lavinia's *mudder* and *dat* were sitting at the table drinking coffee when she walked into the kitchen.

"You look tired," Rachel said as Lavinia bent to kiss her cheek, then her *dat*'s. "I saved you a plate. It's in the oven."

"*Danki.*" She took off her bonnet and hung it on a peg by the door. After she set her purse on the bench there, she walked over and washed her hands.

"I had a sandwich while Abe ate his supper, but that was hours ago so I'm hungry again."

She dried her hands on a dish towel and peeled the foil from the plate as she carried it to the table. "Mmm, looks *gut*."

"I hope a sandwich wasn't all you had to eat today."

"*Nee*. I had lunch with Abe's *eldres*. I was concerned they hadn't eaten much on the trip home."

She took a bite of her *mudder*'s baked chicken and sighed. "The hospital food was *gut*, but there's nothing to compare with your cooking, *Mamm*."

Rachel patted her arm. "*Danki*, sweetheart. So tell us about Abe. Has he been able to move his legs yet?"

Lavinia winced. "*Nee*. He had more tests today. The doctor told him not to get discouraged, but I can tell Abe is worried."

Amos rose to refill their coffee cups. "Lavinia? Want coffee?"

She shook her head. "*Nee, danki*. I had too much at the hospital." She got up and poured herself a glass of iced tea from the refrigerator.

"*Mamm*, Abe asked me to make him some brownies. Is it *allrecht* if I do that tonight?"

"*Schur*."

"As long as you leave one for me," her *dat* spoke up, his blue eyes twinkling.

She smiled at him as she sat again and resumed eating. "That goes without saying. My favorite guy always gets the first of whatever sweet I bake."

He nodded. "That's as it should be."

"I think he married me because of my peach pie," Rachel said, giving him a fond smile.

"And your pot roast," he told her. "The first time you invited me to your house for supper and made pot roast, I knew you were the *maedel* for me." Then he shook his head. "I'm joking. It's not true that the way to a man's heart is through his stomach, although mine has been happy I'm married to such a *gut* cook."

He patted his plump stomach and grinned. "We can be fickle creatures, loving the comfort of a delicious meal, the comfort of a well-kept home. But a wise man looks for a *maedel* with a heart that shines with love for God, for all His children and creatures."

He looked at his *fraa*. "Your *mudder* was that woman for me. She's even prettier now than she was when we married, but it was her heart that won me." He reached for her hand and squeezed it.

Lavinia stared at her *dat* and blinked against the tears that threatened to fall. He was a man of few words, but when he spoke they were always wise and wonderful.

Her *mudder*'s face was smooth and unlined and her hair still a rich brown, although her *dat*'s beard and hair were beginning to show streaks of silver. They were a handsome couple in their fifties—younger than Abe's parents.

"Well, it's time to take a last walk around in the barn, see that all our creatures are ready for a night's rest." He stood, set his mug in the kitchen sink, and left them.

Rachel turned to her and must have seen the emotion Lavinia was feeling. She nodded and gave Lavinia a gentle smile. "He's such a *wunderbaar* man. What he doesn't realize is that he couldn't have thought I had a *gut* heart if he didn't have one himself."

"Abe has a *gut* heart," she said slowly. "That's why it hurts so much to see what he's going through. It's not fair that he works so hard and helps others so much and he's feeling so broken right now."

"He's going to be *allrecht*," Rachel said. "You need to believe that."

"I know." She sighed and rose to put her plate in the sink. Then she turned on the oven to preheat, reached into a cabinet, and found a big pottery bowl. She mixed the ingredients for brownies, poured the batter into a greased pan, then set it in the oven. As she walked over to place the bowl in the sink, her *dat* came in from the barn. He grabbed the wooden spoon from her and she shook her head at him.

"Just in time," he said with a chuckle, as he licked the spoon then put it into the sink.

"Just like a little *bu*," her *mudde*r said.

He sauntered off to the living room, where he'd sit in his recliner and read *The Budget*, and her *mudder* would find him dozing off when she went to tell him it was time to go to bed.

"I sold three of your rag rugs today," Rachel said as she turned the gas flame on under the teakettle. "The big brown-and-black oval one and two of the smaller round red ones."

"That's *wunderbaar*." She'd begun making rugs from scraps of cloth as a *kind* and hadn't thought much of it. She'd gone into town with her *mudder* during the holidays and summers when she was little. After she'd helped dust and sweep the shop and straighten shelves, she'd entertained herself by playing with some fabric left over from whatever quilt her *mudder* was sewing.

Then one day an *Englisch* woman had walked into the shop, seen her working on a simple rag rug, and exclaimed over it.

"My grandmother made these during the Great Depression," she'd told Rachel. "Back then, nothing went to waste."

Lavinia hadn't known what she meant. Wasn't depression what people felt when they were sad? The woman had explained when she saw Lavinia's confused expression, and then she continued to watch her wind the fabric strips into the circular rug.

And so Lavinia's rugs joined the dozens of crafts that lined the shelves of her *mudder*'s shop, which featured the works of Amish men and women in their community. Her skill had improved as she grew older, of course, but the rugs remained a simple but lovely way to use up scraps of material and provide a warm, decorative splash of color on a floor.

Lavinia washed up the dishes in the sink, then sat for a cup of tea with her *mudder* and waited for the brownies to bake. She was yawning by the time the oven timer went off. After they cooled, she cut them into squares, served one to each of her *eldres*, then set the rest in a plastic container.

"Better hide those, or you won't have any to take to Abe tomorrow," her *mudder* warned when Amos came into the kitchen wanting a second brownie. After he left the room with one, she turned to Lavinia. "On second thought, take the container up to your room. You know how he is with sweets."

Lavinia chuckled and did as she suggested. After all these years, her *mudder* knew her *mann*. She climbed the stairs to her room and set the container on her dresser.

After she'd changed into a cool cotton nightgown, Lavinia sat on her bed to brush out her hair and yawned again. She slipped between her sheets and breathed in the gentle scent of the lavender sachet she kept under her pillow. Her thoughts went to Abe. She should take one of the sachets when she visited him tomorrow. The scent would be soothing to him, and maybe it would help overcome the antiseptic smell of the hospital.

On that thought, she drifted off to sleep.

* * *

Abe sighed.

"I can tell you're feeling better," Jodie, his night nurse, said as she checked his temperature.

She was his favorite nurse. She had the same brisk, efficient air about her as his day nurse, Susan, but she spent more time explaining things to him in a calm way that reassured him. He didn't know if it was because she had more years of experience or because things were quieter on the unit at night or what. Although *he* didn't think it was quieter at night. Maybe Jodie's other patients slept during the night, but since he'd had various nurses and people coming in and out at all hours, he didn't think so.

"You really think I'm better? How can you tell that?" Because he *schur* didn't feel much different than when he'd first woken up in the hospital.

"You're bored." She tapped keys on her laptop. Then she looked at him and gave him a sympathetic smile. "No visitors this evening?"

"I sent them home." He told her about his *eldres* and Lavinia and how tired they'd looked, and before he knew what he was doing, he sighed again.

"That was very loving of you, but now the hours are moving like molasses, aren't they?"

He nodded, and this time managed not to sigh. "I tried to read the paper Lavinia brought me, but I'm having a little double vision."

Her fingers stopped the tapping. She frowned as she looked at the laptop screen. "I don't see where you complained of this earlier."

"Not today, no."

"I'll make a note of it for the doctor, and if it gets more severe tonight, I want you to tell me, all right?"

"I will."

"Best to avoid too much television," she said as he began playing with the remote.

"Because I'm Amish?"

"Because it might aggravate the double vision."

"Oh."

"You can try it if you want."

"Maybe later."

"Well, if it's any consolation, if you keep doing as well as you are now, I think the doctor will be moving you to a regular room in another day or so. Then you can have more visitors and for longer. That's something to look forward to, right?"

"It is."

She smiled. "You let me know if there's anything you need."

"I will. Thanks."

He sighed again, then looked at the clock on the wall. Lavinia was probably getting ready for bed now. She hadn't eaten much at supper when she sat with him while he ate. Susan had said she could send for a tray for her, but Lavinia thanked her and said she'd picked up a sandwich from the cafeteria. But he noticed she didn't eat much of it.

Was she making brownies? He knew he'd been selfish to ask her to make him some. She'd already done so much for him since the accident. Had he thanked her enough for looking out for his *eldres* since they'd arrived?

He picked up the remote and figured out how to turn the television on and then adjust the sound when it blared. There were many channels to choose from: news, movies, programs for *kinner*, sports. He settled on watching a volleyball game. It was a favorite pastime of his, one he enjoyed playing with other young men from his community.

But watching it proved painful. His gaze went from the television mounted on the wall to his arm encased in plaster and suspended from the ceiling. The broken bone would heal, but would he ever be able to move his legs? He forced his attention on them, sent all the power of his thought to them.

They didn't move. Not one little inch.

So he prayed, prayed harder than he'd done since he fell off the roof, prayed harder than he ever had his entire life.

Nothing.

Frustrated, he wanted to throw something, but the only thing within reach was the remote, and that belonged to the hospital.

He changed the channel, tried to lose himself in a movie about a man stuck on an island. He hadn't seen a movie in years—not since his *rumschpringe*. He frowned. The man was talking to a volleyball he'd drawn a face on. Abe squinted, blinked. Surely he was seeing things.

Nee, that's what was happening.

Well, he might be having a hard time with things, but so far he hadn't gotten to talking to things like that poor man in the movie. He yawned as he watched and yawned again.

How beautiful the island looked. He'd never been to an island. Never been outside Lancaster County. Dairy farming didn't lend itself to vacations, although his *eldres* had traveled to Pinecraft in Florida last year when his *dat* retired. His *mudder* had sent him postcards.

He marveled at how blue and vast the ocean was, and as he drifted off to sleep, he felt rocked by its gentle waves....

The sand was pleasantly warm under his feet as he walked over to join the man and the volleyball on the beach. The man introduced himself as Chuck and invited him to share his drink in a coconut.

Abe turned to the volleyball.

"So your name is Wilson?"

The ball just sat silently.

He turned to Chuck. "He won't talk to me."

"That's because he's my friend, not yours."

"Well, I have friends back home," Abe said, feeling a little defensive.

He looked around at the island and the blue sweep of the ocean. He'd never seen the ocean. It was so very pleasant to sit and watch the waves roll in, roll out.

But he didn't want to be here.

"This is a nice place, but I want to go home."

"Don't we all. It's not as easy as it was for Dorothy," Chuck said sadly as he opened another FedEx package, took out some papers, and looked disappointed. "You know what everyone told her. Go follow the yellow brick road."

"The yellow brick road?" He stood and searched for it. "All I see is sand."

Then he heard mooing. He had to be close to home. That was Bessie he heard, wasn't it?

"Bessie?"

* * *

Abe opened his eyes and stared into the face of a cow.

"Bessie?" he whispered, and blinked hard.

Nee, not Bessie. It was the stuffed cow Lavinia had brought him. Wow. What a dream…nightmare. Whatever.

The television was still on. The man on the island was home now, in his *Englisch* home, off the island with no volleyball in sight.

Home. Abe had a sudden, overwhelming desire to be home. Surely everything would be *allrecht* when he got home.

He knew some of his friends who farmed plant crops like corn and wheat and vegetables didn't understand his love for dairy farming. That was fine. Lancaster County was the biggest producer of milk in the state, and dairy farms such as his made up a third of all farms locally. So he had plenty of fellow dairy farmers—Amish and *Englisch*—who loved it the way he did, and they met every so often for support and friendship. A card signed by a number of them had already been delivered here to the hospital, and it was propped on a nearby table with a vase of flowers.

Jodie came in and glanced at the television, then at Abe. "How's the vision doing? You're not seeing double?"

"No."

"I saw that movie when it first came out. Great story." She sat and flexed her feet. "Makes a good point."

"Point?"

"Sure. Chuck spends years trying to survive on the island. And we see surviving isn't just about living, is it? Or getting through the physical challenges. It's about surviving emotionally. Chuck finally realizes he has to find a way off the island or he won't survive emotionally."

They both watched the movie for a few minutes.

Then she turned to him. "You're going to get well," she said kindly. "You'll get to go home."

"But will I walk again?"

She met his gaze directly. "I don't know. Your doctor seems to feel the paralysis is temporary, and he's usually right. But you know it's not in his hands."

Another nurse poked her head into the room. "I need your help."

"Be right there." Jodie stood, looked at Abe. "What if you can't walk again? Would that be the worst thing for you? Or would you try to find a way to get home the way he did?" she asked, jerking her head toward the TV.

She didn't wait to hear his answer but hurried out of the room, leaving him to think about what she'd said.

Chapter Six

Feels *gut* to be back to work," Lavinia said as she walked into the shop with her *mudder* the next morning.

She flicked on the lights and made sure the door was locked behind them. They wouldn't open for another half hour.

She'd always loved the time she spent in the shop filled with the artistic handmade crafts of her fellow Amish. Her *mudder*'s loom sat in one corner with the latest throw she was weaving, and Lavinia had her own little table where she wove her rag rugs when business was slow. Shelves were filled with creative wooden and fabric items.

She took her *mudder*'s lunch tote with her to put in the back room and make a pot of coffee. When she returned to the front of the shop, she put both mugs on the counter.

"Anything special you want me to do before we open?"

"We got some new stock in just before closing

yesterday. It needs to be unpacked and priced. Then we'll put it out for display."

"I'm sorry I wasn't here to help when it came in." She sipped her coffee and watched her *mudder* pull the shop ledger out from a shelf under the counter.

"It was more important for you to be there with Abe and his *familye*."

"Waneta and Faron looked so tired when they arrived," she said, nodding. "And Waneta was trying to hide how worried she was. It was hard to get them to go home and get some rest." Lavinia stared into her coffee. "But nobody was trying to hide how worried they were more than Abe. He still can't feel his legs." She sighed. "He told me to go home, but then he asked me to stay. That's why I called and asked you if I could stay yesterday." Her lips trembled and she pressed her fingers to them. "Oh, *Mamm*, I'm so worried about him."

Rachel reached over and squeezed her hand. "I know. But Lavinia, remember what my friend Phoebe, your old teacher, used to say."

" 'Worry is arrogant. God knows what He's doing.' "

"*Ya*. So let's pray. And then we'll do the work we're supposed to do and let God do His."

Lavinia nodded and smiled. Her *mudder* was such a wise woman. After they prayed, Lavinia went into the back room and slit open the cartons of new stock that had come in.

She lifted out a big, hand-carved wooden bowl and ran her hand over its satiny surface. Naiman, her *schweschder* Sadie's *mann*, did such beautiful work. She found six other bowls, each unique, and carried them to the front counter. There, she and her *mudder* recorded them in the inventory and priced them so that Lavinia could put them on display with Naiman's other work.

The shop was filled with the colorful handmade work of men and women in their community. Her *mudder* was a fabric artist who wove beautiful throws that she'd sold on her own before starting the shop years ago. Gradually she'd filled it with the work of other Amish craftspeople, and now the shelves were full of traditional handwoven baskets, handmade candles, and jars of homemade preserves, jam, pickled vegetables, chow chow, and local honey. More canned goods would join them, as the summer harvest had many women in the community canning for hours.

Lavinia straightened the display of lavender sachets, chose two that were made of a simple muslin fabric—no flowers for Abe—and carried them over to the counter.

"Put these on my tab, *Mamm*. I was thinking I'd take them to Abe to put under his pillow to help him sleep. And maybe they'll banish some of the antiseptic smell of the hospital."

"*Gut* idea. I think they'll be as welcome as the brownies."

Customers began streaming in and time sped by. Before she knew it, Lavinia glanced at the clock and saw it was time for lunch. Rachel went into the back to eat while Lavinia manned the counter, and then they reversed their roles so Lavinia could eat. She took the sachets and tucked them into her purse to take to Abe later.

Liz, the *Englisch* woman some Amish hired to drive

them where they needed to go, arrived and honked as she parked in front of the shop. Lavinia hugged her *mudder* and gathered up her purse and the container of brownies.

"*Danki* for letting me leave early so I can spend some time with Abe."

"You're *wilkumm*. Tell Abe I said hello. And Waneta and Faron. I'm *schur* they'll be at the hospital today, too."

"I will."

She started for the door, then turned when she heard her *mudder* call her name.

"Here." Rachel pressed two twenty-dollar bills into her hand. "I don't want you to run out of money."

"I have enough."

Rachel shook her head. "I think you didn't have enough money for supper at the hospital, or you wouldn't have come home and eaten it at our house last night."

"All I wanted was a sandwich there at suppertime. And I don't know anyone who could turn down your baked chicken."

"Go!" her *mudder* ordered, but there was a smile in her voice. "Liz is waiting."

"I'm going," Lavinia said, as she grinned and left the shop.

"How is Abe doing?" Liz asked, after Lavinia climbed into the van and buckled her seat belt. Lavinia figured she knew all the Amish in Lancaster County after decades of driving them around.

"He's doing well, but I don't know when he'll get to go home." Lavinia didn't mention the paralysis. That was too personal.

"It's hard for a man to be laid up in the hospital," Liz said as she checked for traffic and pulled out onto the road. "I remember when my Jim had his knee replacement. Oh my, you'd have thought that he was going to be confined to the hospital for a month."

Lavinia considered that. Just how long might Abe be in the hospital? And how expensive was the type of care he was getting in the ICU?

"Don't you go worrying," Liz told her as their gazes met in the rearview mirror. "Everyone who knows what happened is praying for Abe. And no one gets behind someone in need like the Amish. I've lived here all my life, and I've seen them help not just their own kind but my community, too. Why, they even had fundraisers for people in Haiti after the earthquake."

"I know."

"So, you taking him a little treat?"

"Brownies. He loves brownies."

Liz laughed. "Who doesn't?"

"Would you like one?"

She shook her head. "Don't you tempt me. I'm on a diet. Again."

"My father ate two last night."

"He can do that. The man's a farmer and works a lot harder than me just sitting in this van driving people around all day."

"Dad *is* a hard worker," she agreed. But then again, what farmer wasn't? She didn't think there was such a thing as a lazy farmer.

Liz asked her about her *mudder* and they chatted until

the hospital came into view. "You let me know when you're ready to go home," the driver said. "And tell Abe I'm looking forward to when I can drive him back to his farm."

Touched, Lavinia nodded. "I will." She unbuckled her seat belt and leaned forward to pay Liz, then picked up her purse and the plastic container with the brownies and got out of the van.

She rode up the elevator with other visitors and stepped out onto Abe's floor. But when she went by his room, his bed was empty. Telling herself he was probably somewhere having yet another test, she stopped at the nurse's station. A new nurse was behind the counter, typing on a computer. She looked up at Lavinia and smiled. "How can I help you?"

"I'm here to see Abe Stoltzfus."

"I'm sorry, but he's not with us anymore."

Her blood ran cold and her fingers clutched the counter. "What? What happened to him?" she cried, and her voice sounded like someone else's—high pitched and full of nerves.

* * *

Abe didn't like change much.

So when one of his nurses came in after lunch and said she was sorry she was going to lose him as a patient, he wasn't happy. Until she told him he didn't need to be in the ICU and could be in a regular room.

That was *gut* news. Even better news was remembering that it meant he could have visitors for longer periods.

"I thought that would put a grin on your face," Pam,

one of the daytime ICU nurses, said as she unhooked the blood pressure cuff. "More time to spend with your wife and family. They can let your friends know they can visit."

"Friends." He thought about that. It meant that Lavinia didn't have to pretend she was his *fraa*.

She nodded, picked the stuffed cow up from the bed where she'd set it when she readied him for transfer, and set it on the bedside table.

"She's not actually my wife."

"Hmm?" she asked, smoothing the blanket over him.

"Lavinia isn't my wife."

She paused. "Oh?"

"The paramedics thought she was my wife when they came to my house. Since my parents were away, she got in the ambulance and came with me. Then she kept visiting me until they got here."

"I see. Sort of like *While You Were Sleeping*."

"What? I was unconscious, not sleeping."

"It's a movie," she explained. "Well, we wouldn't have told her she couldn't see you."

"She didn't want to take the chance."

"Sounds like she's a really good friend."

"I don't know what I'd have done without her." It was out before he could stop himself.

"It's wonderful to have someone who cares for us when we need them so much," Pam said quietly. Then she gave him a mischievous smile. "Maybe she's more than a good friend?"

He felt his face redden.

"Well, Abe, we're going to miss you in ICU, but we

always love it when our patients leave us because they got better."

Abe heard what she didn't say. Some of the ICU patients didn't get better.

"Maybe you can come say hi sometime," he said. "And when Jodie comes on duty tonight, will you tell her I'm sorry I didn't get to say goodbye?"

"Will do. Take care."

After she left, he glanced around the room and decided it was a *gut* move. No more machines that beeped and blinked. More privacy. Longer visits with Lavinia and his *eldres*. And it meant that he was getting better, even if he didn't feel he'd made any big improvement. That was something he should be grateful for.

Abe met new nurses, and after they took his temperature and his blood pressure and such, he faced the monotony of lying in bed and watching the clock on the wall. The minutes didn't pass any faster in this room than in the last one. His *eldres* hadn't been by yet, but he figured his *dat* needed some time to rest. Lavinia had to work but had promised to come in the early afternoon.

He dozed off, and when he woke, he found Lavinia sitting in a chair beside the bed. He smiled. "It's *gut* to see you."

"It's *gut* to see you, too."

Something in her tone was different. "Something wrong?"

She let out a shaky breath. "I just overreacted and made a fool of myself."

"You? You're the calmest *maedel* I know."

"I didn't know you'd been transferred, and I misunderstood the new nurse at the ICU nursing station."

"Oh. I'd have told you, but it was a surprise to me, too."

"How long have you been here?"

He glanced at the clock. "Couple hours."

"I used a hospital phone to call your *eldres* and gave them your new room number. Your *mudder* said she's bringing your cell phone and charger with her when they come."

"I hope that's not all she's bringing. I've missed her cooking since they've been gone."

She handed him the plastic container she'd brought. "Maybe you'd like one of my brownies while you wait for her."

"*Schur.* But I'm more interested in talking to you."

Her cheeks went pink and she looked surprised. "Well, that's a nice thing to say."

Abe decided he didn't say enough nice things if this one caused such a reaction. "Tell me about your day."

So she told him about what it had involved and let him know her *mudder* and Liz had asked her to tell him they were thinking of him. She had a funny story about a woman who'd come into the shop and tried out some Pennsylvania *Deitsch* words she was getting from an online dictionary on her phone. Lavinia had finally figured out what the woman was asking for, and they had a good laugh over it.

"Why are you staring at me?" he asked. "Have I got chocolate on my chin?"

She shook her head. "I haven't heard you laugh since before the accident."

"There hasn't been much to laugh about."

"*Nee*," she agreed. "But there's much to be grateful for."

He gave her a skeptical look. "Like what?"

She glanced around the room. "You're out of intensive care, so that means the doctor feels you're getting better, *ya*?"

"*Ya*." He frowned and then sighed. "I guess I haven't been grateful enough."

"I can't say I understand, because that wouldn't be fair," she said. "I've never been in the same position. But I can imagine it's hard lying here when you're used to being so active. And I know you're worried." She bit her lip. "I told *Mamm* I was worried about you, and she reminded me of something our teacher Phoebe used to say. She said worry's arrogant. That God knows what He's doing."

"I'm having a little trouble believing that right now."

"Do you think it would help to talk to someone?"

"Like who?"

"The bishop. You like him, don't you?"

"Not as much as I did Abram. He's *allrecht*."

She knew the late bishop and Abe's *dat* had been very close friends, and so Abe had missed Abram since he died.

"Maybe talk to your *dat*. He's such a wise man. He's had big changes in his life with the MS, so I'm *schur* he understands how you're feeling now more than anyone else."

"He's got enough to deal with."

There was a commotion at the door. Even before Abe glanced over, he knew it was his *eldres*.

"*Mamm*, *Daed*, it's *gut* to see you!" He put on a welcoming smile but was sorry that his time with Lavinia was cut short.

Chapter Seven

Life got busier.

Harvest meant long, hot days for those living on farms. For years, Lavinia and her *mudder* had worked their schedules so that they could be at the shop in town but still have time to pick and can the kitchen garden in summer. Now Lavinia added in trips to the hospital to see Abe.

Twice she'd fallen asleep in the van as Liz drove her home and the woman had had to wake her up.

She and her *mudder* sometimes hired someone part-time during the summer and holiday months. The other day Lavinia had started to say it was time to get someone, but then they'd gotten busy and didn't get to talk about it. She told herself that they needed to hire someone soon. It was getting busier as tourists enjoyed exploring the area and shopping. New arts and crafts arrived almost daily, and she and her *mudder* were constantly unpacking, pricing, and stocking the shelves. And her *mudder* was already working with her artists and craftspeople on plans for Christmas merchandise.

It was never too soon to plan for Christmas when you owned a shop.

Many of the tourists liked shopping ahead for the holidays while they were vacationing, and Amish and *Englisch* businesses in town were happy to tempt them to buy their goods.

"You look tired," Abe told her when she settled in a chair beside his bed.

"*Danki*," she said, and glared at him. "Just what a *maedel* wants to hear."

"Sorry."

"You're looking tired, too," she said after a moment. And, she thought, in some pain.

"I had physical therapy this morning. I didn't think I was going to make it through the session," he said, shifting in the bed. "It was pure torture. I thought it was supposed to be gentle and help get feeling back in my legs. She *hurt* me. And she's coming back later this afternoon." He looked hopefully at her. "Maybe you can sneak me out of here so she can't torture me."

"*Schur*," she said. "It should be easy to hide a six-foot man in pajamas walking out of here." Then she bit her lip as she realized what she'd said. "Did the doctor give you any idea when you can go home?" she rushed to ask.

"He thinks the end of the week." Abe frowned. "But I'll be in a wheelchair, and I'll have a physical therapist come to work with me at the house for a couple of weeks."

Joy burst through her. "Abe! End of the week? That's *wunderbaar*!"

"Didn't you hear me? In a wheelchair. And more therapy."

Joy evaporated. She swallowed hard against the lump in her throat. He looked miserable. *Please, God, help me say something to cheer him up*, she prayed.

There was a knock on the doorjamb. She glanced over. The bishop stood in the doorway, his straw hat in his hand.

"Leroy! *Gut* to see you. Abe, look who's here to see you." She vacated her chair and gestured at it. "Please, sit."

"Are you feeling up to a visit?" he asked Abe as he sat.

"*Ya*," Abe said politely.

Lavinia bit her lip. In his current mood, she was *schur* Leroy was the last person Abe wanted to see—and the person he most needed to talk to. And he'd be forced to talk if she wasn't in the room. She cast about for an excuse to leave them alone.

"Leroy, can I get you something to drink?"

"That would be *wunderbaar*."

"Coffee? Or something cold?"

"What will you have, Abe?" Leroy asked, giving him a genial smile. He was in his forties, younger than the last bishop, but had a calm, wise air about him.

"Coffee would be great. But I don't want you to go to any trouble."

"It's no trouble. I can get you both some coffee. Leroy, how do you take it?"

"Cream and two sugars, *danki*, Lavinia."

As she picked up her purse and escaped from the room, she avoided looking at Abe. She knew him and knew he probably didn't want to talk to the bishop right now. Well, sometimes medicine was hard to take. She had a feeling that Leroy was just what Abe needed today. He always had a positive message about faith and life, but it wasn't always an easy one to hear.

She took her time getting the coffee, and on her way back with the cardboard cup container, she saw Faron and Waneta walking toward Abe's room. She called out to them and they turned.

"Leroy is visiting Abe," she explained. "I was just taking coffee in to them. I thought I'd give them a few minutes to talk, just the two of them. Abe's not in a very *gut* mood today. He says he's in pain from his physical therapy session, poor guy."

Waneta put her hand on her *mann*'s arm. "Faron, let's give them some time."

"They've got peach pie in the cafeteria," Lavinia told Faron when he hesitated.

"Guess we could wait there," Faron said as he gave Waneta a considering look. "You know, so that the bishop can talk to Abe."

Waneta gave him a look. "*Ya*, right. Have you forgotten you had a piece of cake for dessert at lunch?" She turned to Lavinia. "Man's got such a sweet tooth."

"My *dat*, too," Lavinia told her. "Do you suppose it's just Amish men, or do you think it's all men?"

Waneta chuckled. "I think it's all men. *Kumm*, Faron, let's go have some coffee."

"I'll join you as soon as I take Abe and Leroy theirs."

She returned to Abe's room, and he gave her a look of such gratitude she felt guilty. Then he frowned when she set the coffee down on the bedside table and backed away.

"Excuse me, I'll be right back," she said, and slipped out of the room before Abe could object. She paused at the doorway and was reminded of the story of Lot's wife when she looked back and saw Abe's beseeching look. She forced herself to walk away.

She joined Faron and Waneta in the cafeteria. They had a piece of pie and a cup of coffee waiting for her. "*Danki*, this is a nice treat."

"Has the shop been busy?"

Lavinia nodded as she put a bite of pie in her mouth. "My *schweschder*'s been a great help to *Mamm* and me. She's been canning a lot of the vegetables and fruit from our kitchen garden this summer since I've been visiting Abe."

"I've been enjoying doing ours, even though the heat seems worse every summer," Waneta said. "As usual, we have much more zucchini than we can use."

"Don't go sneaking it into a cake again like you did last summer," Faron said as he washed down a bite of pie with a gulp of coffee.

"You mean like in the chocolate cake you had at lunch?"

He stared at her for a long moment and then he chuckled. “Well, you fooled me again.”

They lingered over the pie and coffee and talked. Well, she and Waneta talked. Faron was too busy with his pie. And when he thought his *fraa* wasn’t paying attention, he sneaked a bite or two from her plate. The smile that quirked the corner of Waneta’s mouth told Lavinia that she was well aware of the theft.

“Well, I suppose we should be going up to see Abe,” Faron said when he finally pushed his empty plate aside. “Seems we gave him and Leroy enough time to talk.”

Lavinia rose. She hoped the bishop had said something to Abe to help him feel a little more positive.

* * *

Abe knew he wasn’t in the best of moods because of his pain and not getting to talk to Lavinia, but his *mudder* had taught him to be polite. So he fixed a pleasant expression on his face and sipped his coffee and told himself to be polite if Leroy launched into a sermon about enduring hardship or some such.

“It’s hard to be laid up,” the older man said as he swirled a wooden stirrer in his cup.

Abe wanted to roll his eyes. People always said they understood when they’d never experienced the same thing, he wanted to say. But he didn’t know how to do that without being rude.

“I don’t imagine you remember when I was here in

this hospital after a buggy accident years ago. Guess you'd have been too young."

He sipped his coffee and frowned. "It was a terrible time. My *fraa* was killed in the accident. Our *dochder* was just three."

"I'm sorry."

"*Danki.* What made things really hard was that I was in the hospital for weeks and I couldn't take care of my *dochder*. My *eldres* did, of course, but it was so hard not seeing her."

He looked down at the cup in his hand for a long moment, and then his gaze shifted to meet Abe's. "I know it must be hard not being able to take care of your cows. I know they're more than a business to you. Your farm is home. You want to be there. All in *gut* time, Abe. All in *gut* time."

"This was just the worst time for this to happen. What with milk prices."

"It's a concern, for *schur*." He paused, looked thoughtful. "But remember, 'I know the plans I have for you, says the Lord. They are plans for good and not for disaster, to give you a future and a hope.'" He finished his coffee and tossed the cup into the wastepaper basket. "I stopped by and took a look for myself, and Wayne is doing a *wunderbaar* job in your absence and not letting your *dat* overdo helping."

"I'm *schur* you're right."

"Remember, we Amish take care of our own." He stood. "Maybe it would help if you thought of yourself less as Job and more as Joseph." He glanced at the door as some people walked past. "Well, I'm going to be on my way so that Lavinia can visit with you."

"*Danki* for coming," Abe said. And meant it. Hearing that things were running as they should on the farm—and hearing it from someone other than his *dat*—reassured him and made him feel a little bit better. He held out his good hand and they shook hands.

"I enjoyed talking with you," Leroy said.

"I enjoyed talking with you, too."

"I'll be praying you get to go home soon."

Abe nodded. "*Danki*," he said again.

Leroy nodded and left him.

Lavinia came in a few minutes later with his *eldres*. His *mudder* bent down to kiss him, smelling of cinnamon and sugar. She set a plastic container down on the bedside table. "Snickerdoodles," she said as she took a seat.

His *dat* patted his shoulder and gave the container a longing look.

"Faron! Don't even think about it!"

He chuckled before he sat beside her.

Waneta turned to Abe. "Man had cake for lunch and pie just now. Never gains an ounce." She sighed as she smoothed her apron over her lap. "Well, Lavinia tells us you'll be coming home soon."

"That's the plan. It just won't be the way I'd hoped."

"Give it time," his *dat* said, then lapsed into silence.

That was his *dat*...a man of few words, but the words he did say always made Abe think. And it struck him that hearing words similar to the bishop's meant he was supposed to learn something. His schoolteacher Phoebe had always said there was no such thing as coincidence—such things were messages from God.

He became aware that Lavinia lingered near the door. A nurse came in and offered to get her a chair, but she shook her head and said she didn't need one. After the nurse left, he watched as Lavinia wandered from door to window and back again as his *mudder* chattered.

Abe wasn't *schur* if Lavinia was trying to give him time with his *eldres* or if he had created some distance by being moody with her earlier. She gave him an uncertain smile when she saw he was looking in her direction. He carried on a conversation with his *eldres*, but he couldn't help glancing in Lavinia's direction over and over. His *mudder* must have noticed, because she turned to his *dat* and told him they needed to go.

"We just got here," he protested.

She elbowed him and jerked her head toward Lavinia. "Let's go so the young people can visit."

"Oh," he said, and as he stood and leaned on his cane, his faded blue eyes twinkled as he grinned at Abe. "I remember being a young man."

"You don't remember your reading glasses when they're on your head," Waneta said, but she gave him an indulgent smile when his hand reached for his head with a grin.

Abe's *mudder* gave him another kiss on the cheek and he got another pat on the shoulder from his *dat* and then they were walking out of the room. He felt his spirits dip lower as he watched his *dat*'s awkward stride. They were getting older, and his *dat* had the MS, and here they had to be coming out to the hospital to see him. Worry about him.

He frowned. It wasn't fair. It just wasn't fair.

"Maybe I should leave, too," said Lavinia.

He felt a moment of panic. "If you have to go," he said, trying not to show his feelings.

"I don't have to, but I don't think you're in the mood for visitors."

"I wasn't in the mood for a sermon from Leroy."

She approached the chair beside his bed and sat on its edge. "Is that what he did? Gave you a sermon?"

"Not exactly." He shrugged and pulled his blanket higher. "Why do they have to keep this place so cold?" He shook his head at the way he sounded so irritable. But he couldn't help it.

He frowned when Lavinia tucked the blanket up around his shoulder.

"You don't have to do that," he said.

"I don't mind. Are your feet warm enough? Mine get cold so easy."

"How would I know? I can't feel them."

He watched, appalled, as she burst into tears and fled the room.

"Lavinia!"

But she disappeared from view, and there wasn't a thing he could do about it. Frustrated, he grabbed the plastic cup on the bedside table and threw it.

A nurse passing by the room stopped, picked up

the cup, and walked into the room. "Do you need some help?"

Miserable, he shook his head. "I just got mad at something. I'm sorry. That was childish."

"I need to go wipe up the water before someone slips in it," she said in a neutral tone. She grabbed some tissues from a box on the table and walked off to take care of it.

"I'm sorry!" he called after her, and she waved her hand as if it didn't matter.

Minutes passed and Lavinia didn't return. He finally decided she wasn't coming back—and he didn't deserve for her to do so.

And then he saw her purse lying on the chair. She couldn't go home without it, could she? She'd need money to pay a driver. And women couldn't be without their purses. His *mudder* never went anywhere without hers. Hope struggled with despair. What if she found a way to leave without coming back and before he could apologize?

And then, just when he began to give up hope, she walked in with something in her hands.

"I talked to one of the nurses at the nursing station," she said as she held out a pair of bright red socks. "I can put them on your feet if you want."

"That would be really nice," he said, putting as much warmth and politeness into his voice as he could. "I'm sorry I took out my frustration on you."

"It's *allrecht*." She lifted the blanket from his feet and began to put a sock on one foot.

"*Nee*, it's not. I'll try not to do it again."

"*Gut*."

"You're tickling me," he said as he tried to pull himself up in bed.

"I didn't mean to," she told him. Then she looked up and met his gaze. "Abe, you can feel me putting your sock on this foot?"

He nodded slowly, his eyes widening as he took in what that meant.

She ran from the room, and when she came back, she brought a nurse.

"So, you have some ticklish socks, do you?" the nurse asked, and bent over his foot. She pulled off the sock and ran her hand over his toes.

"I can feel that," he cried, and then yelped in pain. "That didn't tickle."

"Wasn't meant to," she said, but she was smiling. "I'm going to go call your doctor."

Abe watched Lavinia finish putting the socks on his feet and then tuck the blanket over them. She walked over and picked up her purse, then sat down, looking unsteady.

"It tickled," she whispered.

"*Ya*," he said. And he smiled at her and sank back against his pillow. "It tickled."

Chapter Eight

Lavinia felt giddy riding the elevator down from Abe's room.

Abe was feeling something in his legs!

She'd been in the room when his doctor had come in with a big grin, saying, "I told you so!"

"It's only a sort of a tingling," Abe explained as the doctor approached the bed. "I thought Lavinia was tickling my foot when she put a sock on it."

Lavinia slipped from the room while the doctor performed an exam. When she was allowed back in, she could have sworn Abe was blinking hard to hold back tears.

She would've liked to stay longer, but she'd asked Liz to pick her up at eight p.m. and she had to hurry to make it to the front door of the hospital on time.

Liz was waiting and grinning at her when she climbed inside the van. "Well, you're in a good mood."

She nodded. "Abe is doing well. We hope he'll get to go home soon. Maybe end of the week."

Then she fell silent. She didn't feel she should say more. She'd been taught from childhood that discussing personal things wasn't done, and besides, this was Abe's business. Only her *familye* and Abe's knew that the fall had caused temporary paralysis.

"You let me know if I can be of help driving him home, all right? My treat."

"That's very generous of you. I'll tell Abe. I know he's looking forward to being back home."

She watched the passing scenery and debated stopping by Waneta and Faron's house to talk to them.

"Liz, would you mind dropping me off at Abe's house instead of mine? I think I'll visit with his parents for a few minutes before I go home tonight."

"Sure."

Liz glanced in the rearview mirror and their gazes met. Then Liz glanced back at the road.

Lavinia figured that the woman guessed something was going on, since she didn't usually ask to be taken to Abe's house. But the *Englisch* who drove the Amish respected their privacy and didn't ask personal questions.

As Liz pulled up at Abe's house, Lavinia felt her heart beat faster. She fairly jumped out of the van the minute Liz stopped, and then felt herself blushing when she turned back and handed her the fare.

Liz just grinned. "See you tomorrow morning!"

"Tomorrow!"

She started up the walk to the house, but Liz tapped on her horn. When Lavinia turned around, Liz pointed to the back seat. Lavinia looked in the window and saw her lunch tote sitting there. Now she was really embarrassed. She collected it, said thanks, and walked up to the house. Usually she just called out as she entered, but since it was getting dark and they weren't expecting her, Lavinia knocked.

Waneta opened the door. "Lavinia! What a surprise." She threw open the door. "Abe just called to tell us the *wunderbaar* news!" She hugged Lavinia, then called over her shoulder, "Faron! Lavinia's here!"

"Well, have her come on in!" he yelled from the back of the house.

"We were just having a snack in the kitchen," Waneta told her as she shut the door. She kept her arm around Lavinia's waist as they walked to the kitchen.

"I was hoping you and Faron were still up."

The older woman chuckled. "Lavinia, it's not late."

Faron looked up with a smile as he sat at the kitchen table. "So we finally got some *gut* news, eh?"

She nodded and smiled. "I wanted to make *schur* you knew."

Waneta urged her into a chair. "Sit. I'll make you a cup of tea." She walked over to the stove to turn the gas on under the kettle. "We're just so grateful for all you've done to help our *sohn*."

"I didn't do anything," she said quickly. "But there

is something I'd like to do. I wanted to see what you thought about it."

They listened, absorbed, as she began to tell them of her plan. Waneta held up her hand to pause Lavinia when the teakettle whistled. She quickly made a cup of tea for Lavinia and then resumed her seat. "Go on," she urged.

They both beamed at her when she finished. Lavinia drank the tea and then stood. "I need to get home. I'll call you tomorrow and we can talk some more."

"I'll walk you to the door," Waneta said, and heaved herself to her feet. She turned and gave Faron a look. "And no more cookies."

He held up his hands. "Haven't touched them."

Waneta rolled her eyes. "Now you can't say Abe ate them like you always do," she said as they started out of the kitchen.

"Woman counts them in the cookie jar," Faron complained as they walked out of the room.

Lavinia thought she heard the scrape of a chair, the clank of pottery.

"*Ya*," Waneta said with a grin when Lavinia glanced at her. "He's in the cookie jar again. I hate to warn you, dear, but men don't grow up."

She chuckled, and as Lavinia left their house, her mind raced. Now that they'd approved what she had in mind, she needed to get others on board.

She hurried to get home and talk to her own *eldres*.

* * *

Abe woke up feeling like ants were crawling all over his legs.

He tried to raise himself in his bed and slap at them, but with his broken arm still on the pulley, it was just too awkward. Desperate, he hit the call button for his nurse and asked for help.

Doreen came in a few minutes later. "Ants? Oh my goodness."

"They're crawling on both legs, but the right one seems worse."

She peeled back the sheet and blanket covering his leg and inspected it. "No ants. I think it's the tingling getting worse. I know it's irritating, but it's a good sign, remember? Feeling is coming back." She covered his leg again and gave him an encouraging smile. "I can get some lotion and put it on your legs if you want, but the feeling you're having is inside, not on your skin."

He shook his head. "No, thanks. Sorry to bother you."

"No bother at all. You're doing physical therapy this morning, right? That'll help some as they get the circulation moving."

"Then it'll feel like bigger ants?"

She laughed. "Let's hope not. Is there anything else I can do for you?"

He glanced at the clock. It was way too early for Lavinia to visit.

"I know boredom's the worst part of being here. But you won't be our guest for much longer."

Inherent good manners kept him from saying he was glad for that. She left him to take care of other patients, and he tried to find something to take his mind off the ants.

Breakfast came. He poked at it. His appetite was off. No doubt it would pick up when he got home and his *mudder*—one of the best cooks in his community—cooked some of his favorites.

A staff member, a lanky young man who liked to talk about baseball, came to collect the tray and frowned. "Not a fan of sausage gravy on biscuits, eh?"

"Not real hungry today.

"I noticed you always order milk."

"Grew up with it. I own a dairy farm."

"That's cool." He jerked his head toward the stuffed cow Lavinia had bought him. "Your cows look like that?"

"Not exactly." Looking at Molly, he found himself missing old Bessie, who was as cranky as she could be.

Two physical therapists came for him a few minutes later. Double trouble, he couldn't help thinking. They performed their torture, and the crawling ants on his legs became biting flies.

The therapists beamed. "This means your body is healing itself," one proclaimed, and the other nodded vigorously. "Nerve endings are waking up."

By the time it was over, he was exhausted and sweaty. He was never so grateful for the male nurse who helped him clean himself since he couldn't take a shower because of the cast. He wondered what he was going to do about bathing once he got home.

Worn out, he slept, then woke when something

tickled his nose. He batted at it with his hand and it tickled again. He opened his eyes, and his *dat* was leaning over him, using the stuffed cow to tickle him.

"Faron, leave the *bu* alone," he heard his *mudder* saying.

His *dat* just grinned at him. "It's boring sitting here watching him sleeping away the day."

"I'm awake," he said, and his *dat* sat back in his chair, looking pleased.

His *mudder* stood and leaned over him to brush her lips against his cheek. "It was so *gut* to hear your news. Lavinia stopped by the house yesterday to make *schur* you'd called and we knew."

"She did?"

Waneta nodded and sat again. "Such a sweet, considerate *maedel*."

He nodded and glanced at the clock. He saw he'd slept two hours, but it would be hours still before Lavinia would be visiting.

"He's counting the hours until he sees her," his *dat* said.

Abe's gaze flew to him. Was he that easy to read?

"I was a young man myself once," Faron told him with a wink.

Waneta chuckled and patted her *mann*'s hand. "Many, many years ago."

"Seems like yesterday."

"Oh, Faron, when you say things like that, I remember what it was like to be a *maedel*." She sighed and gave him a fond smile.

Abe had seen them showing their love for each other, but somehow it touched him more today than usual. He wanted this for himself—this love and support between a *mann* and his *fraa*. A bond that lasted decades through so many *gut* times and not-so-*gut* times, forged with love and faith.

Would he be able to recover enough to keep his farm afloat and to have a life one day with Lavinia?

"Abe? What's going on in that busy mind of yours?" his *mudder* asked.

"Sorry. Just a little distracted." He told them about the sensation of crawling ants, the physical therapy, and his concern about how he was going to manage when he got home.

"Well now, you know we're going to be right there in the *dawdi haus* to help you, *sohn*."

"I don't want to be a burden, *Mamm*. You shouldn't have to be taking care of me."

"That's what *familye* does, Abe. We help each other. And it won't be long before you're back on your feet."

"Wayne is doing a fine job," Faron added. "He said he can keep giving you the hours he's been working while you're here for as long as you need him."

"That's *gut*, but it's not going to be easy to pay him if milk prices continue to fall."

"Well, we'll take it one day at a time and know God's got a plan."

She reached into her tote bag and pulled out a container. "I brought you a treat."

He enjoyed the treat—chocolate chip cookies this time—and their visit. His *mudder* did most of the talking, like usual, but he enjoyed hearing what was going on in the community. They left when hospital staff began delivering supper trays.

They hadn't been gone long when his doctor came in. "Well, are you looking forward to going home?"

"Am I ever!"

"How does tomorrow sound?"

"Tomorrow? I thought you said end of week."

"Well, if you're enjoying it here that much," he teased.

"No! I want to go home!"

The doctor smiled. "Then let your family know they should expect to come bail you out of here around two or three o'clock tomorrow." With that bit of good news, he turned to leave. He nodded as he passed Lavinia entering the room.

"You'll never guess," Abe said as she approached the bed. "The doctor just said I can go home tomorrow."

"Tomorrow?" Her steps faltered. "But—"

"I know. It was a surprise to me, too. I can't wait to call my *eldres* and tell them. They left a little while ago."

She sat and seemed quiet, but maybe that was because he couldn't stop talking about how excited he was to be going home. He was disappointed when she didn't stay as long as usual, but he understood when she said she wanted to go by his farm and see if his *eldres* needed any help getting things ready for him.

"Ready?"

"Well, you know, you'll be staying in the downstairs front bedroom," she said as she stood and picked up her purse. "I'll make *schur* the bed's made, whatever your *mudder* needs done."

"Oh, *ya*, right."

"Liz said she'd be happy to give you a ride home free of charge. So I'll see you tomorrow at your house after work."

"Two o'clock can't come soon enough."

"Two o'clock," she repeated. "I'll make *schur* they know."

Abe lay wide awake most of the night, wondering if it was really going to happen...if he was really going to be discharged the next day.

Bright and early the next morning, his day nurse came in and began talking about him going home. His physical therapists visited for another session and explained that an outpatient physical therapist would visit him at home to continue the work.

It was really going to happen. He was going home.

And Lavinia showed up instead of his *eldres*. She said they stayed home to get things ready for him. He didn't think that was necessary—all he figured they had to do was put sheets on the bed in the downstairs bedroom like she'd said the day before—but he was glad she'd come.

A nurse helped him into a wheelchair and pushed him in it as Lavinia walked alongside. Liz was waiting in her van in front of the hospital.

It was really happening. It was not a dream.

It seemed to Abe that Lavinia had an air of suppressed excitement about her. Her cheeks were pink, her eyes sparkled, and her hands fluttered as she talked to the nurse wheeling him to the front door of the hospital.

The automatic doors slid open, and as he was pushed toward Liz's van, he took a deep breath. The day was warm and humid, but the air smelled fresh—not antiseptic like it did inside the hospital. The sun was shining and there wasn't a cloud in sight. It felt like freedom, even though he was still trapped in a body that wasn't working normally for him and he had to ride in a wheelchair.

It took some doing, but he was helped inside the van and buckled in with the stuffed cow beside him on the seat and Lavinia in the front with Liz.

And then they were on their way. He leaned back against the seat, exhausted from the effort.

"Okay back there?" Liz asked.

"More than okay, thanks."

Lavinia was quiet on the drive home, and Abe thought she seemed distracted. "Are you all right?"

"I'm fine. Your parents will be so happy to see you."

Before he knew it, Liz was pulling up in front of the farmhouse. Abe peered out his window, wondering why there were so many cars and buggies parked in the drive and people crowded on the lawn and porch.

And then he saw the banner stretched across the front porch. It read **WELCOME HOME, ABE!**

Chapter Nine

Abe looked at Lavinia. "What is all this? Did you plan this?"

She smiled. "Welcome home, Abe."

He was speechless.

Liz shut off the engine. "Sit tight. I'll get your wheelchair."

She was barely out of the van before Wayne and Leroy were already unloading it and wheeling it to the door. The two men helped Abe move from his seat to the chair.

Wayne pushed the chair up the walk to the house. Lavinia followed, carrying the stuffed cow she'd given Abe at the hospital.

One by one, many of the dairy farmers he knew stepped forward, welcomed him home, and offered help to him.

An *Englisch* man did so as well. "My name is Philip Smith—we met at the Dairymen's Association. Paul Bryant and Mel Miller are here as well. We want you to call on us for anything, anything at all that you need."

Abe swallowed hard. "Thank you. That means a lot."

More men stepped up, friends of Abe's from church who were farmers, carpenters, craftsmen, and construction workers. Their *fraas* joined them in greeting Abe and offering their help. His hand was shaken, his shoulders patted, and by the time the last of them greeted him, he was overwhelmed.

When the people before him parted, Abe saw that a ramp had been built over the steps to the porch and the front door.

"Wayne and I built the ramp when we heard you were coming home," Leroy told him. "We'll be over the minute you don't need it anymore and can dismantle it in two shakes."

"There's another off the back porch," Wayne said.

"That's *gut*, *danki*," he said, and heard the tremor in his voice. They'd gone to so much trouble, and wood wasn't cheap these days.

He glanced at Lavinia as she walked beside him. Then he looked closer. "Are you crying?"

"*Nee*," she said, blinking hard.

As his chair was rolled onto the porch, he saw his *eldres*. His *mudder* rushed forward to hug him. His *dat* gave him a big grin as he sat in a rocking chair he'd built himself years ago. One hand rested on his cane. The other held a cookie.

"Do you feel up to staying out here for a few minutes? Maybe have some cake and coffee?" Lavinia bent close to ask after she set the stuffed cow and her purse aside.

She gestured at the table that had been set up. It held a fancy cake with **Welcome Home, Abe** written across it in blue icing. There were several plates of cookies and a big coffeepot.

"Of course." He grinned. "When have I ever turned down cake?"

Soon everyone was standing around, eating and drinking and offering their help. Wayne, Abe's helper, surprised him by bringing Bessie to the side of the porch. She didn't look all that impressed at seeing him, but that was her way.

As Wayne led her back to the barn, Lavinia brought Abe a plate with a brownie. "I baked some for you."

He took it and bit in. "Best part of the day."

"*Nee*, it's not. I saw how you looked at Bessie."

"Old, cranky Bessie," he said, chuckling. "I did miss her."

He gazed around at the men and women chatting with each other. Both Amish and *Englisch*, from all walks of life. He knew they didn't associate with each other as much in other communities, but it had always been this way in Lancaster County—two groups that did business together, made friends with each other, helped each other in times of need.

He turned to Lavinia. "Whose idea was this gathering?"

"Depends on if you like the idea or not," she told him cautiously.

"How could I not like it? I'd be pretty ungrateful, wouldn't I?"

"Well, not everyone likes a surprise."

"I don't, usually. But it got a little lonely sometimes at the hospital." He felt himself color at the admission.

"I can imagine. I'm sorry I couldn't spend more time there."

"You were there a lot," he said. "You got me through the worst time in my life."

"That's what friends are for," she told him quietly.

But something passed between them, something deeper, more intimate. He didn't know how long they might have looked at each other without a care that anyone around them might notice, but then someone cleared her throat.

"Abe, people are leaving," his *mudder* said. "You should be thanking them for coming, say goodbye."

He tore his gaze from Lavinia and did as his *mudder* directed. When he watched the last of them walk to their cars and buggies, he realized how exhausted he felt.

"Time to get you inside and into bed for a nap."

"*Mamm*, I'm not a *kind*."

"Are you telling me you're not tired?"

Since he'd just had to smother a yawn, he couldn't deny it. But who wanted his *mudder* to talk like she was going to tuck him into bed when Lavinia was standing nearby?

"Lavinia helped me make up the bed in the downstairs

bedroom," his *mudder* was saying as Lavinia hurried ahead to hold the front door open.

Abe had slept in this bedroom once before when he'd taken a tumble from a tree as a boy and hadn't been able to climb the stairs to his second-floor bedroom. He remembered he hadn't liked it much back then. It had felt too far from the rest of the family. He'd heard noises from outside the house he'd never heard in the quiet upstairs room.

But he was an adult now, even if his *mudder* was bustling around caring for him as though he were a *kind* again. She and Lavinia helped him move from the wheelchair to the bed and take his shoes off, then offered him a pain pill and a glass of water.

He hated it. Hated having to need the help of two women to get into his bed. *Nee*, if he was honest, he hated needing Lavinia's help. It felt awful being so vulnerable when he'd always been healthy and taken care of himself.

When she moved to the bedside table to turn on a battery-operated fan, his frustration got the better of him.

"*Mamm* can do it." He knew he sounded a little irritable, but he was embarrassed and exhausted and couldn't help it. "I'll see you tomorrow."

"Abe," his *mudder* said, in that tone *mudders* used.

"He's tired. I'll go," Lavinia said softly.

And she rushed from the room.

His *mudder* switched on the fan to send a gentle breeze across him, laid a hand on his forehead, then left the room.

Home. He was home at last.

His eyes were already closing. He sank into the comfort of the bed and the quiet of the old house and knew no more.

* * *

A light rain began falling on her way home. Lavinia didn't mind. The weather had been uncomfortably hot, and it would cool things off. Besides, getting wet just added to her misery.

She tried not to feel sorry for herself for the way Abe had behaved just before she left. She told herself it was just because the day had been a lot for him. He had to be overtired and overstimulated. She knew that. Still, tears slipped down her cheeks and mixed with the raindrops. It hurt her feelings a little.

The rain was mercifully brief. This was the time of year when farmers hurried to get crops harvested.

When she walked into the kitchen of her home, she winced at the wave of heat that hit her. Two battery-operated fans were aimed at the stove and the kitchen window was open, but it didn't do much to help cool things off. The scent of tomato sauce hung heavy on the air.

"Great timing," her *schweschder* Sadie said as she turned from the stove. She wiped the back of her hand across her forehead. "I canned a big batch of the tomatoes from the kitchen garden." She gestured at the rows of glass mason jars sitting on the kitchen counter.

Lavinia went straight for the pitcher of iced tea in the refrigerator and got two glasses from the cupboard. "Sit," she said as she poured the tea. "You look exhausted."

"Happy to get off my feet," Sadie said, taking a seat at the table. She rubbed her baby bump under her apron, then ran the cold glass over her forehead before she took a sip. "You look wet. Is it raining?"

"*Ya.* It felt *gut*, though, to walk home in it. It was hot today."

"So did Abe get to come home today?"

She nodded. "He was surprised at all the people who showed up to welcome him home." Remembering, she pressed her lips together. "I don't think he had any idea so many people cared about him."

She told Sadie about the turnout of Amish and *Englisch*, about the offers of help.

Sadie nodded. "That's Lancaster County. Full of *gut* hearts." She tilted her head and studied Lavinia. "How are you feeling?"

"Me? I'm fine."

"Are you? I know you've been so worried about Abe. If you looked in a mirror, you'd see you're the one who looks exhausted."

She shrugged. "He's home now, so I won't be going out to the hospital to see him. I'll be working at the shop more, be home more."

"It looked like the two of you were getting serious about each other before this happened."

Emotion swamped her. "He's become my whole

world," she blurted out, then pressed her fingers to her lips.

She took a deep breath, forced herself to think positively. "He's getting better. Feeling's coming back in his legs. He'll be having physical therapy at home. And his *eldres* are back from their visit out of state. I'm taking things one day at a time. I don't know what will happen now."

Sadie reached over, grasped her hand, and squeezed it. "I had the feeling he was going to ask you to marry him before this."

"I did, too." She sighed. "But Sadie, he's been so worried about his farm. What happened to him…complicates things."

"It seems like it's even more important for people to be together when times are hard."

She smiled. "Seems like the happily married always want to see everyone else married."

Sadie laughed and stood. "You should listen to us." She set her glass in the sink. "I'm going home now to fix supper for my *familye*."

"*Mamm* should be home from work soon," Lavinia said as she glanced at the clock. "I need to start supper, too."

She waved a hand in front of her face. "I'm thinking something cold. Maybe haystacks."

Sadie picked up several jars of tomato sauce and gave Lavinia a rueful glance. "After canning this all day, I don't think I'll be making spaghetti for supper."

After she left, Lavinia sat there staring at the jars of

ruby-red tomato sauce lined up on the kitchen counter. It was harvest time, so it was no wonder Sadie had brought up Lavinia's relationship with Abe. After the hard work of harvest was over, couples were free to marry. She knew there would be wedding after wedding after wedding.

In the deep chambers of her heart, she'd had hopes Abe would ask her to marry him. Now she had to lock away that hope, set aside that dream. A man and a woman took a vow for better or worse, for richer or poorer, in sickness and health. She was willing to marry Abe no matter what, but she didn't know how he felt. Would Abe want to marry before he was on his feet and back to working his farm? He needed to concentrate on his recovery. She couldn't see him asking her until things were better.

She sighed. Would it matter if they had to wait a year to get married? If they loved each other, it shouldn't matter, should it? But she knew the answer to that question. Married couples got to be together, spend more time with each other. They *belonged* to each other. Worked together. Shared dreams. Had *kinner* together.

She sighed again and forced herself to get up and start supper. Soon she was browning hamburger with some chopped onion and garlic and cutting big, ripe tomatoes and a just-picked head of lettuce.

The kitchen door opened and her *dat* came in. He took off his hat, hung it on a peg, and walked to the sink to wash his hands. "Something smells *gut*."

"I thought haystacks would be nice on a hot day like this."

He nodded. "I could eat one a mountain high."

She set the glass before him as he sat at the table. "*Mamm* should be home soon. Do you need a snack to tide you over? Maybe some cheese and crackers?" She knew he'd worked hard all day out in the hot sun.

"Sounds *gut* to me."

She quickly put together a plate of cheese cubes, crackers, and slices of apple. He munched happily while she finished browning and draining the hamburger and set it aside.

"So did Abe make it home from the hospital today? I was sorry I couldn't make it there."

"*Ya.*" She sat at the table to chop fresh vegetables for the haystacks and told him about the gathering at Abe's house. "We really surprised him." She blinked hard at the tears that threatened to fall.

He laid a big, work-roughened hand over hers and patted it. "Now, now, no need to cry. Everything's going to be *allrecht*."

She sniffed. "I know. It's just the onions making me cry."

"*Schur.* Except you haven't started chopping them yet," he said gently.

Lavinia looked down and saw he was right. The onion sat at the corner of the cutting board and hadn't been touched.

She shook her head. "I know I should be grateful he's getting back the feeling in his legs. That he's home now. But I was hoping things would be so much better. It feels like he has a mountain to climb."

"Seems to me that he's been blessed to have you as a *gut* friend. That he has so many other friends as well who welcomed him home and offered help." He popped the last cheese cube in his mouth and reached for one of the black olives in the dish before Lavinia.

"He has." She took a deep breath and resumed chopping the head of lettuce. Such a bounty of fresh, delicious vegetables this time of year.

By the time her *mudder* walked in the door, Lavinia had gathered and chopped all the ingredients and had them sitting on a lazy Susan her *dat* had made for his *fraa* one Christmas.

"It's a nice night," Amos said with satisfaction as the three of them gathered at the table and they bent their heads in prayer. "Both of you home for supper."

Lavinia broke up a handful of tortilla chips and put them in the bowl in front of her, then layered beef, rice, and all the chopped vegetables—except green pepper. She'd never liked the taste of green pepper. Shredded cheese went next, then salsa last. Lavinia always thought of haystacks as summer in a bowl.

She knew without looking how her *eldres* assembled their haystacks. Her *mudder* favored lots of black olives on hers, and her *dat* was particularly fond of the extra-hot salsa. That was what made it a favorite of her *familye* as well as other Amish *familyes*: everyone got to make the haystack to their liking. And it was a nice cooling supper during the hot harvest season.

Lavinia took a smaller amount of each of the ingredients than usual tonight and poked at it more than ate it. She didn't have much of an appetite. Her mood was too unsettled and she felt too tired to eat, even though it was only seven o'clock.

If her *eldres* noticed, they didn't say anything. Her *mudder* chatted about her day and her *dat* talked about how the harvesting had gone.

When he was done, her *dat* pushed away from the table and stood. "That was delicious, Lavinia. Rachel, I'm going out to the barn to finish up chores."

Lavinia rose and began clearing the table. Her *mudder* reached out to touch her arm. "Sit, Lavinia. Talk to me. I can see something is wrong."

"I'm just tired, *Mamm*. It's been a long day."

Rachel shook her head. "I think your spirit is tired more than your body."

"Maybe. We're both tired. You've had more work on you because I've been with Abe. Why don't you go sit in the living room, put your feet up, and relax?"

Rachel studied her and then sighed. "*Allrecht*, I'll do that if you really don't want to talk now. When you're ready, let me know." She stood and hugged Lavinia, then left the room.

Lavinia filled the sink with water and dishwashing liquid and barely noticed when tears slid down her cheeks and plopped into it. The day felt like an anticlimax, not like the high she'd expected.

Chapter Ten

Rachel raised her eyebrows at Lavinia as she descended the stairs the next morning and walked into the kitchen with her work tote. She set it on the bench by the kitchen door.

"What's in that?" she asked, looking over as she stood at the stove.

"Finished the rug I was working on last night," she said. "Couldn't sleep."

She walked over and kissed her *mudder*'s cheek before pouring herself a cup of coffee. "Mmm, pancakes."

Rachel flipped two pancakes onto a plate and handed it to her. Amos came in, sniffed the air, and grinned.

"Mmm. Pancakes." He washed his hands quickly, grabbed a cup of coffee, and sat at the head of the table.

Lavinia pushed the little pitcher of maple syrup

toward him and watched as he buttered his pancakes before lavishly pouring the syrup over them. Simple pleasures, she thought. Coffee and pancakes at a big wooden table. Dawn sending pink fingers of light in the window. A day of work you loved to look forward to. New people to greet and regulars to see again. Seemingly ordinary days that had a quiet satisfaction to them.

She was looking forward to no longer visiting the hospital. Those days had never been quite without worry, no matter how much she tried.

Rachel settled herself at the table with her own plate of pancakes and a cup of coffee. When Lavinia saw that her *dat* had finished his stack and looked hopefully at the stove, she rose and took his plate over to add more from the sheet pan piled with pancakes that her *mudder* had kept warming in the oven.

"I made a pitcher of tea and sandwiches and left them in the refrigerator for you for lunch," Rachel told him. "Don't get so busy you forget to get out of the sun and take a break."

"Now there's no need to talk to me like I'm your *kind*," he said, but Lavinia saw him give his *fraa* a fond look.

"I know you."

He squeezed her hand and set about demolishing his second helping of pancakes.

They left for work a little while later. Lavinia carried her purse, her lunch, and the tote bag with the new rug as well. At least she had something tangible to show for the hours she hadn't been able to sleep.

"Another rug?" Liz asked when they climbed into the van for the ride to the shop. "Can I see it?"

Lavinia took it out and held it up for her to see. She'd made an oval rug with fabric scraps in pastel colors.

"So pretty. I can just see that in a girl's bedroom." She checked for traffic and pulled out onto the road. "I have to find time to drop by your shop soon. I have lots of family to buy Christmas gifts for this year."

"Never too early to start," Rachel said.

Lavinia helped open up and set about unpacking and pricing new crafts before displaying them on the shelves and in the front shop window. This was the part of the job she had always enjoyed the most. Working on displays in the shop was a *wunderbaar* way to be creative.

Remembering what Liz had said about the rug looking like something that belonged in a girl's room, she took one of the cloth Amish dolls that Sarah, one of their vendors, made and set it on top of the rug.

"That looks pretty," her *mudder* said as she came to stand beside her.

"I just need a few things," Lavinia murmured. "Things aren't quite the way I want them yet."

"I can just see those wheels spinning around in your head. Why don't you take a break, get some air?"

"I've taken too much time away lately. You and Sadie have had to take on more so that I could be with Abe."

"Life isn't just about *familye* and work and community, Lavinia," Rachel said gently. "We need to find time to renew ourselves, to fill the well inside us, or we have nothing left to give to others."

Lavinia sighed. "You're right. But after I come back, then you have to do the same."

Rachel smiled. "I will."

So Lavinia took her purse and went for a walk.

It was already warm, but not as muggy as it had been the day before. She cast a glance at the sky and, with the skill of a farmer's daughter, judged the day would get hotter but there would be no rain—*gut* for farmers harvesting their crops.

She found herself heading toward the quilt shop owned by her friend Hannah to see what she was doing.

Hannah looked up from sewing a quilt as Lavinia walked into the shop and greeted her with a smile. A loud shriek came from the crib in the corner. Hannah's new *boppli* looked up and waved a chubby fist at her.

Lavinia detoured to pick her up and give her a hug. "She's getting so big."

"Had her six-month checkup yesterday. The doctor says she's doing very well."

She hugged her close. How *wunderbaar* it felt to hold such a sweet little *boppli*.

Hannah got up to ring up a purchase for a customer, then returned to her seat at the quilting table. "So did Abe go home yesterday as planned?"

"He did."

"I wish I could have attended his welcome-home party."

"*Danki* for sending over so many cookies for the refreshment table. It couldn't have been easy to make them after a long day of work and with a *kind*."

"Gideon helped." She grinned. "Of course, he ate a number of them while he helped. Said he was quality control."

Lavinia laughed. She glanced around at the shop. It was so cheerful with all the colorful bolts of fabric and completed quilts hung on the walls and displayed on tables.

"Say, would you be willing to loan us a few skeins of yarn and some knitting needles? I want to use them for a display. I'll put your business card in with it."

"*Schur.* Pick out what you want." Hannah picked up her *boppli* and walked with her around the shop.

Lavinia grabbed a wicker shopping basket and walked over to the shelves of yarn, determinedly looking away from the table of fine fabrics prominently displayed for Amish brides this time of year.

"I'm thinking of stopping at Gideon's shop, too." She selected several skeins and put them in the basket.

"Eli and Emma are there today while Gideon is working on some Christmas orders."

She picked up two sets of knitting needles and carried her basket to the checkout counter. "I want to fill a big wooden bowl Naiman made with these, and another with fruit."

"Clever." Hannah put the items in a shopping bag and added her card.

They chatted for a few minutes more, and then Lavinia left to visit the toy shop. There John sat in a corner, playing with some cars his *onkel* had carved from wood, making zoom-zoom noises as he raced them along the floor.

Eli, Gideon's *zwillingboppli bruder*, was on the phone. He waved at Lavinia as she walked down the aisles to look at the toys.

How quickly time passed, she thought. It seemed like it was only yesterday when Emma Graber had come back to town with her *boppli* John, wanting Eli, his *dat*, to take responsibility for him, give him a home. Eli hadn't been ready to be a *dat* when Emma told him she was pregnant. So Emma had done the only thing she thought she could do and moved away.

When she came back, Eli had realized what he'd missed, and they'd worked things out. Now he and Emma and John were a *familye* living in the *familye* farmhouse, with Gideon and his *fraa* Hannah in their own home nearby on the property.

She sighed. It helped to remember that things could turn out well. It was such a bad time for Abe right now. She understood that. She needed to be a friend to him, and maybe one day they could be more. And maybe they'd have their own happy ending.

Yesterday, after the party, had felt like a setback. But it was natural to have setbacks in this...whatever this relationship was. She had to take it one day at a time. With a sigh, she chose two cloth dolls and took them up to Eli at the counter.

* * *

Abe's first day at home started out so differently from those in the hospital. He woke up surprised to see sunlight coming in his window. He'd slept through the night. It took a minute for him to realize he was in the downstairs bedroom of his home. And that he'd slept soundly because a nurse hadn't come in to take his blood pressure—and sometimes vials of his blood—in the middle of the night.

The clock on the bedside table said eight o'clock. While he was in the hospital, he'd gotten out of the habit of waking before the sun came up to do his chores. He needed to get back on that schedule, even if he couldn't do the chores for a while.

He smelled coffee. Levering himself up, he reached for his wheelchair and pulled it closer. The therapists at the hospital had worked with him on transferring safely from bed to chair. He locked the wheels and worked at maneuvering himself into the chair. It wasn't easy. He had most of the feeling back in his legs, but they still were like rubber, and he had to be careful not to use the arm in the cast. But he was determined to do it without calling for his *mudder*.

By the time he was seated in the chair and rolling out the door, his face was damp with perspiration. He grabbed a washcloth in the bathroom, dampened it and wiped his face, ran a comb through his hair, and decided he needed coffee before he tried changing from pajamas to regular clothes.

"Well, look who decided to finally get up." His *dat* grinned at him. "If it isn't Rip Van Winkle."

"Very funny." He pushed his wheelchair over to the end of the table where he usually sat and noticed his regular chair had been removed so that he could pull up to it.

"I looked in earlier and you were sleeping, so I decided to let you be," his *mudder* said as she put a mug of coffee in front of him.

"*Danki.* You don't get much sleep in the hospital."

He noticed his *dat* had pushed his empty plate aside and was drinking coffee. Abe had a funny feeling his *dat* had gotten a later start to his morning than back when he'd had to be up early to milk the cows.

Waneta set a plate of bacon, *dippy* eggs, and fried potatoes in front of him. He thanked her and began eating, thinking how the day seemed so ordinary, so much like so many other days he'd started in this old farmhouse.

And yet it was so very different. He sat here feeling trapped in his chair, needing to ask his *mudder* for more coffee instead of jumping up to pour it himself, for a cloth when he spilled his coffee and had to wipe it up. He wouldn't be out milking his cows and doing his morning chores.

Wayne came in, hung his straw hat on a peg by the door, then nodded at him as he washed his hands. Waneta rose to fix him a plate, and it felt as if they were a *familye* enjoying a meal instead of Wayne being an employee. It had always been so. Wayne's *familye* owned a farm that raised vegetables, but one day after *schul*, he'd stopped by and watched Abe and his *dat* working with the dairy cows and asked for a job. He'd started off working after *schul*, and now, in his early twenties like Abe, was a tall, lanky man who Abe had come to feel was a friend, not just a helper.

He ate quickly, not talking much. That was no surprise. He'd been up since before dawn, and this was his first meal of the day. Waneta poured him a second cup of coffee, resting a hand on his shoulder as comfortably as she had Abe's, and asked if he wanted anything else. He shook his head, thanked her, and then looked at Abe.

"Do you want to go out and see how things are going?" he asked politely.

Abe felt his spirits rise. "If you don't mind pushing the chair."

Wayne rose and walked over. "Don't mind a'tall."

The cows were grazing in the pasture and didn't pay him much mind. Wayne pushed the chair into the cow barn, and the sights and scents of it made Abe feel more at home than his house had. There had been times when he lay in the hospital and wondered if he'd ever see it again.

"Everything looks *gut*," he told Wayne.

"*Danki.* Your *dat* helped a lot."

He pushed the chair back outside, and Bessie wandered over to the fence. She gave Abe a glance, then returned to chewing her cud.

"I think she missed you," Wayne said, giving her an affectionate pat.

"I can't thank you enough for all you've done while I was in the hospital."

"Enjoyed it." He pushed the wheelchair back toward the house. "Does it feel *gut* to be back?"

"It *schur* does."

"No climbing on the roof for a while."

"*Nee.*"

He would have said more, but he saw a car pull up in the drive. He sighed. "And the morning was going so well."

"Visitor?"

"Torturer," Abe muttered as a woman who looked to be in her forties got out of the car. "Quick, push me back in the barn."

"Huh?"

Before Wayne could act, the woman, dressed in scrubs and carrying a folder in her hands, glanced over and saw them. "Abe Stoltzfus?"

He could hardly deny it. "That's me."

"Bess Thurman. Your at-home physical therapist." She looked at Wayne. "I can push him into the house."

"Yes, ma'am."

Bess pushed Abe's chair up the backdoor ramp and into the kitchen. Waneta stood at the sink, washing dishes. Bess introduced herself and turned down the offer of coffee.

"Where are we going to work?" she asked Abe.

"My bedroom's in the front," he said, and she pushed him in that direction.

Bess helped him go from the chair to the bed, which his *mudder* had come in and made up. She took a seat on the chair beside the bed and opened his file. She laid out what she called his therapy plan in a brisk, no-nonsense manner, and then proceeded to do the same type of manipulations on his legs that his hospital therapists had done, but with more vigor.

He was exhausted when she finished and barely able to thank her as she left—his *mudder* had taught him manners—before he felt himself conking out.

When he woke, the room felt warm in spite of the battery-operated fan his *mudder* must have come into the room to turn on. The muscles in his legs ached as he struggled into his chair again. When he wheeled through the living room, his *dat* looked up from his newspaper.

"Well, sleepyhead. Wondered when you'd stir."

He folded the paper and got up, reaching for his cane. "Your *mudder* has your lunch waiting for you in the kitchen. I'll have a glass of iced tea and keep you company while you eat."

Abe had just finished his sandwich when he had a sudden thought. "Wayne. He hasn't been paid."

"I asked him if he'd been paid since you were in the hospital, and he said he could wait until you got home," Faron told him.

Abe shook his head. "Grab my checkbook and my bill folder from the drawer there, would you, please?" Armed with it, he wheeled himself out onto the front porch and spent the next hour writing checks and balancing his checkbook.

When Wayne came to report that the afternoon milking had been done and asked if he needed anything else, Abe shook his head and handed him his check.

"I'm so sorry you had to wait for this."

"I told your *dat* it was no problem."

"Well, I appreciate that, but I'm sorry there was a delay. And thanks for the extra hours you've been putting in."

Wayne nodded. "Glad to help. You just think about getting well and don't worry about things."

Ya, he was a friend, not an employee, Abe thought as Wayne left to go home.

Abe felt depression falling onto his shoulders as heavily as a blanket as he stared out at the road and felt life passing him by. Buggies rolled down it. Cars whizzed past. Everyone was going somewhere. And here he sat thinking about how empty his bank account was and how useless he felt.

His *mudder* came out with a glass of iced tea and a plate of cookies, and he thanked her for the snack. She sat in the rocking chair and rocked silently.

"What time is it?" he asked her.

"Just after three."

Hours yet before Lavinia got off work. And he'd acted less friendly than he should have yesterday after the welcome-home party—who knew if she'd even stop by to see him?

"Well, you just gonna sit here and brood?" his *mudder* asked.

No sympathy for the pitiful here, he thought. "What else can I do?"

"You can help me with some canning in the kitchen," she told him.

He took a deep breath and nodded. "*Schur*, I'll help you." As she pushed his chair inside, he figured doing something might make him feel a little more positive.

Chapter Eleven

Lavinia couldn't help looking for Abe on the front porch of his house as Liz drove past it that evening.

She wasn't surprised when she saw him sitting there in his wheelchair. What *did* surprise her was seeing what he was doing. He wasn't snapping green beans, was he? She craned her neck to look back as the van passed the farmhouse.

"See something interesting?" her *mudder* asked, keeping her voice low.

Lavinia turned and saw the twinkle in her eye. She shrugged. "Just surprised to see Abe on his porch."

"I'm *schur* Liz would stop and let you out if you want to visit with him."

"Maybe later. We need to get supper on the table. *Daed* will be starved after working in the fields. And I should do a little work in the garden before it gets dark, since Sadie didn't come today."

She didn't want to tell her *mudder* that she thought it might be best to let Abe settle in more first. She hadn't told her that he'd hurt her feelings snapping at her yesterday when she and his *mudder* helped him into bed after the welcome-home party. She knew he was tired and she shouldn't have let it bother her, but it did.

When they walked into the kitchen, they found Amos poking in the refrigerator. He backed away from it, looking guilty.

"Amos Fisher! What are you up to?"

He grinned and brought his hand out from behind his back and took a bite out of a chicken leg. "I got hungry. Couldn't wait for supper."

Lavinia turned to her *mudder*. "Told you."

Rachel chuckled. "So you did." After putting her purse and lunch tote down on the bench by the door, she walked over to the refrigerator. She kissed her *mann* on the cheek. "Sit and I'll get something on the table as quick as I can."

Lavinia put down her own things and went to the sink to wash her hands. She set the table and poured glasses of tea, then hurried outside with a basket to gather up several tomatoes and cucumbers. Then, after checking to see if her *mudder* needed any help, she set the table and chatted with her *dat*.

As soon as she'd eaten supper, she looked to her *mudder*, and Rachel chuckled. "Our *dochder* can't wait to leave us. Go," she said. "Your *dat* and I will do the dishes."

"We will?" he asked.

"We did before she got old enough to help," she reminded him.

"*Ya*, we did," he said, and his eyes twinkled as he leaned over and kissed her cheek. "I remember how we used to—"

"Amos!"

Lavinia shot to her feet and started for the door. "Bye!"

She heard her *dat*'s chuckle as she rushed out the kitchen door.

The evening was still warm, but the walk to Abe's house was short. Honeysuckle and jasmine scented the air. Her steps slowed as she reached the house, and she hesitated when she saw him sitting on the front porch. Should she have waited another day? Called first?

"Lavinia!" Abe called.

Taking a deep breath, she walked up the ramp and stepped onto the porch. "How are you?"

"*Gut*. How are you?"

"*Gut*."

They stared at each other.

"Are you going to sit down?" he asked.

"I wasn't *schur* if I should come."

"Why not?"

She bit her lip. "Yesterday—"

"I'm sorry," he said quickly. "I was tired, and it felt awkward having you tend me like a *kind*. I'm really sorry."

"I didn't tend you like a *kind*," she countered. "You needed help and I wanted to give it to you."

Abe looked down at his hands, then up at her. "I know. I sound ungrateful. I don't like needing help. Bad enough my *mudder* had to be there, but—"

"But then a female friend," she finished for him.

He nodded. "Will you sit? Please?"

Lavinia took a seat in the rocking chair beside his wheelchair. Neither spoke. Silence stretched between them, punctuated by the creak of the rocking chair as she set it into motion with a push of her foot.

"So how was your day?" she asked finally.

"A little boring," he confessed, after glancing over his shoulder at the front door. "Wayne took me out to the cow barn, but I can't help much," he amended. "But it's *gut* to see the cows."

"Especially cranky Bessie."

He chuckled. "Especially cranky Bessie." He rolled his shoulders. "And I met the physical therapist who'll be coming to the house. She was . . . strict. I'm feeling a little sore."

She might have offered some sympathy, but the front screen door opened and Waneta stepped out with a glass of iced tea.

"Why, Lavinia, what a nice surprise!" she said as she set the glass on the table beside Abe. "Can I get you a glass of tea?"

"I don't want to put you to any trouble."

"It's no trouble." She bustled off and returned with the tea and a plate of sugar cookies.

"How are your *eldres*?" she asked Lavinia.

"They're *gut*. We've been busy at the shop. *Daed* has been working hard in the fields like usual."

They chatted for a few minutes until Waneta glanced at Abe, then excused herself and went back inside the house.

Silence hung on the warm summer air.

"Well, I guess I should go. You're probably tired."

Abe laid his hand on hers, and, startled, she jerked her head and stared at him.

"Don't go," he said quietly, so quietly it was almost as if he whispered the words. "Please."

Abe studied the way his hand looked on Lavinia's. He'd watched Liz's van drive past earlier and found himself wondering if she would stop by to see him. After all, he knew he'd snapped at her yesterday as she helped him. He was usually even-tempered, not known for being irritable or out of sorts. But he'd been exhausted, stressed, and overwhelmed at seeing all those people who'd come to welcome him home. He was a quiet man, used to spending his days working on his farm, his only company Wayne... and his cows. He was probably better at talking to his cows than to people. So he'd talked to those who'd come, shook hand after hand, and made conversation. It was a lot after days of lying in a bed staring at the ceiling, his only company the brief times Lavinia and his *eldres* could visit.

"Tell me about your day," he said.

"My day?" She smiled. "It wasn't all that interesting."

He stared out at the fields across from the house. "I've come to appreciate little things more since the accident."

She nodded. "I call them simple pleasures. I was

sitting at the table this morning eating the pancakes *Mamm* made us for breakfast and thinking how much I appreciated something that simple."

"I didn't think I took them for granted before, but I did."

He reluctantly took his hand from hers and rubbed at a muscle in his thigh that chose that moment to spasm. "I'll think of something I want to do, start to get up, and realize I can't. I took the simple act of walking, of doing things for myself, for granted."

"You'll be able to do them again soon."

He nodded. "I know. But things have changed. Money was tight before this, and now..." He trailed off, glancing at the stack of bills the mail carrier had brought that afternoon.

"What is it?" she asked, obviously seeing the direction of his gaze.

"Bills from the hospital. I haven't had the courage to open them."

"You shouldn't worry. You know we help each other out here."

"There's that word 'help' again. I hate to ask for the help. We had a lot of hospital and doctor bills this past year, what with one member having a buggy accident and the chemotherapy for another—"

"It's part of being a community," she reminded him. "We found a way. God provided." She picked up the plate of cookies and offered it to him. "Don't you remember what our teacher Phoebe used to say?"

"'Abe, stop running in the classroom'?"

She laughed. "Well, *schur*, she said that a lot to you when you were a *bu*. You had only one speed and that was fast. *Nee*, I'm talking about what she said about worry. Do you remember?"

"'God knows what He's doing.'"

"*Ya.*"

"So let's talk about something else," he said. "Tell me about your day."

She shrugged. "It wasn't much different than usual. I unpacked new stock, set it out on shelves. Did a new display window." She took a sip of her tea. "Oh, I walked to Hannah's and saw her and her new *boppli*. Then I went to Gideon's shop and saw John. He's growing so fast!"

"Did you have many customers?"

She nodded. "We stayed busy. People are already talking about buying Christmas presents."

Christmas felt so far away sitting here.

The whole world felt far away right now. He listened to her talk about the people she'd encountered that day, what they'd said, what she'd seen as she walked around town. Her face grew animated, her eyes sparkled, and her hands moved so expressively.

He'd always thought she was pretty, but at that moment, in the fading glow of sunset, she looked beautiful.

And so out of his reach.

"Abe?"

"Hmm?"

"I'm sorry, I'm rattling on."

"*Nee*, I like listening to you," he said quickly. "You love your work and it shows."

"I know you love yours, too. And you'll get to do it again soon."

He flexed the fingers on his left hand. His legs weren't his only hindrance. The broken arm also made him feel trapped in his own body. He shook away the thoughts. Now wasn't the time to brood when he had this woman he'd waited to see all day here with him.

"So do you think you'll be attending church on Sunday?" she asked him.

"Church?"

She smiled. "*Ya.* You do remember church, don't you?"

"*Ya.* Of course."

"Everyone will be glad to see you, see that you're doing well."

He flashed back to the welcome-home party again, remembering how it had felt to suddenly be in the midst of all those people.

"I'm not *schur* I'm ready to go yet."

"Well, you have a couple of days to think about it. There's a singing later that evening, but that might be a long day for you."

He heard the wistful note in her voice. They'd attended singings often before the accident and enjoyed sharing the music of their faith. He'd enjoyed even more giving her a ride home and taking the long way there. They'd begun dating after the first time he asked if he could give her a lift.

"We'll see," he found himself saying, and he hoped he'd be able to manage going to church—a three-hour-long service—and then the singing in the evening. Maybe if he rested in between…

"Well, I should be going," she said.

He wanted to ask her to stay, but she'd had a long day and *schur* hadn't had a nap like he had.

"See you tomorrow?" he asked.

She nodded. "Tomorrow."

"*Danki* for coming," he told her. "It was so *gut* to see you."

He was rewarded with a big smile before she left. He watched her walk away, so slim and graceful, and craned his neck as she disappeared in the gathering indigo shadows of evening.

Chapter Twelve

Lavinia leaned forward and put her hand on her *dat*'s shoulder. "*Daed!* That's Abe's buggy!"

He glanced back as their horse pulled their buggy into the drive of the Lapp house, where church services would take place today. "*Ya*, it is. So?"

She held her breath as she watched two of the men from church walk over to join Abe. One pulled a wheelchair from the buggy and unfolded it. Then the men reached inside, lifted Abe out, and settled him into the chair. One pushed it up the walk, and when they reached the stairs to the porch, other men joined them and they lifted Abe in the chair up the stairs onto the porch.

Lavinia couldn't see Abe's face. She wondered how he felt about having to accept the help of his fellow church members after what he'd said about needing help right now.

By the time her *dat* had pulled up to the front of the house to let her and her *mudder* out, Abe had disappeared inside.

Rachel glanced at her as they went up the walk. "You seem surprised Abe is here today."

Lavinia nodded. "He didn't sound like he wanted to come when I talked to him a couple days ago. He didn't want to ask for help."

It was her *mudder*'s turn to nod. "Most men find it hard to ask for help."

They climbed the stairs and went inside the house. Benches had been set up in two sections—one for women, one for men. Lavinia saw that Abe's wheelchair sat at the back of the men's section. Chairs had been used to fill out the rest of the space a bench would have taken. The men who'd helped him from the buggy and carried the chair up the stairs sat beside him talking.

Abe glanced up just then, and their gazes locked. He looked pale, but he smiled and nodded at her. Relieved, she smiled and stopped by to say hello to her *schweschder* Sadie, who was sitting in the back row with her *dochder*, little Anna Mae.

"You go ahead and sit up front like usual," Sadie whispered to her. "I have to be back here so I can be close to the bathroom." Her hand rested on her baby bump.

Lavinia leaned down and kissed Anna Mae's cheek.

She looked just like her *mudder* with her flyaway blond hair and big blue eyes. Then she turned her attention back to Sadie, who was just glowing in her second pregnancy. "Hope you can come to supper later this week. We don't see enough of you."

Sadie nodded. "See you later."

Lavinia and her *mudder* proceeded to the front of the women's section and sat on the bench next to each other.

She glanced back and saw that everyone who walked in stopped to say hello to Abe. It felt *gut* that they were happy to see him attending church. Peace settled over her as the service began. Lay minister Elmer always had a message that resonated with her, and the singing . . . well, Lavinia loved singing the old hymns.

Which reminded her that she'd asked Abe if he'd attend the singing the young people enjoyed on church Sundays. She cast a furtive glance in his direction to see how well he was faring and saw him shifting in his chair and rubbing his thigh with his free hand. She frowned and wondered if he'd be able to last the three hours of the service. No one would blame him if he needed to leave early.

Relief swept over her when the service ended and she glanced back and saw Abe had made it through and didn't look the worse for wear. She rose and made her way to the back of the room to congratulate him, but several people stood talking to him, so she walked to the kitchen to help with serving coffee and the light meal.

The first chance she got, she carried a cup of coffee and a plate with a slice of bread covered with church spread out to Abe. He'd always loved the sweet mixture of peanut butter and marshmallow creme on a slice of bread.

"*Danki*," he said as she put the coffee cup and the plate down on the bench beside him.

"I wasn't *schur* you'd come today."

He looked over to where his *mudder* stood talking with his *dat*. "*Mamm* had a lot to do with it," he said quietly, keeping an eye on her. "She said I could sit here as well as I could sit at home and maybe I'd hear something I should."

"And did you?"

"Nothing quite as *gut* as what the bishop said when he visited me in the hospital."

"Oh? And what was that?"

"He said maybe I should think of myself more as Joseph than Job."

She was prevented from saying anything when Elmer came up and greeted Abe. She left them to talk and went back to the kitchen. There she picked up a pot and went back out to roam the room, pouring coffee and chatting with friends.

"Lavinia, I'd love some coffee," Ben, a classmate of hers and Abe's, said with a warm smile as he held out his cup. "You look well," he told her as his gaze swept over her.

She blushed. Ben had been a charmer all his life. "*Danki*, Ben. You do as well."

"I was wondering if you're going to the singing tonight?"

"I am," she said, and tried not to look in Abe's direction.

"Then I'll see you there."

She nodded and turned when her *dat* hailed her from his seat a few feet away.

"Any coffee left for your old *dat*?" he asked, holding his cup out. His blue eyes twinkled. "I see you have another young man's attention."

She frowned, not understanding at first. "Ben? I went to *schul* with him and he constantly teased me, remember?"

"He's not looking at you like the *bu* who pulled your pigtails when you were little."

"Don't be silly." But when she glanced back at him, she saw Ben was indeed looking at her the way a man did a woman he was attracted to. She wondered if she had missed that look before today.

Well, it didn't matter. She was interested in Abe. She looked over at him and saw that he was watching her with a thoughtful look on his face.

She poured more coffee and worked her way over to him. "So, did you think about going to the singing this evening? I could pick you up."

He stared at her for a long moment, then looked past her. "Sorry, I don't think so. I'm feeling really tired."

"Maybe you'll feel like it after you have a rest." She gave him an encouraging smile.

"I don't think so. Maybe next time."

Disappointed, she nodded. "Just give me a call if you change your mind."

He looked past her. "Have you seen my *dat*? I want to go home now."

"I'll find him. Take care."

She hurried away, feeling let down and chiding herself for it. It couldn't have been easy for Abe to come to church today when he hadn't been out of the hospital long. It was important for her to remember that she needed to be grateful he was looking better each day, that he had come through so much.

"There you are!" she said when she spotted Waneta and Faron at the back of the room. "Abe says he wants to go home now."

Faron nodded. "Would you mind telling him I'm going to get the buggy? I'll ask a few friends to help us get him down the stairs and into it."

"*Schur.* Oh, and I asked him if he'd like to go to the singing later, and he said he was tired. I'm hoping he'll change his mind. I can pick him up. I think it'd be *gut* for him to get out."

"I'll work on him," Waneta said with a conspiratorial wink.

She blushed. "*Danki*, Waneta."

Maybe it wasn't fair to use his *mudder* like that, but Lavinia told herself she was just thinking of Abe. He had always so enjoyed singing, and she loved hearing his rich baritone singing songs of faith. He needed those more than ever before. When she sang hymns, she always felt the words reverberate through her, making her heart-strong and confident all would be well with her world.

* * *

"You doing *allrecht* back there?" Waneta called over her shoulder as the *familye* rode home in their buggy.

"Fine." He was stretched out in the back seat, worn out with exhaustion after the long church service and talking with so many people. The rolling motion of the buggy was lulling him to sleep.

"Tell me you're glad you went," Waneta said.

"Don't nag the *bu*," Faron told her.

"Not nagging. Asking."

Abe would have made a face, but he didn't dare. He'd learned years ago that his *mudder* had eyes in the back of her head.

"*Ya.*" It wasn't a lie. He'd been glad he'd gone to the effort of going to the service for a while...he'd gotten a chance to see Lavinia, even if it was only briefly.

Then he frowned, remembering how he'd watched Ben flirting with her. Ben had made plenty of plays for her attention, but she'd never been interested in him. Abe had never figured out why she'd been attracted to him rather than Ben. He thought Ben was better-looking, with dark brown hair and blue eyes and a way of charming the *maedels* Abe had never had. Ben also had a prosperous farm and no obvious money problems. Why, Abe had heard that Ben had invested a lot of money on more livestock and equipment recently.

Meanwhile, Abe sat in the back seat of the buggy, being carted home by his *eldres*, aching all over from the enforced hours of sitting and pretending he was fine when he felt distant from all those around him.

He slumped in his seat and felt himself sinking into a depression. It was going to be a long haul back to normal for him. Even after he recovered his physical health, he wasn't *schur* he would be able to pull his farm back to prosperity with the milk market the way it was.

If he was a *gut* man—an unselfish one—he'd tell Lavinia she should take a second look at Ben. Was he *gut*? Unselfish? They'd been friends for years before they'd realized they were attracted to one another and started dating. If he was really a *gut* friend, he'd want the best for her.

Right now he wasn't.

He sighed heavily.

"Abe?"

"I'm fine, *Mamm*. Just tired."

"A nap will put you right," she stated confidently.

Ya, *a nap would cure everything*, he wanted to say, but that was rude. So he kept his mouth shut and lapsed into a bit of a doze until his *dat* pulled into their drive. He roused himself and wondered how he was going to get himself out of the buggy without the help of his *eldres* when Wayne walked up.

"Where'd you come from?" he asked, relieved and struggling to wake up.

"Saw you leave church. Thought you might need

some help," he said as he got the wheelchair out. Together, Wayne and Faron got Abe out of the buggy, into the house, and onto his bed.

"*Danki*, Wayne. Hope you didn't leave early just for me."

Wayne shrugged. "I was ready to leave. Got some chores to attend to at home, and then I'll be back for the afternoon milking. Need anything else?"

"*Nee, danki.* See you later."

Abe managed to get his boots off and lie down before his *mudder* came in with a glass of iced tea and set it on the bedside table. "Thought you could use a cold drink before you take a nap," she said as she bustled around, opening the bedroom window and turning on the fan.

"*Danki.*" Too tired to pick the glass up, he was asleep before she left the room.

He woke to her shaking his good arm. "Abe, you have company."

"Huh?"

"Says he's your doctor."

She helped him get into his chair and his boots. When she came at him with his comb, he held up his good hand. "*Mamm*, I can do that myself."

"Fine." She stood there waiting until he used it and then pushed him into the living room.

"Abe, hope you don't mind us dropping in," Dr. Hamilton said as he rose from a chair. "We happened to be out this way, and I thought I'd check on you. I've never seen a dairy farm. Wondered if you'd mind showing us around." He gestured to the little girl who stood beside him. "This is Piper, my youngest."

"Nice to meet you, Piper."

She smiled shyly at Abe. "Daddy says you have cows."

"I sure do. Let's go see them." He looked up at the doctor. "Mind giving me a push?"

"No problem. How's your PT going?"

"Good. Hoping I won't be in this chair much longer."

They went out the back door and out to the cow barn.

"Can I touch one?" Piper asked him.

"Sure." He took her hand and put it on the flank of the nearest cow, and Piper's eyes grew huge.

"She feels rough and scratchy!" the girl said.

The cow just swished her tail and ignored them.

"Which ones give us choc-lit milk?"

"Chocolate milk?" Abe held back a laugh at the familiar question.

"My daughter thinks some cows have white milk and some have chocolate milk."

Abe bit back a smile. "I've had adults think the same thing." He turned to Piper. "Cows give us white milk, and chocolate is added later."

"Oh." Piper looked disappointed.

Wayne strolled in and looked surprised to see them. Abe introduced him to the doctor and his daughter.

Abe turned to Dr. Hamilton. "Wayne can show Piper how to milk Annie here, if it's okay with you," he suggested, gesturing to a cow that hadn't been hooked up yet. "We do it with machinery these days, but I learned how to milk one by hand when I was about Piper's age."

"Can I, Daddy? Please?"

"Sure."

Wayne helped her wash her hands in a nearby sink, then set a small stool down beside Annie so Piper could sit.

Piper bit her bottom lip, hesitant to touch the cow's teats, her face reflecting her mixed feelings when she did. But she stuck with it and frowned in concentration as she worked them as Wayne directed. She squealed when a stream of milk spurted into the pail. "Daddy! It's milk!"

He grinned and took a photo with his phone camera. "Wait until your mom sees this!"

She giggled. "Can I drink it?"

Abe had drunk raw milk as a *kind* and never had any ill effects, but he knew before he looked at the doctor he wouldn't approve.

"We pasteurize it for people," Abe told her. "It's like we boil it to make it safe, get rid of any germs," he explained. "But you can give it to Mary, our barn cat. She likes fresh milk."

"Tell Wayne thank you for showing you how to milk the cow," her father prompted.

"Thank you, Wayne." She turned to the cow. "And thank you, Annie."

She washed her hands again and they headed over to the house, with Piper carefully clutching the handle of the pail. Abe took the pail and told her to run into the house and ask his mother for a bowl for the cat, and she ran to fetch it. When she returned, she carefully poured the milk into the bowl without spilling a drop.

Dr. Hamilton looked around as Piper talked to the cat. "Great place to raise kids."

Abe nodded. "It is." He frowned. "Well, used to be. It's getting harder and harder to make a profit. Milk prices have fallen in the last few years as people drink milk made of rice and almonds and such."

"Yes, the wife favors almond or rice milk."

Abe decided it would be rude to say he didn't feel it was milk if it didn't come from a cow.

"I would like to take home some of the cheese you make here on the farm. Both of us are usually working when you have the farm stand open."

"Be happy to give you some." He shook his head as the doctor reached for his wallet. "Your money's not good here. My mother will be happy to give you some cheese for all you've done for me."

"Have you considered selling it at the local stores? Maybe on the internet?"

"Considered a lot of things, and then I fell off the roof."

"Were you trying to be Superman?" Piper piped up. "One day when me and my friends were playing at Jason Felder's house, he said he was gonna go up on his roof and try to fly like Superman. I told his mom and she sent him to his room."

Abe bit the inside of his cheek to keep from laughing. "No, I was fixing my roof." He held up his arm in the cast. "Your dad had to operate on me and fix me."

"He didn't fix your legs?"

"They're almost well."

She beamed. "My daddy's a smart doctor."

"He is."

They went into the house and found his *eldres* in the kitchen.

"Can I get you some coffee or something cold to drink?" Waneta asked the doctor.

"No, thanks."

"He'd like to take some of our cheese home," Abe told her.

"Why, I should have thought of that!" Waneta said. "Haven't had time to have the farm stand up since Abe's accident, but I intend to start up again this week."

She bustled about getting several blocks of cheese from the refrigerator and putting it in a woven basket along with a loaf of her bread.

She handed the basket to Piper with a big smile. "You come again soon, both of you. And maybe you can bring your mother next time."

Abe's *dat* stood and held out his hand to shake the doctor's. "You stop by anytime," he told him. "We're just so grateful for what you and everyone at the hospital did for our son."

"It was our pleasure." He turned to Abe. "I hope the next time I see you that you'll be on your feet."

"Me too. My therapist plans for me to be out of the wheelchair soon. I can't wait."

His *dat* walked their guests to the door.

"Want something to drink?" his *mudder* asked Abe.

"Yeah, *danki*. I fell asleep before I could drink the glass of tea you put on my bedside table."

"I'll fix you a fresh glass."

She filled a glass with ice and tea and set it before him, then added a plate of cookies before she sat at the table. "What's that look about?"

"Look?"

"You're looking sad. Something the doctor said upset you? You know you'll be on your feet soon."

"I know. Just doesn't feel fast enough."

His *dat* came in then and asked what was for supper, so he didn't have to tell his *mudder* the thing that the doctor had said that had made his mood turn blue. He'd agreed with the doctor that the farm was a great place to raise *kinner*. It had been for generations. But Abe didn't know if he could hold on to it long enough to raise the next generation.

Chapter Thirteen

Lavinia wanted to call Abe and find out if he wanted to go to the singing, but she felt that would be pressuring him. She told herself that she'd done all she could to persuade him and resolved to let it go. It was like the saying "You can lead a horse to water but you can't make him drink."

So she went by herself and caught herself looking up hopefully every time she heard a buggy approach.

Groups of young men and women gathered on the lawn of her friend Arnita's house and milled around talking to each other.

"Lavinia! You're looking lovely," Ben said as he walked toward her. "I'm glad you came tonight."

"*Danki*."

Lester, an old friend from *schul*, walked up behind him. "Lavinia, is Abe coming tonight?"

"I don't know. When I talked to him after church today, he sounded tired."

She wished now that she'd called him.

After Lester walked away, Lavinia glanced around. It felt *gut* to be here tonight with others her age and enjoy some free time with those she'd known all her life.

She was looking forward to seeing Arnita. They'd been friends for years since they attended *schul* together. But Lavinia had been so busy seeing Abe at the hospital, and Arnita was occupied helping her *mudder* while she cared for her *mann* as he went through chemotherapy.

Arnita walked over and placed a stack of hymnals on a table that had been set out on the lawn. "Help me pass these out?"

"*Schur.*"

"How is Abe doing?" she asked quietly.

"He's doing well. Church tired him out, or he'd be here tonight."

Arnita nodded. "He's been through a lot." She touched Lavinia's arm. "You, too."

"We're just *gut* friends."

"Really, really *gut* friends," Arnita said with a mischievous smile.

Dating was kept confidential in their community until engagements were announced. It just worked out better that way for all concerned. If a relationship didn't work out, others didn't know about it. But after each singing, when it was time to leave, it was easy to see who was pairing off into couples as they walked to buggies and began a long, romantic ride home.

"So where is Saul?" Lavinia asked Arnita in turn. She knew the two were "*gut* friends" as well, and she expected that they would be announcing their engagement after harvest.

"He's in the house talking to my *eldres*." She sighed. "My *dat* had a hard day. He had chemo this morning and isn't feeling so well."

"I'm sorry."

"Saul seems to be a comfort to *Daed* when he's not well." She stared back at the house for a moment. "I'm going inside to check on snacks. *Mamm* was baking some cookies for us."

Lavinia was glad Arnita's *dat* had Saul to sit with him when he wasn't feeling well. She saw Wayne talking to a few men on the other side of the lawn. He was a friend as well. But he hadn't been able to come to the hospital to visit Abe because he was so busy caring for the dairy farm. Lavinia had noticed the way Wayne had quietly helped Abe at church this morning. Now she wondered if she should have asked Wayne to bring Abe to the singing.

She shook her head. Time to stop trying to help Abe. He'd resume his old activities as he felt better. She was *schur* of it.

Arnita came back out of the house looking concerned.

"Something wrong?"

"*Daed* seems worse," Arnita said as she chewed on her thumbnail. "*Mamm* and I are worried about him."

"Maybe we should cancel the singing."

She shook her head. "*Nee. Daed*'s resting in the front

bedroom, and I think he'll enjoy hearing the hymns we sing."

Lavinia nodded. "*Allrecht*, let's get started then." She motioned to their friends and they assembled, waiting to be told which hymn to begin with. Soon the gentle harmonies and uplifting lyrics drifted on the breeze. Lavinia hoped Arnita's *dat* could hear them and that they gave him some comfort.

They were just singing the last notes of the third hymn when the front door of the house slammed open and Arnita's *mudder* called out sharply for her.

She dropped her hymnal and ran to her. Then she went inside the house with her *mudder*.

"What should we do?" Lester asked Lavinia.

"Let's give it a few minutes," she began, but then Arnita came out of the house and walked over to them. Lavinia saw that her friend had been crying, and her heart sank.

"*Daed* has to go to the hospital," she said, her lips trembling. "*Mamm* called the doctor, and he told her to call nine-one-one. They're sending an ambulance."

Lavinia turned to the group standing there looking expectantly at them. "I think we should pray for Arnita's *dat* and then go home."

There were nods, and then the group prayed briefly. Afterward, they left their hymnals on the table before talking quietly as they walked to their buggies.

"I'm going back inside to be with *Mamm*," Arnita said.

Lavinia nodded, helped scoop up the hymnals, and

carried them up to the porch. Arnita took them inside, then stepped out again.

Lavinia gave her a big hug. "I'll pray for your *dat*. You call me and let me know how he is later, *allrecht*?"

Arnita nodded. "*Danki.*" She walked into the house and closed the door.

Lavinia stood on the porch for a moment, thinking how quickly life could change. One moment they'd been singing praise, and the next, praying for the father of their friend who was fighting cancer. With a sigh, she descended the steps and crossed the lawn.

"I thought you might need a lift," Ben said, startling her.

She'd been so lost in thought she hadn't seen him. "Oh, I can walk home."

"It's getting dark. Not safe. *Kumm*, let me give you a ride."

When he reached for her hand, she wouldn't let him take it. That was too forward of him. She felt a moment's unease, then told herself she was being silly. This was Ben. She'd known him since they attended *schul*.

She got into the buggy and settled back for the ride.

"Too bad we had to stop the singing," he said as he guided the buggy down the drive and onto the road.

He pulled over as an ambulance came speeding up behind them and turned into the driveway.

"It wouldn't have been right to stay," she pointed out as she glanced back to see paramedics getting out of the ambulance.

"*Ya.* I guess." He shrugged.

"Arnita was so worried about her *dat*."

"I'm *schur* he'll be fine."

She turned and stared straight ahead. It took her a moment before she realized the direction he was headed in.

"You're going the wrong way," she said.

"*Nee*, just taking the long way home."

"Why?"

"Give us a chance to catch up."

She supposed it would be less than gracious not to chat with him when he was giving her a ride. But when he reached for her hand again, she shrank back against the window on her side.

"So, what's been going on with you?" he asked conversationally, not appearing to be offended by her not wanting his touch.

"Been busy working. You?"

"Same. *Daed*'s been making me work too hard, as usual."

She remembered now how he didn't care for working very hard on the family farm. "Anyway, since we're not having the singing I'd just like to get home," she said. "I could do some work on a rug."

"Aw, relax. Life isn't supposed to be all work, you know."

Lavinia tried not to roll her eyes at him. A few minutes later, he pulled off the road and turned to her. He reached over and traced the line of her cheek with his finger. "What do you say to us going out some evening?"

Why hadn't she seen this coming? "I'm sorry, I'm not interested in dating right now."

"I bet I could make you interested," he said.

"I want you to take me home. Now."

"Is this about Abe?"

"What are you talking about?"

"Look, I know you like the guy. You always did. But, Lavinia, think about it. I've got a lot more to offer you than he does."

She gave him a pitying look. "Abe can offer a lot more than you, Ben. He's never made me feel uncomfortable."

Looking pained, Ben shifted back to his side of the buggy and picked up the reins. "Fine. Giddyap, Max. Let's take her home."

He sulked all the way to her house. She thanked him as she got out and was barely out of the way before he was driving off.

With a sigh, she made her way into the house. Her *dat* was sitting at the kitchen table drinking a cup of coffee when she walked in.

"You're home early," he said, smiling at her.

She threw her arms around his neck and hugged him.

"Whoa, what's this about?"

"I love you," she said.

"I love you, too. Something wrong?"

She stood back and nodded. "We canceled the singing. Arnita's *dat* had chemo earlier today and felt so ill tonight that he went to the hospital in an ambulance."

"I'm sorry to hear that."

"Arnita said she'd call me and let me know how he's doing. She hasn't called, has she?"

He shook his head, then tilted it as he studied her. "Did Abe go tonight?"

"*Nee.* He said he was tired after church and didn't think he'd come." She sighed and put the teakettle on the stove, then sat at the table. "I guess it's just as well, with what happened. He'd have gone to a lot of trouble for nothing."

Her *dat* patted her hand. "Things work out for the best, Lavinia."

"I guess." Then, seeing him looking at her, she nodded. "I know."

She decided she wouldn't tell him about her ride home.

* * *

Abe knew he was hiding like a little *bu* in his room. He'd have stayed there for hours after he woke from a nap, but hunger won out. So he got up, struggled into his wheelchair, and rolled out to the kitchen.

His *mudder* turned from the sink where she was washing dishes and frowned at him. "I tried to wake you. I thought you'd want to go to the singing."

"*Nee.*" He'd heard her come into his room and call his name, but he'd pretended he was asleep.

She put her hands on her hips and looked at him. "Wayne came by to say he'd be happy to take you. I told him I couldn't wake you."

Abe shook his head. "Too tired. I went to church."

"And you should have gone to the singing. It would be *gut* to get out."

"Leave the *bu* alone," his *dat* said as he walked into the kitchen.

"He spends too much of his time with us," she said as she walked to the refrigerator and got out a plate covered with clear wrap.

"Looks *wunderbaar*," he said as she put the plate on the table in front of him and took off the wrap. Supper was cold baked chicken, macaroni salad, and sliced tomatoes. Perfect meal on a warm evening.

"Changing the subject," she muttered. "*Hungerich?*" she asked as she poured a glass of iced tea and set it beside his plate.

"*Bu*'s always *hungerich*," his *dat* said as he poured a glass of iced tea and set it on the table.

"Like *dat*, like *sohn*," she retorted, but she smiled. "I'm going to sit down in the living room and read for a while."

"*Danki* for supper, *Mamm*." Abe dug into the meal as she walked out of the room.

"She worries about you."

"I know." He took a sip of his tea and avoided his *dat*'s gaze. It was tempting to say she worried about her *mann*, too, but he didn't think it was polite to point that out. "I'm sorry."

"Wasn't easy to go out the first time, but it'll get easier," Faron said quietly.

"I know." Abe set his fork down. "I just didn't feel

like pretending everything is *allrecht*. Does that make sense?"

His *dat* rested his hand on his cane at his side. "*Ya*, it does."

Abe nodded. He knew how difficult the diagnosis of MS had been for his *dat*. There were days Faron didn't want his *fraa* to know were hard for him, times Abe saw him struggling privately to put on a brave face for her. He felt guilty that his own injuries gave them worry they didn't need after a lifetime of working hard on the farm.

There was a brief knock on the kitchen door, and then Wayne walked in.

"Singing got canceled," he told Abe. "Thought I'd stop in and see if you needed anything before I go home."

"Canceled? Why?"

"Arnita's *dat* wasn't feeling well." Wayne got a glass from the cupboard and filled it with water from the faucet. He drank thirstily. "He went to the hospital in an ambulance. So we decided to go home."

Faron frowned. "I'm sorry to hear that. He's had a rough time with chemo."

Wayne nodded. "So, Abe, need anything?"

He shook his head. "*Nee, danki*."

Wayne set the glass in the sink. "Some of the men are going to go back tomorrow to take care of chores on his farm."

The men in the community always helped each other with such work. Abe knew the women would do their part, too, see if they could bring meals or do laundry or housework.

Wayne left, and Abe and his *dat* sat in silence.

"I know it's weighing on you, not being able to take care of the farm," his *dat* said finally. "But sometimes we have to accept help."

"I can't lose this place after all you put into it," Abe blurted out, then wished he could cut off his tongue.

"You're not going to lose it. We've had tough times, but we've always survived," his *dat* said firmly. "You were young so you wouldn't remember the tough times, when we had bad weather and lost a crop. When it was hard to pay the tax bill."

He got up, got out a lemon icebox pie from the refrigerator, and brought it to the table.

"Finish your supper and you can have a piece of pie," he said.

Abe found it easy to do so as he watched his *dat* cut a slice for each of them. Nothing was better on a warm, late spring evening than a cold supper and a slice of his *mudder*'s lemon icebox pie.

"We've had it easier in some ways during the rough times," Faron said as he forked up a bite of pie and savored it. "Living off the land, we grow much of what we need. And we need a lot less of the things that some people think they must have."

Abe knew he meant those who were not Amish.

"My *dat* told me about the hard times so many experienced during the Great Depression," he said as he ate. "He said there was a lot of food, milk, and such that the country produced. But many people had no money to buy it. My *dat* said he remembered your *grossdaadi* giving milk to *familyes* that needed it, giving work to everyone he could." He looked off into the distance for a long moment, then turned his gaze to Abe. "The farm survived then. It'll survive this hard time. You'll heal and get strong again. You'll find a way to make the farm thrive. Your *mudder* and I and everyone in the community will help however we can."

Abe had to swallow hard against the lump that rose in his throat. He was glad now that he hadn't gone to the singing. His *dat* was a man of few words, but when he spoke, he revealed a deep faith and wisdom Abe hoped he'd have one day. "*Danki, Daed,*" he said quietly.

His *mudder* came in a little while later and clucked her tongue disapprovingly when she saw her *mann* was eating a slice of pie.

"Had to keep the *bu* company while he ate his supper," Faron said. "You go on back to your reading. We'll take care of our dishes when we're done."

"Let's not make the pie dish one of them," she told him pertly as she scooped up the pie and returned it to the refrigerator. "That makes your third piece today."

Faron winked at Abe as she left the room.

Chapter Fourteen

The next day, the shop was so busy Lavinia barely had time to quickly eat a sandwich at the front counter as she helped customers. When it came time to turn the sign from **Open** to **Closed** on the shop door, she and her *mudder* looked at each other and sighed with relief.

"It's nice to be busy, but my, I will be happy to sit down," her *mudder* said as she locked the door.

Lavinia nodded as she finished up the day's deposit slip. She'd barely finished when Liz honked as she pulled up outside.

"I've got your things," her *mudder* cried. "Let's go!"

She followed her to the door, locked up, and, when she climbed into the van, sank gratefully into a seat. *Ya*, it was *gut* indeed to sit down.

As Liz pulled out onto the road and drove, Lavinia

realized she'd been so busy she hadn't had a chance to think of Abe all day. She wondered how his day had been. Had he gone out to the barn with Wayne to see his cows? Worked with his physical therapist? Had a nice lunch or a visit from a friend?

Had he thought of her?

She stared out the window at the passing scenery and wondered if she should call him or stop by to see him after supper. It seemed to her that he'd been a little distant the day before at church, and that troubled her. She'd put it down to it being his first time out of the house since his accident, but it would be *gut* to make *schur* that he was *allrecht*.

"Tired?" her *mudder* asked quietly.

She nodded. "You're right. It feels *gut* to sit down."

But there was still work to be done when they got home. Supper wouldn't cook itself, and dishes wouldn't wash themselves. Sadie had called the shop to say she hadn't felt well today, so she hadn't been over to water the kitchen garden, and she and her *familye* wouldn't be coming for supper as planned.

Ah, well, it was *gut* to have work to do and a home to go to in the evening, Lavinia reminded herself.

She glanced out the van window as they passed Abe's dairy farm but was disappointed when she didn't see him sitting out on the porch.

When she turned from the window, she saw that her *mudder* was smiling gently at her. "Maybe you'll have the energy to take a walk after supper," she whispered, which made Lavinia smile.

"Maybe."

Liz pulled up in front of their house, and they said goodbye to her and got out.

"I don't see *Daed* out in the fields," Lavinia told her *mudder*. "Maybe he got finished early and he's making supper."

They looked at each other and laughed. Amos always said he was *gut* at eating but terrible at cooking, and his womenfolk could attest to that. But he was always appreciative of whatever they put on the table.

Amos came in a few minutes later as Rachel set a big bowl of potato salad on the table. She'd boiled the potatoes the night before as she did the dishes and left them to chill in the refrigerator. Tonight she added cubes of ham and cheddar cheese to the potato salad to make it hearty.

Lavinia went out to the kitchen garden, gave it a quick soak with water from the hose, then brought in several big, juicy, ripe tomatoes to slice up.

They ate the simple meal with the fan stirring up the warm breeze, enjoying glasses of cold tea with it.

"Nothing better than ice cream after a hot day working in the fields," Amos said with satisfaction as Lavinia scooped up big bowls of it and added some cookies from the cookie jar. He had two bowls before he pushed away from the table.

Lavinia insisted on doing the dishes—not that there were a lot of them, since there hadn't really been any cooking. She glanced at the kitchen window. Still time for a walk before it got dark. She walked into the living room where her *eldres* were sitting reading.

"*Mamm*, I think I'll go for a walk."

"Tell Abe and Faron and Waneta I said hello."

"I will."

She stopped in the living room. "*Daed*, do you mind if I take one of your books to Abe? I'm thinking he might enjoy reading since there's not a lot he can do right now."

"*Schur.* Which one?"

"You pick."

He put down the book he was reading and got up from his recliner. Lavinia found herself fidgeting while he took his time looking over the books in the bookcase that lined one wall. She hadn't thought it would take so long just to pick out a book.

Finally he pulled one from a shelf, gave it a long look, then handed it to her. "Steinbeck's a favorite of mine," he said thoughtfully. "I think he'll like that one. We've talked about this author. We both enjoy his writing."

She nodded. "*Danki.*" She had no idea what Abe liked to read, so she figured she should trust her *dat*'s choice.

"Tell him to let me know if it's not something he cares for," he said. "It won't offend me. A particular book's not for everyone."

"I will." She kissed his cheek. "I'll see you later."

She tucked it into the pocket in her dress and left the house. It felt *gut* to be outdoors after being cooped up indoors all day at the shop. The air was still warm, but there was a breeze as she walked. It carried the sweet scent of honeysuckle twining over a fence beside the road. Some of her neighbors were sitting on their porches enjoying the weather after supper. She waved to them as she walked.

Abe's house came into view. She saw him sitting on his front porch. Her heart sped up as she walked toward it, but as she drew closer she saw his shoulders were slumped and he was staring at his arm in the cast and frowning.

Oh my, she thought. *Someone looks like he isn't having a* gut *day.* She hesitated, debating whether she should stop and visit. She decided to stop. She'd missed seeing him at the singing the night before and wanted to know how he was doing. It had to be hard sitting around the house not being able to do much.

* * *

Abe sat on his front porch and tried to shake off a bad mood that had lasted all day. He'd started it with a morning doctor appointment. Not his favorite start, by any means. He'd much rather have been working with Wayne in the cow barn, no matter how hard the work or what the weather.

And he had to go to the appointment with his *mudder*. Like he was a little *bu*. She'd insisted, and since Wayne was busy, it wasn't like he could argue with her. He needed help with navigating in his wheelchair, and she had so many questions about his injuries that he'd given in. At least his *dat* wasn't coming along. He'd decided to help Wayne in the cow barn, and Wayne had told Abe privately that he wouldn't let the older man overdo.

So after Liz had delivered her morning passengers to their jobs in town, she stopped and drove Abe and his *mudder* to the doctor's appointment. The drive turned out to be the only bright spot in the morning. Abe hadn't been for a drive since he'd come home from the hospital, and it was nice to get out and about.

But after X-rays, the doctor had come into the exam room frowning and said the break in his arm was taking longer to heal than he expected and the cast might have to be on longer than he'd estimated.

Abe had ridden home feeling depressed, and his *mudder*'s offer to fix him his favorite meal for lunch hadn't brightened his spirits. He'd gone to his room to rest and, *ya*, to sulk.

A drizzly rain began falling and instead of cooling things off, it made the afternoon more humid. The battery-operated fan wasn't of much help. He fell asleep but tossed and turned and had a bad dream of being held down. No wonder, he thought. The heavy cast weighing down his arm was surely what had caused the bad dream.

With a sigh, he sat up and got himself into his wheelchair. Wayne was taking a break and having a cold drink with Faron at the kitchen table. Waneta walked in carrying a battery-operated ice-cream maker and grinning from ear to ear.

"What are you going to do with that?" Abe asked her.

She gave him a quizzical smile. "Make ice cream. I always do this time of year."

"It's just a lot of trouble. Isn't it easier to just buy it at the store?"

"It's a *gut* way to use up milk," she reminded him. "Which we happen to have a lot of. Back when I came to the farm as a new *fraa*, I made ice cream and sold it in a stand at the front of the house. My fresh strawberry was the top seller."

"It was the best," Faron said with a nod.

"Brought in some extra money that helped out." Waneta set the pinewood bucket on the table and went to the sink to wet a dishrag and begin wiping it off.

"*Mamm*, you don't need to be doing that," Abe said. "We'll be fine. You already do so much making the cheese and selling it at the farm stand."

"It'll be fun," she told him. "Hand me that recipe box behind you."

Waneta began flipping through the box that was as old as he was. "I think I'll start off with the strawberry, since they're ripening." She pulled a pad and pencil from a kitchen drawer and began making a list. "Wayne, can you set up some things for me on Saturday?"

"*Schur.*"

Abe figured his *dat* must have caught his expression. He shook his head at Abe. "Don't try to stop her. Once she gets an idea in her head, she won't let go of it."

He sighed. His *dat* knew his *fraa* for *schur*.

Abe scooped up the mail, tucked it at his side in the wheelchair, and rolled himself out onto the front porch. He began opening the mail and found it was mostly bills. The thick envelope from the hospital made his hands shake. For a long moment, he couldn't open it, just as he hadn't been able to open one that had come sometime back. This one was bigger in size—likely the final hospital bill. Then he forced himself to do it. There was no putting it off.

Reading through page after page of charges for things he didn't understand made his head hurt. The total on the last page made his eyes widen.

His *dat* wandered out to the porch to take a seat in a rocking chair.

Wordlessly, Abe handed him the bill and watched his *dat*'s expression.

"Wow."

"*Ya*," Abe agreed.

"Well, I'll see that the bishop gets this," his *dat* said as he folded the sheets of paper and stuck them back into the envelope. He gave Abe a sharp look. "You're not to worry about this, *sohn*. You know the community takes care of its own. We've all gotten together and helped with hospital and doctor bills like this in the past. Now it's your turn to be helped."

"Don't want to be a burden," Abe muttered.

"Did you think Luke was a burden when he was kicked by one of his horses and had to have surgery? Or Lovina when she had appendicitis?"

"*Nee*."

"*Nee*. You and your *mudder* and I contributed to the fund to pay those bills, and we'll do so again in the future as church members need it."

Waneta walked out to join them on the porch. She wore a frown as she sat in the rocking chair next to her *mann*. "Abe, I went upstairs to bring some of my fabric down from my old sewing room, and I found that the roof is leaking again. I put a bucket under it, and Wayne said he'd get up on the roof tomorrow when it's had a chance to dry out."

Abe sighed and shook his head. "What else?"

"We should have had Wayne check to see if the repair Abe went up to fix was done before he fell," Faron said. "Didn't think of it."

"I didn't either," Abe said slowly. "I wasn't finished."

Faron patted Abe's hand on the arm of his wheelchair. "Wayne and some of the men from church will take care of it."

His *eldres* went into the house a little while later, leaving him to sit and watch the cars and buggies traveling the road in front of the house.

After some time, Wayne came to talk to him about the day. He sat in one of the rocking chairs and told Abe about the milking totals and the new driver who'd picked up the day's output.

He stopped suddenly. "Say, I think that was Lavinia waving to you."

"What? Where?"

"There, in Liz's van."

Abe glanced down at the road and saw the back of Liz's van.

"You should have gone to the singing last night," Wayne said slowly. "Ben was flirting with her."

"*Ya?*"

Wayne frowned. "I was driving Katie Ann home, or I'd have offered her a ride." He stopped and looked like he didn't know what to say.

"What?"

"Ben took her home in his buggy." He stared at his hands resting on his knees. "I know the two of you have been looking close lately."

Abe shrugged. "We're friends." He held out his arm in the cast. "She came to see me a lot at the hospital. She was here when I fell off the roof."

Waneta stuck her head out the front door. "Supper's ready."

Wayne pushed the wheelchair inside the house and left them. Abe tried to eat but wasn't much interested in eating. He let his *mudder*'s chatter wash over him and escaped as soon as he could.

Sheer boredom sent Abe back out onto the porch after he ate. That, and it was cooler than inside the house. At least the drizzling rain had stopped.

"Hello there!"

Lavinia climbed the steps to the porch.

"Hi."

"Thought I'd stop over and see how you're doing."

He shrugged. "Just watching the world go by."

She nodded. "I know it's hard sitting here not getting to do anything but wait to heal."

"*Nee*, you don't," he said.

Surprised, she nodded. "*Nee*, you're right. I haven't had anything as bad as what happened to you. Few people have. Is there anything I can do to make you feel better?"

"You can't fix me, Lavinia. Even the doctors can't."

Alarmed, she stared at him. "Did you get bad news?"

Abe shook his head. "I haven't had any new bad news, if that's what you mean." He sighed and looked out at the road. "I'm sorry, I'm not feeling well, and I'm just not *gut* company right now. I need to lie down. Maybe we can see each other tomorrow." He began wheeling himself toward the door.

"Let me help you," she said.

"I can do it myself." He banged his arm struggling with the door, but pride wouldn't let her hold it for him.

"Abe, what's going on?" His *mudder* hurried toward him.

"It's nothing." He headed toward his room. He heard his *mudder* talking to Lavinia, but he pushed himself forward and shut the door.

Chapter Fifteen

Lavinia felt tears slipping down her cheeks as she walked home.

She brushed impatiently at them, telling herself it was silly to get upset over the way Abe had behaved. He was obviously not feeling well and having a bad day, and that was no surprise. It had to be hard being in the condition he was in and not being able to do anything about it.

But it hurt.

She managed to get the tears under control by the time she reached her house, and when she let herself in, she was relieved to find that her *eldres* were in the living room.

"I'm back!" she called to them from the kitchen. "I'm going up to bed."

"'Night!" her *dat* called.

She climbed the stairs to her bedroom and changed into a nightgown, took off her *kapp*, and unpinned her hair. Then she sat on her bed, her brush in her hand, and just stared at it.

There was a knock on her door. "*Kumm!*"

Her *mudder* came in and sat on the bed beside her. "You *allrecht*? You weren't gone long."

Lavinia bit her bottom lip to stop it trembling. "Abe wasn't in the mood for a visit. He cut our visit short, so I came home."

"I'm sorry. It hurt your feelings?"

She nodded and blinked back tears.

Her *mudder* took the brush and began drawing it through Lavinia's hair in long strokes. "I'm sorry."

Lavinia sighed and relaxed as the brushing soothed her. She'd always loved it when her *mudder* brushed her hair when she was a *kind*. "I could tell he wasn't having a *gut* day when I got to his house."

"He shouldn't have taken it out on you, but that's what we do with the people we love sometimes."

"He didn't exactly take it out on me," she admitted. "He was just abrupt about not wanting to talk to me, and it hurt. And *Mamm*, he doesn't love me. We're just *gut* friends."

"I know. But friends can love friends, can't they?"

"I—I guess."

Her *mudder* finished brushing her hair and began braiding it, then bound it with the stretchy tie wound around the brush handle. She hugged Lavinia, then rose. "Try not to worry about Abe. God is holding him in His arms, even when it seems He isn't."

She paused by the door. "And Lavinia?"

"*Ya?*"

"Your *dat* and I were best friends before we married. Still are." She walked out and shut the door.

Lavinia thought about that for a long moment and then climbed between her sheets. It took a long time to fall asleep. The first pale fingers of dawn light were slipping into the window before she finally dozed off.

Several sharp raps on her bedroom door woke her.

"Lavinia! Time to get up!" her *dat* called.

Jerking awake, she sat up in bed, and her eyes widened when she looked at the clock on her bedside table. She hadn't set the alarm because she always woke up on time. She never overslept!

Throwing the sheets aside, she rushed through dressing, fixing her hair, and putting on a fresh *kapp*. It was hard to leave the room without making her bed, but there just wasn't time.

She clattered down the steps and ran into the kitchen. "I'm so sorry, *Mamm*. I overslept."

Her *mudder* turned from the stove. "You don't look like you slept well."

Lavinia grimaced. She'd seen the lavender circles under her eyes. "I didn't." She didn't usually let things get to her. She figured maybe she was just tired and had been concerned about Abe since the accident.

"Well, there's still time to eat breakfast if you're

quick." Her *mudder* picked up a plate she'd kept warm on the back of the stove and set it on the table.

While she ate her pancakes, Lavinia watched her *mudder* put the lunches they'd packed the night before in their insulated totes. She added apples, cookies, and a thermos of lemonade to each. The two of them were waiting on the front porch for their ride just minutes before Liz came for them.

"I'll set my alarm tonight," Lavinia told her *mudder* as they walked to the van. "I don't want to rush like that again."

"We're not late."

"Only because you had my breakfast ready and put our lunches in our totes," Lavinia said, feeling guilty. "I didn't do my part this morning."

"Once isn't worth worrying about."

They got into the van and greeted Liz as they buckled their seat belts.

Two women were peering into the window when they arrived at the shop. "Guess we're too early," one said as they got out of the van.

"No problem," Rachel said as Lavinia unlocked the shop door. "You're welcome to come on in."

Their early bird shoppers walked out twenty minutes later, their shopping bags loaded with purchases.

"Well, that was a fine start to the morning," Rachel said with satisfaction.

Lavinia brought them both mugs of coffee she'd just made, then walked over to the table in the corner where she worked on her rag rugs when there was time.

Arnita came in a short time later. "*Mamm* and I came into town to run some errands. We have to pick up prescriptions for *Daed* and more canning jars. Just can't have enough canning jars at harvest time. *Mamm*'s getting some fabric for a new quilt, so I decided to run over and say hi."

Rachel stood up. "Sarah's at Hannah's?"

"*Ya.*"

Rachel turned to Lavinia. "I'm going to run over and say hello. I'll be back in a few minutes."

Lavinia nodded, then turned to Arnita. "I'm so glad you came by. I've missed you so much."

"Maybe we can get together soon."

Arnita nodded. "My *mamm* was so upset we had to cancel the singing that night *Daed* got sick."

"Everyone understood. I'm glad he's feeling better. Listen, if you're not busy later, why don't you come for supper?"

"I will if I don't have to help *Mamm*." She watched Lavinia as she twisted strips of fabric into her current rug. "I should have remembered to bring a bag of scraps from *Mamm*'s quilt work for you. I'll bring it this evening if I come to supper."

"That would be great. I can always use them."

Rachel returned. "Arnita, your *mudder* says she's ready to go."

"See you later," Arnita said, and she flew out the door.

"It was so *gut* to see Sarah, even if it was just for a few minutes."

"I know. I felt the same way about Arnita stopping

by. I invited her for supper later. She said she'll come if her *mudder* doesn't need her."

"Sarah said her *mann* is much better. The chemo treatment was rough on him that day, but he's feeling better."

"I'm glad."

The rest of the day passed quickly, and as soon as they got home, Lavinia insisted on fixing supper, so her *mudder* went out to her kitchen garden in the backyard and puttered in it. She came in a while later with a basket filled with fruit and vegetables. After she washed off a leafy head of lettuce and some ripe, red tomatoes, she made a big salad to go with the ham left over from Sunday supper.

"Sadie said she'd do some more canning for me since we've been too busy at the shop to spare one of us to do it."

The *familye* depended heavily on what it grew in the garden, so canning and preserving had to be done no matter how many hours were spent working outside the home like Rachel and Lavinia did. When winter came, they'd be grateful for the jars of green beans and corn and carrots. And there was nothing better than strawberry preserves on a hot biscuit on a cold day.

Arnita came for supper with the bag of fabric scraps she'd promised. Lavinia's *dat* sat and ate quietly, smiling indulgently as the three women chattered nonstop through supper. Lavinia gave him a second scoop of ice cream on his slice of pie for dessert and kissed his cheek.

"What's that for?" he asked, surprised.

"For being you," she responded. "You let us talk all through supper without saying a word."

He shrugged. "You and your *mudder* don't get much time to visit with friends since you work in town all day."

"Like you get any time with yours when you work out in the fields?"

"I manage to see them, especially this time of year when we help each other with harvesting."

He helped his *fraa* with the dishes so Arnita and Lavinia could sit on the front porch and visit. They had a *gut* time catching up on all the news. Lavinia hadn't heard that Wayne was seeing Katie Ann and that Katie Ann's bakery was doing well. Arnita listened raptly to Lavinia talking about the customers who'd visited the shop and what was going on in town.

After Arnita left to walk home, Lavinia sat there for a long moment in the rocking chair. This was the first day she hadn't seen Abe. Was he sitting on his porch enjoying the evening as dusk fell? Gradually the stars came out in the sky, and when cars passed on the road in front of the house, they had their headlights on. Few buggies rolled by, as most Amish tried to be home before dark.

Lavinia told herself she should get up and go inside. Abe *schur* wasn't going to stop by. And if she'd hoped he'd call and apologize for his behavior the evening before…well, apparently it wasn't going to happen. She got up and went inside.

* * *

Abe found the paperback book on the table on the front porch the next morning. For a minute he stared at it. Where had it come from? Then he realized it was written by an author he and Lavinia's *dat* enjoyed reading. She must have brought it for him last night when he hadn't been in a *gut* mood. He hadn't seen her set it down on the table.

Fortunately, it had been protected from the weather by the front porch roof. Abe knew how much Amos valued his books, and he wouldn't have wanted to explain any damage when he returned it. As he sat with it in his hand, he wished he could take back how he'd behaved. Lavinia had been such a support to him since he'd fallen off the roof.

He needed to make it up to her, but how was he going to do that? It didn't seem right to just call her on the phone. But he didn't have the ability to just walk over to her house in his condition.

His *mudder* came out holding a towel and a pair of scissors. "You're looking shaggy. Thought I'd give you a haircut."

Appalled, he stared at her. "Not out here where people can see!"

"I just mopped the kitchen floor. Don't want hair all over the place."

"Then let's go out on the back porch."

"Fine." She walked behind his chair and began pushing it toward the front door.

He hated that she had to push his chair. He couldn't wait until he wasn't a burden to other people.

Then he chided himself for being a little cranky. With all she did, she was making time to cut his hair, and here he was complaining. The woman had raised a *familye*, worked hard to help her *mann* with the farm, and now, when she should get some time to take it easy, she was helping him. His *mudder* was busy as a bee doing something every minute he turned around.

"Is the floor dry?" he asked as they approached the kitchen. He didn't want her to fall and break a hip. Then there would be two of them laid up.

"It's dry. Are you trying to get out of a haircut?"

"*Nee.* Just didn't want you to slip."

They went out onto the back porch, and Waneta tucked the towel around his neck and began clipping. Soon, clumps of hair littered the wooden porch floor. It made him remember all the times she'd cut his hair as a *kind*. He tried not to feel like he'd gone back to that time as she worked, humming a hymn.

"Is *Daed* next?"

"Hmm? *Nee*, I cut his before I came for you."

"You've had a busy morning."

"Same as usual. You know what they say about idle hands."

He stared at his hand, the one he was unable to use since his arm was in a cast. He flexed the fingers and daydreamed about what it would be like when he got the awkward cast off.

"You falling asleep on me there?" Waneta asked wryly.

He shook his head, then got a tap on the crown as she chided him for moving while she was cutting his hair. She muttered under her breath about nearly nicking his ear.

Finally she finished and flicked off the towel, scattering hair. "Stay put while I get the broom."

He watched his *dat* walk out of the cow barn and make his way across toward the house. He'd been worried about his *mudder* slipping on the kitchen floor, and here his *dat* was maneuvering awkwardly with his cane.

His mood plummeted at the thought of what a burden he was on his *eldres*. Even Wayne was taking on more than his usual job.

"What's that you're reading?" his *mudder* asked when she returned with the broom.

He held it up. "Lavinia brought it over last night."

Waneta sniffed. "She didn't take it back after you weren't so nice to her?"

Abe reddened. "*Nee.*"

"What was the problem?"

He ducked his head. "I wasn't feeling well, wasn't in a *gut* mood. So I decided I should go to my room and see her another time, that's all."

Waneta frowned and stared at him, her lips pursed. Then she began sweeping hair clippings from around his feet and off the porch. "Lavinia's a sweet *maedel*. I never interfere, but seems to me you need to apologize." Another sweep of the broom sent more off the porch.

Before he could say anything, she'd marched over to the back door, walked inside, and let the screen door slam behind her.

Well, he guessed he'd been told.

"Your *mudder* riled up about something?" Faron asked as he slowly climbed the stairs to the porch.

"Seems so."

Faron settled into a rocking chair. "What's the problem?"

"Me and my not-so-*gut* mood yesterday. I just decided I should cut short a visit with Lavinia, that's all. *Mamm* thought it wasn't polite."

His *dat* gave him a long look. "So what are you going to do about it?"

"What do you do when you mess up with *Mamm*?"

"Who says I do?"

Abe thought about it. Actually, he couldn't remember a time when his *eldres* had argued.

"Well, there were a few times early on when I got on the wrong side of her," Faron admitted. "I remember talking to Abram. You know he was my friend as well as the bishop before he died. He told me about a quote from Ephesians that he liked. It says be kind to one another, tenderhearted, forgiving one another just as God through Christ has forgiven us." He smiled reminiscently. "Followed that advice for more than thirty years now, and it's served me well." Then he chuckled. "An *Englisch* friend said it a little more plainly than that. He said, 'Happy wife, happy life.'"

Abe hadn't heard that one, but it made sense. But he and Lavinia weren't married... and with all that was happening, marriage looked far in the future.

"So what did you do to make it up to *Mamm* when you did mess up?"

Faron grinned. "Went into town and bought her a box of her favorite chocolates. She's partial to turtles."

"Turtles?"

"*Ya.* They pour chocolate on top of caramel, with pecans sticking out like little legs. Looks like a little brown turtle." He looked thoughtful. "Been a while since I bought her some."

Abe didn't think he'd ever seen them, but they sounded *gut*. Then he frowned. "Well, chocolates won't work." Abe waved his *gut* hand at his wheelchair. "Can't get myself anywhere to buy them."

"Could be someone might be persuaded to pick them up while he's in town getting a few things we need this afternoon."

"*Ya?*"

"*Ya.*"

"Deal. Then all I have to do is persuade Lavinia to come over and apologize to her."

Faron grinned. "I have faith in you." He stood. "Be thinking about what kind of chocolates you want me to get while I ask your *mudder* for her supply list."

Abe thought about the only time he'd seen Lavinia sampling chocolate from the candy shop. He realized he'd been more interested in watching her rosy lips than what she was eating.

Maybe he'd better ask his *dat* to get a sampler.

Chapter Sixteen

Lavinia checked the answering machine in the phone shanty and shook her head.

"Please call me, Lavinia. We need to talk."

Abe had left messages for her three days in a row now. Her hand hovered over the erase button and then, with a heavy sigh, she hit it. She sat there for a moment in the chair beside the machine. *Ya*, she heard a note of apology in his voice. But she shook her head. She had to resist it. Her feelings had been hurt, and she just didn't want to talk to him for a while.

She reminded herself that she'd been raised to forgive. Every fiber of her being called out to her to do so.

Maybe she would. *Allrecht*, she probably would.

Just not today.

But maybe some time apart would do them *gut*.

Her *mudder* looked up from the stove as Lavinia walked into the kitchen. "Any messages?"

Lavinia nodded and handed her the piece of paper she'd scribbled a message on.

Rachel read it and nodded. "I think I'll go call her. I was about to mash the potatoes, and the meatloaf is nearly done. Can you—"

"Go!" Lavinia said with a smile. "I can finish supper."

She busied herself draining the potatoes and worked the potato masher through them in the pot, then added butter and a little milk. Her *mudder* had already started a pan of butter browning, so she stirred it and kept it warm to top the potatoes at the last minute when she put the bowl on the supper table.

Her *dat* walked into the kitchen and sniffed the air. "Mmm, meatloaf. Where's your *mudder*?"

"Returning a phone call."

The oven timer dinged. Lavinia turned it off, then made *schur* the oven and all burners were off as well. Using pot holders, she set the pan with the meatloaf on the top of the stove. When her *dat* approached with a fork to get a taste, she shooed him aside.

"Just checking that it's done," he said with a chuckle. "After all, I might not have put it in the oven at the right time."

Lavinia plucked the sticky note from the kitchen counter. "I don't see how you could mess up with the note *Mamm* left on it this morning in the refrigerator. 'Put in oven at 350 degrees for one hour fifteen minutes,'" she read. But she took the fork he held and used it to break off a bite for him to try. "There," she said, offering it to him. "Taste done to you, Chef?"

Actually, he was pretty *gut* about helping occasionally in the kitchen, unlike some of the men his age who tended to avoid the room unless it was to eat. While he mostly put a casserole or other meal that just needed baking in the oven so they didn't have to wait until Lavinia or her *mudder* got home from work, it often helped them eat supper on time.

"Tastes *gut*," he said, and walked over to sit at the table.

Her *mudder* returned from making her phone call. "Sorry, that took a little longer than I thought it would."

"Sit down. I have everything ready." She handed her *mudder* the basket of sliced bread to put on the table.

Rachel sat as Lavinia sliced the meatloaf and arranged it on a platter. She piled the potatoes in a big bowl and drizzled the browned butter on top before setting it and the platter on the table. A bowl of chow chow was a nice cold addition with its tart, vinegary chopped vegetables.

As she retrieved the pitcher of cold tea from the refrigerator, Lavinia turned and saw her *eldres* chatting quietly, their attention totally on each other. There was such warmth in her *dat*'s eyes as he listened to her *mudder*. She wondered if they ever minded that their youngest chick hadn't left the nest yet.

Her *mudder* glanced up. "Lavinia? Are you *allrecht*?"

She nodded and poured tea into glasses. "Just

thinking you two must look forward to a time when you'll have the house to yourselves."

Her *mudder* stared at her. "What a thing to say. Your *dat* and I love having you. Used to be pretty noisy at suppertime. But sometimes I miss my two *dochders* gathered around this table."

Lavinia sat and felt especially grateful for the meal with them.

They were just finishing up when there was a knock on the front door.

Rachel rose to see who it was, and Lavinia stared with disbelief as she welcomed Ben into the kitchen.

"Sorry to interrupt your supper," he said. He looked uncomfortable as he stood there holding his straw hat in his hands.

"We just finished," her *dat* said. He waved a hand at an empty chair. "Sit."

"Have you eaten?" Rachel asked.

"*Ya, danki.*" He looked at Lavinia. "Hello."

"Hi."

"Amos, let's take our tea and go watch the sunset on the front porch." Rachel rose and stood next to his chair.

"Huh?" he said, and then understanding dawned as she gave him a look.

They took their glasses and walked out of the room.

Lavinia watched them leave, then just sat there. It was so quiet she could hear the kitchen clock ticking away the minutes.

"Can I get you something to drink?" she asked politely.

He shook his head. "*Nee.* I wanted to come by and apologize for my behavior the night I drove you home," he said without meeting her eyes.

Lavinia wondered why she had to have the misfortune of two men who behaved badly in her life.

"That wasn't very nice of you to do that," she said.

"I know."

She sighed. "I'm very upset with you."

"I know I behaved badly, but it won't happen again. Please say you'll give me another chance. Let me take you to lunch."

"*Nee,*" she said firmly. Even if she never went out with Abe again, she didn't want to be with Ben.

He sighed. "It's not like you not to forgive me."

Lavinia gave him a level look. "This is not the same as the time you pulled my braids in *schul* when we were ten."

He gave her a winning smile. "You forgave me then."

Lavinia sat there and told herself she was supposed to forgive him. Her church taught her to forgive. She just didn't think today was the day she was going to be able to forgive either Ben or Abe.

* * *

Abe settled himself in the buggy and took a deep breath as he used a bandanna to wipe his forehead.

"You *schur* you don't want me to go with you?" Wayne asked.

He shook his head. It wouldn't do to take another

man with him when he was going to apologize to Lavinia. Wayne had looked curious when he'd asked for his assistance getting the buggy, helping him inside, and loading the wheelchair. But he hadn't asked Abe where he was going. Abe suspected Wayne had figured it out for himself.

"*Allrecht.* You call if you need me," Wayne told him as he loaded the wheelchair into the back of the buggy.

"I will. *Danki.*"

It felt *gut* to be the driver and not a passenger. To be going for a drive to see Lavinia and not a doctor. To be outdoors and feel the breeze and see how the crops were doing and wave as he passed someone he knew.

He hadn't worked out what he was going to do yet when he got to Lavinia's house if no one was in the yard to get her for him. It was the first impulsive thing he'd done in…he couldn't remember. But he'd find a way to see her.

As he neared her house, he saw a buggy in her drive. It wasn't the buggy Lavinia's *familye* owned. He frowned, trying to identify it.

And then the front door opened and he watched Ben walk out of the house. Lavinia stood there in the doorway watching him walk to his buggy.

Abe called to Star and urged her to move faster so that Lavinia wouldn't see him passing the house. What was Ben doing here? Had Lavinia already decided to move on? Was that why she wasn't returning his calls or accepting his apology?

Discouraged, Abe slumped in his seat and debated going home. He sighed. Home. Another evening to sit by himself on the front porch or lie on his bed in his room or talk with his *eldres*, who surely must be sick of him by now. What did you do when you didn't know what to do? If God had a plan for him, as he'd been told all his life, he *schur* wished He'd show him what it was.

Reluctant to go straight back home, he called to his horse to slow and let him meander his way along the road. They passed the farms of church members and friends of his. The community was a beehive of activity, as it was every day but Sunday. Farmers worked their fields. Women weeded and watered their kitchen gardens. *Kinner* who weren't old enough for *schul* played in their yards.

Abe couldn't help noticing how prosperous and well kept the farmhouses looked, and felt guilty that his own needed a fresh coat of paint and some work on the roof. So much of his time, energy, and money had gone into keeping his dairy farm afloat the past few years. And with his injuries, the work would wait even longer, since Wayne was taking on so many of his chores.

He sighed and told himself that he needed to focus on something positive. The day was warm and sunny, and he was out and about by himself for the first time in weeks. He'd need Wayne's help getting out of the buggy when he got home, but for now he had an independence he'd lost since he fell off the roof, and that was something.

The bishop looked up from his work in his front yard and hailed him as he approached. Abe pulled over, and the older man walked over to lean in the window and grin at him.

"You're looking well there, young Abraham," he said. "Your *dat* brought the medical bills by. He said you were worried about them. You should know better. The community has always pulled together on such things."

Abe ducked his head. "I know. Just wish it hadn't happened."

"We don't know why such things do," Leroy said. "I know it seems like it's all bad right now. You can't do for yourself. But maybe it's time to let others help you and know that it's all part of a plan we don't always understand at the time."

"I guess." Abe met his gaze.

"So you're out for a drive by yourself. How's that feel?"

"Pretty *gut*. When I get home, Wayne will have to help me out, but for now it's just Star here and me."

Leroy stepped back. "I'll let you get back to it." He tilted his head and studied Abe. "Maybe you should stop by a certain *maedel*'s house and see if she'd like to go along for a drive."

Abe felt his spirits fall. But he wasn't about to share with Leroy what he'd just seen. "Maybe."

"Giddyap," he called to Star, and he waved to the bishop as they got rolling.

They passed more farmhouses, more fields. Abe felt

himself relaxing. Star didn't need much guidance, so he let the reins rest in his lap.

Naomi Zook was taking down the sign in front of her house and glanced out at the road as he approached. She smiled and waved at him.

Abe pulled over and stopped. "Done for the day?"

She nodded. "Did real *gut*. Sold all the vegetables we had for sale." Then she grinned. "Well, had a few zucchinis left. There's always too much zucchini."

"Maybe your *mudder* will sneak it into cake or muffins the way mine does."

Naomi laughed. "She's already been doing that. So, are you out for a drive?"

"*Ya.* Can't do a whole lot else right now."

"You will soon," she said kindly. "Nothing better than a drive on a day like this."

He felt his spirits lifting in response to her friendly, open face. Naomi had always been friendly to him when they attended *schul* and church.

"Would you like to join me?" he found himself asking impulsively.

"I'd love to. Just let me tell *Mamm* where I'm going."

She rushed off, and when she returned, she climbed into the buggy and turned to him with a smile. "So, did you have someplace special you were going, or are you just moseying along?"

"Moseying?"

Naomi laughed. "That's what Daniel and I call it when we don't have any particular destination in mind."

"I guess we'll just mosey then." He checked for

traffic and decided to make a U-turn and go back the way he'd come. "How's Daniel doing?"

"*Gut.*" She took in a deep breath and let it out in a satisfied sigh. "Such a nice time of year. It's not too hot just yet."

She chattered as they rode along—most of it gossip—and now he remembered how much she'd always liked that sort of thing. He listened with half an ear and then realized that he was coming up on Lavinia's house. She was standing out in front by her mailbox chatting with a neighbor, and as Abe passed, she glanced over and their gazes locked. Then she looked over and saw Naomi, and she stiffened.

The buggy rolled on and he frowned. He suddenly realized she might misunderstand seeing Naomi in the buggy. Lavinia had been his whole world after he was injured, and he didn't want that to change.

"Are you *allrecht*?"

"Hmm?"

"Is everything *allrecht*? You're being awfully quiet."

Her pretty face was marred with a frown as she stared at him. "I know I talk a lot. *Mamm* says a *maedel* shouldn't talk so much. That she should get the man to talk about himself. So, Abe, talk to me. Tell me what you've been doing since you fell off the roof." She clapped a hand over her mouth and looked repentant. "Sorry, that didn't sound nice."

"It's *allrecht*. I *did* fall off the roof." He told her about his physical therapy sessions and how he hoped he'd be back to normal soon. She plied him with questions as they rode along, and he realized they were all about the farm and how well it was doing.

"Daniel's taking over the farm, you know," she said.

Daniel had been a year ahead of them in *schul*, and the two had not made a secret of their attraction to each other.

"So I'm looking forward to after harvest," she said, sounding happier than he'd ever heard her. "Like I'm *schur* you and Lavinia are, right?"

Abe didn't know what to say. Even if things were going well with Lavinia, he wouldn't have felt right telling anyone else their plans.

"It's *allrecht*, you don't have to answer," she told him, and she laughed. "I had a lovely time," she told him when he pulled up in front of her house. "I hope to see you out more soon."

"I'm not getting out much right now," he admitted, holding up his arm in a cast. "Lots of doctor appointments, physical therapy. And trying to do more around the farm as I heal."

She nodded. "You take care and say hello to Lavinia for me. Bye!"

He drove home, taking the long way so he wouldn't pass by Lavinia's house again.

Chapter Seventeen

Lavinia walked slowly back into the house and set the mail down on the kitchen table.

"Anything interesting?" her *mudder* asked.

She shook her head. "I think I'll go for a walk."

"Is something wrong? You look upset."

She shook her head. "I just feel like a walk." She turned and left the room quickly before her *mudder* could ask any more questions.

What a shock it had been seeing Abe driving past in his *familye*'s buggy—and then seeing Naomi Zook in the passenger seat! What was that about? She pressed a hand to her heart as she walked down the road. It hurt so to see him out driving with another woman. And just days after they'd last seen each other and he hadn't been the friendliest to her.

Allrecht, she'd been avoiding talking to him. But did

that mean he should just start seeing someone else so quickly? Had she meant so little to him that he could be so...fickle? *Nee*, he wasn't like that, she told herself. She was jumping to conclusions, and that wasn't like her.

As she walked, she exchanged greetings with neighbors and friends sitting on the porches of their homes, enjoying the breeze and the approaching sunset. So many were couples having a last chat after a long, busy day, she couldn't help noticing. Maybe it was just her mood but it felt like nearly everyone she saw was a part of a couple. Like Noah's ark, two by two.

She walked faster and stared ahead. With harvest almost over, she was going to see more emphasis on couples as the marriage season started. She frowned. While she'd told her *mudder* that she and Abe were just friends, the fact was that he'd become more than that to her. She had to admit that in her heart she'd harbored the hope that he'd ask her to marry him soon.

She saw Phoebe, her teacher from years ago, sitting on the porch of her farmhouse just ahead. She smiled and waved when the woman turned and saw her.

"Lavinia, how lovely to see you!"

"Phoebe, how are you doing?" Lavinia wondered how old the woman was. She had already seemed old back when Lavinia was a *kind* attending *schul*, and Lavinia had noticed Phoebe had some problems with memory when she talked with her at church in recent years.

"*Gut, gut.* Are you off to see Abe?"

Lavinia blushed and shook her head.

"Always had your eye on the *bu*. But he was always racing about."

She frowned. Phoebe hadn't been in church lately. Maybe she hadn't heard about Abe's accident.

"I just finished grading the essays," Phoebe told her. "You did a lovely job on yours."

"I—I did?"

"*Ya*, you got an A on it, just like you always do. Such creative writing." She waved a thin hand at her lined face. "It's a bit warm today, isn't it? Would you like a glass of cold tea?"

Lavinia hesitated. She hadn't intended on staying long when she spotted Phoebe, but this talk of essays when she'd been out of *schul* for years concerned her.

"I don't want to put you to any trouble," she began, but Phoebe was already getting to her feet.

"No trouble at all. I fixed a pitcher before supper tonight."

"Then that would be lovely, *danki*." She frowned as Phoebe shuffled toward the front door. She wore two different-colored shoes.

When Phoebe returned, she carried two glasses of lemonade. She handed one to Lavinia then took her seat again and sipped as she looked out at the road with faded blue eyes.

The front door opened, and Ruth, one of Phoebe's *dochders*, walked out. "Lavinia, I didn't know you were out here. *Mamm*, you didn't tell me."

Phoebe stared at her and frowned. "I didn't?"

Ruth shook her head. Lavinia hadn't seen her in

church in a few weeks and thought she looked tired and strained.

"You know what would be *gut* with this lemonade?" Phoebe asked abruptly.

"*Nee*, what, *Mamm*?"

"Some cookies." She set her glass down on the table beside her chair and shuffled off again.

Ruth stared at her for a long moment and then sighed. "Her dementia is getting worse. This time of day is always hard. The doctor called it sundown syndrome."

"She remembered me, but she told me she'd just finished grading my essay."

"Her oldest *schweschder* doesn't think she has a problem. Said they had a long talk the other day and *Mamm* sounded like her old self. I asked if they talked about something that had just happened or something from a long time ago. She said a long time ago, so that meant her memory was just fine. But *Mamm* can't remember something from a few minutes ago sometimes."

Lavinia stared down at her glass. "She went inside saying she'd get us cold tea and came back with lemonade. I'm sorry. It must be hard after she's been so sharp being a teacher for years and years."

"It hurts to see her confused and trying to remember," Ruth said slowly. "The doctor said not to try to make her remember things because it just makes someone more upset. I'm going to a support group of other caretakers of *eldres* and learning ways to cope." She smoothed her apron and smiled ruefully. "Sometimes she forgets she's lived in the *dawdi haus* for years. I guess it's *gut* that we're both widows. I imagine it would be a shock if she walked into her old bedroom I shared with my *mann* when he was alive and found him there."

Phoebe returned without the cookies she'd gone to fetch, wearing a different dress than she'd had on when she went into the house. She frowned as she looked out at the road. "It's not like Johnny to be late." She walked over to take her seat.

Lavinia glanced at Ruth, who didn't look surprised that Phoebe was looking for her *mann*, who'd died five years earlier.

"I suppose it's no secret we're courting," Phoebe told Lavinia with a smile. Then her frown returned and she turned to stare down at the road again. "I hope nothing's happened. People are so careless driving their cars around buggies."

"Lavinia came to see you," Ruth said quickly, distracting her. "You remember Lavinia."

"Did such a *gut* job on her essay," Phoebe said. She reached over to pat Lavinia's hand. "You worked so hard on it."

"I think we should send Lavinia home now," Ruth told her. "It's getting dark and it's a *schul* night. She needs to get home and go to bed."

Phoebe nodded and rose. "See you at *schul* tomorrow, dear."

Lavinia hugged each of them and left. She looked

back as she reached the bottom of the porch steps and watched Ruth gently leading her *mudder* into the house.

The scent of honeysuckle and late-blooming wild roses drifted on the evening breeze as she walked home. Her headlong rush to get out of the house to walk off her mood hadn't been such a *gut* idea after all. Now she felt sad. Melancholy, even.

Hmm. There was a word she didn't use often to describe how she felt. Phoebe would be proud she'd remembered a word from one of the vocabulary workbooks they used in *schul*.

She went into her house and found her *eldres* sitting in the living room reading.

"Have a nice walk?" her *mudder* asked.

"*Ya.* I'm feeling tired, though. I think I'll go to bed and read for a little while." She kissed them both on the cheek and climbed the stairs to her room. Tomorrow was soon enough to talk to her *mudder* about them finding some time to give Ruth a break from caring for Phoebe.

But while she'd told her *eldres* that she was going to read a book, the one on her bedside table didn't appeal. As she lay in her narrow bed waiting for sleep, she couldn't help thinking about how Phoebe had forgotten she'd gone into the house for cold tea and cookies... but she hadn't forgotten her *mann*.

Lavinia wondered how long Phoebe would look for her Johnny.

And how long she would think about Abe.

* * *

Abe pulled into his driveway and sat there for a long moment.

Going for a drive to see Lavinia hadn't been the best idea. He sighed and turned to get out of the buggy, figuring that might be easier than getting in. He was wrong. He bumped his arm in the cast and then felt pain radiate up to his knee when his left foot landed a little too hard. Gasping, he waited for the pain to subside before trying to pull his wheelchair from the back of the buggy.

"Hey, wait a minute and I'll help you!" Wayne called to him.

Abe decided to let him. As he waited, he realized the gift bag with the box of chocolates had fallen out of the buggy. He bent down to pick it up and managed to smack his forehead.

"Here, let me get that for you." Wayne retrieved the bag and placed it on the front seat before he unloaded the wheelchair and set it beside Abe so he could sit in it. Then he put the gift bag on Abe's lap. "Gift from an admirer?" he teased. When he saw Abe's face, his grin faded. "Sorry. Things didn't go as planned?"

Abe shook his head. He didn't elaborate, and Wayne didn't pursue the subject, telling him that he'd done the evening milking as he pushed him toward the house.

Once inside, Abe thanked him and rolled himself into his bedroom. He didn't want to talk to anyone, but soon after, there was a tap on his door and his *dat* stuck his head in. He started to say something when he saw the gift bag Abe had tossed on the bedroom dresser.

"You didn't give them to Lavinia?"

"She had...company."

"Company?" Then his *dat* understood. "Oh. I'm sorry."

"Yeah. Me too." Abe levered himself onto the bed and used his good hand to push the chair away from him.

"Want to talk about it?"

"*Nee!*" Then he sighed. "Sorry. It's my own fault. It'll teach me to take out a bad mood on someone. Lavinia decided not to put up with me, and I don't blame her."

Faron sat on the end of the bed and stared at the cane he held in his hands. "Well, get some rest. Things have a way of looking different after a *gut* night's sleep."

Abe didn't see how a *gut* night's sleep was going to change the fact that Lavinia was seeing Ben, but there didn't seem to be any point in debating it. His *dat* patted his shoulder and then got up. "Need any help?" he asked, leaning heavily on his cane.

"*Nee*, but *danki*. See you in the morning."

The next morning, Abe woke up before dawn. He couldn't say a night's sleep had changed his depression about Lavinia, but he pushed himself to get up, get dressed, and go out to the barn to help as best as he could.

"Did you check the weather report?" Wayne asked.

"*Nee.* Not today." He'd been too busy feeling upset over Lavinia. A *gut* farmer couldn't do that.

"Some bad weather expected this week."

Abe's spirits plummeted. "Great. Just what we need." He looked out at his fields. Like many dairy farmers, he grew some of the hay, corn, and soybeans he needed to feed his cows.

He remembered seeing a cartoon strip in a newspaper years ago. The main character was a little man who always walked hunched over and had a dark cloud looming over him. He frowned and felt anxiety build in himself in spite of the cloudless blue skies overhead.

Wayne must have sensed his growing tension. "No need to worry before it gets here," he said calmly as he looked up along with Abe. "We can't control the weather. We can only pray and deal with whatever comes."

Abe sighed. "I know. I just don't need anything else to worry about."

"Then don't."

He gave a snort of laughter. "As if it's that easy."

Wayne shrugged. "It is."

"Look, I'm trying not to worry about things."

"Don't try. Do." He went back to checking the milking equipment.

Abe stared at him for a long moment. Wayne had always been so practical about everything, his faith seemingly resolute. They were *gut* friends because they were so much alike—or had been until Abe had fallen off the roof. Now he knew he worried more than he should.

He looked around. "Well, looks like you've got

things under control here. Maybe I should go see if *Mamm* needs my help with the farm stand."

Now it was Wayne's turn to snort. "Your *mudder* can juggle ten things at once."

He knew Wayne was right, but checking on her made him feel like he was doing something, so he rolled out to the front of the house where she'd set up a table with an umbrella to shade it. Partway down the drive, he heard a loud mechanical racket and rolled his eyes.

Schur enough, his *mudder* had gotten his *dat* to set up the contraption that he'd put together to make ice cream back when they'd taken over the farm from his own *dat*. It was a battery-operated whirligig of a thing with a big wheel that turned and churned a bucket of ice cream and made a clamor that could be heard out to the roadside.

"That thing is as noisy as I remember," he shouted over the din.

Faron grinned. "You never complained when you got to eat the ice cream it made. And it always attracts customers."

"How old is it anyway?"

His *dat* shrugged. "Older'n you, but it still works."

The machine coughed and made a whirring noise and then ground to a stop.

"Just needs a little oil," Faron said.

"Needs a decent burial," Abe muttered, and his *mudder* poked him with her elbow. But he thought he saw her grin.

Faron squirted oil in various places and tinkered with it for a few minutes, and the thing belched to life.

Customers began parking their cars and walking up to stare at the machine.

"How're you making it run?" one man asked. "Don't see an electric cord."

"Battery," Faron told him, gesturing at it. "Beats hand cranking."

"Eh?" the man yelled.

"Battery," Faron shouted over the din.

Soon a crowd was gathered around, enjoying the creamy confection Waneta dished up with a big smile. Faron tucked away bill after bill in the small metal cash box.

Abe just shook his head at them. They looked like they were having the time of their lives. He glanced up at the sky and hoped the weather wouldn't be as bad as predicted this week.

Chapter Eighteen

Lavinia watched Abe walking slowly toward the section of benches set up for the men today. Her eyes widened. He was out of the wheelchair and using a walker! Her heart leaped at his progress. Then she frowned. If they'd been speaking, he'd have told her about it.

She'd been wondering if he would attend church services this morning and how she would handle seeing him again. She wasn't looking forward to it. The only thing that had saved her from having to talk to him was the fact that others arrived right behind him so she was able to avoid him and join her friend Rebecca on a bench.

"It was *gut* to see Abe doing so well," Rebecca said. "I didn't know he was out of his wheelchair."

Lavinia didn't want to tell her she hadn't known, either. She nodded and hoped that Elmer would begin the service quickly.

"I heard Wayne and a couple of men had to get up on the roof and repair it," Rebecca went on. "I'm glad they were able to do it safely."

Lavinia hadn't heard about it. She glanced in Abe's direction and saw him staring at her. Quickly she averted her gaze and was grateful when Elmer stepped to the front of the assemblage. She sent up a quick prayer for Abe, hoping that the roof repair hadn't cost him too much. He'd had enough challenges without the expense of losing the crops that fed his dairy cattle.

When she sighed, Rebecca turned to look at her. "Are you *allrecht*?"

She nodded. "Just glad to sit down."

Not that three hours on a hard bench was the most comfortable. Then she thought about how hard it might be for Abe with his injuries. *Nee*, she was not going to think about him. Not when she was still feeling a little tender at the way he'd treated her. And not when she was in a church service.

Peace settled over her. It was always so during church.

When the service was over, she jumped up and went to help the women with the light meal and coffee they'd serve. The men moved the benches to make it more convenient for the churchgoers to sit in groups and share conversation while they ate and sipped coffee.

She was roaming the room with a carafe of coffee

when she had to stop at the table where Abe sat with other men.

"Wayne told me the roof repair was extensive," Lester was saying.

Abe nodded but didn't say anything.

Shocked, she nearly spilled coffee as she filled his cup. More problems?

Their gazes met, locked. She stared at him, filled with sympathy, but he frowned and looked away.

Feeling rebuffed, she moved on, checked the cups of the other men, filled them, and walked away quickly. She needed to compose herself, and the nearly empty carafe was a *gut* excuse to hurry to the kitchen.

She almost ran into Waneta.

"Lavinia? Are you *allrecht*? You look upset." She stared at Lavinia with concern.

"I—*ya*, I'm fine."

Waneta looked past her. "Did Abe say something to upset you?"

"*Nee.*" She hesitated. "Waneta, I overheard him telling the men sitting with him that the roof had to be repaired—that there was a lot of damage."

Waneta nodded. "None of us thought about having it looked at after his accident. Then it started leaking again, so Wayne and some of the men had to fix it."

"I'm sorry to hear that."

"Abe's upset, of course. He didn't need another expense when he's worried about milk prices and medical bills. But the farm's had tough times before. And we've always managed. Faron and I have told Abe that. All will work out. He's doing so well with his therapy, and that's the most important thing. Won't be long and he'll be *gut* as new." She turned back to the bread she was slicing and arranged it on a plate. "Why don't you put some church spread on this while I get more coffee?"

Lavinia got a butter knife and began spreading the bread with the mixture of peanut butter and marshmallow creme that was a favorite for the after-service light meal. It wouldn't be a Sunday service without it, she couldn't help thinking. Since Waneta was still seeing to the coffee, she carried the plate out and began offering it around.

Wayne and Faron had been sitting with Abe, but she saw that they had left the table. Abe sat brooding into his coffee cup.

"Would you like something to eat?" she asked him as she stopped at his table.

He looked up, his dark blue eyes taking a moment to focus on her. "*Schur.* Didn't get much breakfast this morning. I was running late getting ready."

"I'm glad to see you're out of your wheelchair. That must feel *gut*."

He nodded. "Therapist says the next step is a cane."

She held out the plate as she glanced around the crowded room. "Are Wayne and Faron coming back?"

"Eventually. They went off to talk with the other men."

"Your *mudder* said you had to repair the roof."

He frowned. "*Ya.* Listen, Lavinia, we need to talk."

She shook her head. "Not now."

"When?"

Lavinia glanced around and saw several people looking in her direction. "I have to pass out the bread."

He called out her name, but she pretended not to hear him.

She walked over to the table where Rebecca sat with her *dochder*, Lizzie, and the *kind*'s eyes lit up when she saw the plate.

"*Mamm*, can I have some bread?"

" 'May I?' " Rebecca corrected.

"*Schur*, you may, too. Right, Lavinia?" Lizzie laughed and then said, "Sorry, *may* I, *Mamm*?"

"*Ya.* And I'll have a slice, too." She gestured for Lavinia to lean closer and whispered in her ear. "I'm eating for two."

It took a moment for what she'd said to register. Her friend the midwife was going to have a *boppli*. Her eyes widened.

Rebecca nodded and grinned.

"Oh, I'm so happy for you!" Lavinia said quietly.

Rebecca had been a *wittfraa*, losing her *mann* after they'd been married just a few years. Lavinia knew how hard it had been for her friend to continue her work as a midwife after losing her *mann* and the *boppli* she carried.

How *wunderbaar* to see her looking so happy with Lizzie, the *dochder* she'd gained when she married Samuel, the widower who'd moved here several years ago. Lavinia had loved the story of how Lizzie—then six years old—had played matchmaker and gotten the new *mudder* she wanted by finding ways to bring the two together.

Lizzie tugged on Lavinia's skirt so that she'd bend

down. "*Mamm* says we're not telling everyone yet," she whispered, and then gave her a big grin. "*Daedi* and I are so happy!"

Rebecca wiped at the peanut butter on Lizzie's chin. "I didn't hear you say *danki* to Lavinia."

"*Danki*, Lavinia," she said as she swung her legs and munched on her treat.

"You're *wilkumm*." She looked at Rebecca. Lavinia thought about how *wunderbaar* it was that things had turned out well for her friend. She knew the couple had had problems but had worked them out....

"Lavinia?"

She realized she'd been standing there woolgathering as Rebecca stared at her.

"Are you going to talk to him?" Rebecca asked.

"Who?"

"You know who. Abe can't take his eyes off you."

"Do you want me to leave a slice for Samuel?" she asked, pointedly ignoring the question.

Rebecca grinned. "*Schur*, that would be nice. He's off talking to some of the other farmers about getting in the crops."

It was the hot topic of the day, Lavinia thought, glancing back at Abe. She saw that he was watching her, so she quickly turned and offered the bread to those sitting at a nearby table.

He'd said they needed to talk. She knew he probably wanted to apologize.

She just wasn't *schur* she wanted to listen to another apology from another man who'd behaved badly.

* * *

Abe watched Lavinia moving gracefully around the room offering refreshments. He couldn't help feeling a little envious of the sweet smiles she bestowed on others—except, he noted with surprise, Ben. Apparently Ben wasn't getting smiles from her any more than he was. What had happened between them to earn that frown from Lavinia? he wondered.

His *dat* and Wayne returned to the table, talking about what the other farmers were saying about the progress they were having with harvesting their crops. Abe listened with half an ear as he watched Lavinia.

"Samuel Miller said he pulled three big trout from his field."

Abe dragged his attention back to the conversation. "Huh? Trout?"

Faron laughed. "I don't think you're paying attention." He looked at Lavinia walking on the other side of the room. "Wonder what you're looking at. Or should I say who?"

"So, are we going to get enough help bringing in our crops?" he asked his *dat*, hoping to distract him.

"That's not a problem. Everyone wants to help since you've been laid up," his *dat* told him.

That made him feel a little better. He had to believe all the bad things that had happened were over or he was never going to dig himself out of the hole he felt he was in.

His *mudder* stopped by the table. "Your *dat* and I are going to get a ride home with Wayne."

Surprised, he stared at her. "Why?"

Waneta glanced over at Lavinia then back at him. "I think you have some unfinished business."

She knew him too well. "You don't have to get a ride with Wayne. We can go home now. I don't think Lavinia's going to talk to me."

"How is she going to avoid it?" she asked, her eyes sparkling with mischief. "Think about it. You're both going to be in the same place, so it's going to be hard for her to avoid you."

Abe hadn't thought about that.

"I always knew I had a smart *mudder*," he said thoughtfully. "But I had no idea how smart."

"It's how I ended up with your *dat*."

"It's me that's smart," Faron said, and Waneta turned to see him standing behind her. "I went to *schul* with her and saw she wasn't just beautiful, she was the most intelligent *maedel* I knew."

Abe hoped one day he had a woman look at him with the kind of love his *mudder* showed his *dat*. She positively glowed with it.

"See you at home," he said, but he didn't think they heard him as they left him.

A few minutes later, Lavinia stopped by his table with a coffeepot in hand. "I thought I saw your *eldres* leave."

"They did."

"They're coming back for you?"

He shook his head.

"I don't understand."

"Wayne gave them a ride home so I could talk to you."

She put a hand on her hip and met his gaze. "I don't want to talk to you."

Abe wondered what she'd say if he told her he wasn't leaving until they talked. He didn't think he had the nerve. And really, that wasn't the kind of man he was....

"Lavinia. Please," he said quietly.

She turned and left the room. He sat there for a few minutes more and finally decided she wasn't coming back. Nearly everyone else had gone. Giving up, he got to his feet and found he'd gotten stiff from sitting so long. He grasped his walker and made his way carefully from the room.

Just as he reached the front door, he heard Lavinia call his name. He turned.

"Where are you going?" she asked.

"I'm leaving since you won't talk to me."

She walked toward him. "You couldn't expect me to talk to you when there are others around."

"*Allrecht*," he said, careful not to let her see his relief. "Do you want to go for a ride?"

She sighed. "Fine."

They walked outside, and he navigated his way carefully down the stairs.

"I'll go get the buggy."

"Don't be silly," she said crisply. "I sent *Daed* out for it."

Schur enough, her *dat* pulled up in front of the house.

"*Danki*," Abe said as Amos got out of the buggy.

"Have a nice drive," Amos said before walking off.

Abe couldn't tell if the man knew his *dochder* was upset with him, but when Amos walked away without further comment, he decided maybe Lavinia hadn't shared it with him. Most couples didn't talk about who they were dating. Many might suspect, but often the *eldres* didn't know about a decision to marry until right before—or during—the announcement of banns at a church service.

"It feels *gut* to be driving a buggy again," he said after they got into it.

"*Ya*, I saw you out driving around the other day," she told him.

When he heard the chill in her tone, he realized he'd been right to think she might have misunderstood seeing Naomi in his buggy.

"I was just giving her a ride."

"I see."

"Speaking of seeing..."

"What?"

"When I drove past your house, I saw Ben coming out." He hesitated. "Someone told me he drove you home from the singing."

"He did." She frowned. "And if you must know, he had to apologize for not being a gentleman."

"I see."

"Do you?"

He nodded. "I'm not happy he behaved badly, but I'm glad you're not interested in him."

"I've never been interested in anyone else, Abe."

He felt hope rise. Then he saw the gift bag with

the chocolates his *dat* had bought for him. He didn't remember seeing it in the buggy when they left for church earlier.

Had his *dat* or *mudder* put it in the buggy, planning a little matchmaking? he wondered. Glancing over, he saw Lavinia's gaze dart to the bag, and when she realized he was looking at her, she jerked her glance away and stared straight ahead.

"It's for you," he told her.

"Me?"

He nodded.

"What is it?" she asked.

"Take a look."

She picked up the bag as he guided the buggy down the drive, checked for traffic, then pulled out onto the road.

He heard the rustle of the tissue paper, then her murmur of pleasure when she drew out the package. "I love chocolate," she said.

"I know. I remembered."

She opened the box and offered it to him.

"I don't think I'm supposed to eat them," he said.

"Why not?"

"They're part of an apology, so it doesn't seem right. I got them for you because my *dat* says it's a better way to say you're sorry than flowers. Seems he's bought them for my *mudder* a few times when they've had a disagreement and such."

She chose a chocolate and then looked at him, surprised. "So you told him about us?"

"He kind of noticed you weren't coming around."

She popped the chocolate into her mouth and chewed, looking thoughtful.

He turned and looked at her. "I'm really sorry I treated you the way I did, Lavinia. You didn't deserve that just because I was upset with my life."

"You've had a really bad time," she said.

"I don't want your sympathy," he told her. "I wouldn't have gotten through the past weeks without you. I want you to know that."

"I care about you." Her voice was quiet, but he heard every word. And clung to them. "We've been friends for years."

"I want us to be more," he said.

Her gaze flew to him. She took a deep breath and then she nodded. "I want that, too."

The timing couldn't have been better. A covered bridge loomed ahead. The Amish called them kissing bridges because, in the privacy of them, a couple could steal a kiss.

The buggy entered the bridge. In the dim light, he turned to her and saw her eyes grow wide as they leaned toward each other.

He kissed her and her lips tasted of chocolate.

Chapter Nineteen

The shop got busier as the days grew warmer. Summer always brought tourists from all over the country. Lavinia loved hearing the different accents and had gotten quite *gut* at recognizing the origin of a visitor from just a few words—the slow, easy drawl of a Southerner, the brisk, quick speech of someone from New York. She was as curious about them as they were about the Amish but was more of a silent observer.

It was fun to see the reactions of the *kinner* some brought into the shop with their *eldres*. They regarded her with wide eyes, and often she heard them ask their *eldres* questions—sometimes so loudly and inappropriately that they were quickly shushed.

"Mommy, is that a Pilgrim lady?" she heard one ask. "Did she come over on the *Mayflower*?"

Her *mudder* blushed and apologized. "I explained to her who the Amish are, but she's just six. She doesn't understand." She looked at her *dochder*. "Honey, why don't you go sit with your father on the bench outside?"

"It's okay, really. Children are curious." Lavinia smiled at the little girl, who wore a Disney princess dress, as she rang up the woman's purchase. "We came here for the same reason as the Pilgrims all those years ago," she told her. "The people where we lived in Europe were mean to us because of our religion."

"Did you fight with the Indians when you got here?"

She shook her head. "We try to live peacefully." She looked at the *mudder*. "There are some great children's books on the Amish in the local bookstores."

"Thanks. We might get one. She loves to read." The woman studied the rug Lavinia had pushed aside on the counter to take care of the sale. "You really make these yourself?"

She nodded. "I started making them when I wasn't much older than your daughter. It was fun to play with scraps of fabric in different colors and textures. Still is."

"It's too bad you don't sell kits. I'd like to try making one."

"That's a good idea," she said, surprised. "I'll mention it to my mother. Maybe next time you visit we'll have them."

She couldn't wait to tell her *mudder*, who was off on an errand to the post office.

And she couldn't wait until the business day was over. She and Abe had been seeing each other nearly every day since last Sunday, when he'd taken her for a ride, apologized, and kissed her for the first time. They were dating, and this evening they were going to eat at their favorite Italian restaurant. Abe was going to pick her up in his *familye*'s buggy.

They still hadn't talked about the future, but she felt that Abe's accident had taught both of them to appreciate each day more.

She walked to the front door of the shop when there was a lull in customers to look outside. The sky was a vivid blue without a cloud in sight. Tourists and locals wore summer clothes, and some looked a bit overwarm as they strolled the sidewalks. She wore her favorite cotton dress, the one the color of the wild violets that grew abundantly near her home.

Sunny days were ahead. She just felt it. Abe was healing well, according to his doctors. And it was summer, when a young *maedel*'s thoughts turned to the marriage season coming up after the harvest was over....

As much as she loved her job, she wanted the day over so she could spend an hour or two with Abe in the little Italian restaurant, where it could be just the two of them talking about their day, where they could look into each other's eyes and feel the connection they'd had since childhood. She'd begun to hope they'd talk soon about marrying after the harvest.

The many years of growing up together, studying in their one-room *schul*, learning about each other while they were taught reading and writing and arithmetic, as well as Amish history...it gave them a foundation for their relationship. It was no surprise that this foundation, built from childhood friendship and a commitment to stay together through the storms of life, kept couples together in her community.

Not all Amish couples knew each other since childhood, of course. Occasionally someone would move into the area, like Samuel, Rebecca's *mann*. But most of the couples she knew were like her and Abe—first childhood friends, then teens who dated and, in their twenties, realized they loved each other and wanted to be married.

She enjoyed listening to the voices of their customers to figure out where they came from, but she also observed the relationships the *Englisch* couples had. It was a wonder to her that their marriages worked when couples so often didn't know each other for years like the Amish did. She thought of Cassie, one of Rebecca's *Englisch* friends. Cassie hadn't known her *mann* all her life, but Rebecca said the couple was very happy and had recently welcomed a *boppli*.

Did the *Englisch* believe that God set aside someone for them the way the Amish did? she wondered. She studied *Englisch* couples when they visited the store to see if they had the same sense of unity that the married Amish couples she knew had. All she knew for *schur* was that the *Englisch* didn't often work together on farms or businesses the way the Amish did, which she felt gave them a common goal and helped them have more time to be together.

The woman who'd visited the shop a little while ago with her daughter walked past carrying another shopping bag. Lavinia smiled at the Disney princess and found herself musing about how she'd read some *Englisch* fairy tales when she visited the library when she was younger. They had often featured a young woman waiting for her prince to come riding up on a white steed. She hadn't known what to think of such stories. Her *mudder* hadn't told her she couldn't read them, but she'd said they were the kind of thing that just made girls have unrealistic expectations of men.

Well, she didn't have any unrealistic expectations of Abe. She'd known him for too long.

Her *mudder* came bustling into the shop, carrying a bag from a sandwich shop nearby. "Decided to treat us to a sub."

"But we brought our lunch."

"So we'll leave it in the refrigerator and have it tomorrow. Unless you don't want a turkey sub?"

Lavinia laughed. "As if I've ever been able to turn one down. This is a day for treats. Lunch from the sandwich shop and pizza with Abe after work."

"How were things while I was gone?" she asked as they sat behind the counter and ate their sandwiches quickly.

"Busy until a few minutes ago."

Rachel nodded. "Looks like another *gut* summer for us. I'm going to get a glass of lemonade. Do you want one?"

"*Ya, danki.*"

Two customers walked in complaining about the heat, so the glasses of lemonade sat on the counter while Lavinia answered their questions about the carved wooden bowls they'd seen in the display window. Each bought a bowl, and one added a small carved bird by the same artist.

One woman looked at the other. "I think it's time for us to go find a cold drink and have a sit-down."

The other woman lifted the bag with her purchases and nodded. "Sounds good to me."

Rachel smiled at Lavinia as the women left. "I think it's time we had a cold drink, too."

But it was as if a *schul* bus had let out down the street. Customer after customer came in, and the afternoon passed in a blur. By the time they got to sip their drinks, the ice had melted. Lavinia sighed. It was going to be nice to sit down in the restaurant with Abe and enjoy eating and drinking in a leisurely manner. Really nice.

* * *

There she was.

Abe pulled up in front of Rachel's shop just as Lavinia came out, her *mudder* behind her. She looked like summer itself in a dress the color of the wild violets that bloomed along the road, her eyes bright with pleasure as she caught his gaze. Rachel waved at him as she locked the door, but he only had eyes for Lavinia as she walked toward his buggy. Was it possible that she was growing prettier the longer he knew her?

She smiled as she saw him and walked gracefully toward the buggy. A breeze caught her dress and molded it against her slender form.

"Right on time," she said as she got into the buggy.

Her smile warmed his heart. Abe wasn't going to tell her that he'd gotten into town a half hour early and had to drive around for a while. She didn't need to know how much he'd come to want to see her.

He wanted more with this *maedel*. He wanted to see her more than a few hours each day.

He wanted a life with her. He wanted to marry her.

"Are you *allrecht*?" she asked as he stared at her.

"*Ya*," he said slowly, and shook his head as if to clear it.

Careful! he warned himself as he checked for traffic and pulled out onto the road. Precious cargo aboard now. Watch what you're doing.

He frowned as they moved forward slowly. "Traffic's really heavy today."

"Have you forgotten we're in our busiest tourist season?" she asked.

"Guess I've had a lot on my mind."

"I know."

It was growing closer to the time they needed to talk if they were going to marry. The marriage season started right after harvest. If they didn't do it then, they would have to wait a whole year....

"Did you have a *gut* day?"

She nodded. "Busy but pleasant."

Abe stopped for a jaywalking shopper then proceeded

slowly. When he glanced back, he saw Liz guiding her van into the parking space he'd just left.

"How was your day?" she asked him.

"Busy as well. Doctor and physical therapy appointments in the morning. I'm still not much help to Wayne in the cow barn, so I spent a lot of the afternoon working with *Mamm* in the farm stand."

"Is she still making ice cream? I remember how delicious it was."

He rolled his eyes. "She won't listen to me that she's doing too much. And *Daed* gets such a charge out of setting up that noisy ice-cream machine."

"They really enjoy helping you. And doing things together is what makes a happy marriage, don't you think?"

Abe glanced over at her. "I guess. But they're getting older, and I was really hoping they'd take things a little easier, you know?"

"I think staying active makes them young."

He hadn't thought of it that way. "*Daed* does need to be careful, though, with his MS."

"True."

Traffic was heavy, with some of the cars on the road bearing out-of-state license tags. "It's easy to forget how busy it gets in town this time of year when you don't come in often," he said.

"Great for business."

He guided the buggy into the parking lot of the Italian restaurant. He'd left the choice of where they'd eat up to her and wasn't unhappy with it. The pizza was *wunderbaar* and the prices were reasonable, so it was a favorite with locals. But he felt a little guilty that he'd never taken her to one of the fancier places available.

"What?" she asked.

He glanced at her. "What what?"

"I can almost hear you thinking."

"Are you *schur* you don't want to go someplace nicer?"

She shook her head. "This is very nice. And I love pizza. You know that. Come on. They're going to get busy as people get off work." She got out of the buggy and waited for him to join her.

It was great fun to surprise her with the fact that he now used a cane—one with four legs that stuck out at the bottom for balance—instead of the walker.

"You don't have your walker!" she exclaimed.

He grinned. "Hoping to fire my therapist soon."

They went inside and sat in their favorite booth in the back. The waitress, a young Mennonite teenager, brought their soft drinks without needing them to order, even though they hadn't been in since Abe's accident. "Large thin crust, half pepperoni, half mushroom?" she asked as she set the drinks down on the table.

Abe grinned. "You sure remember your customers."

"That I do." She bustled off to put in their order.

He watched Lavinia settle back against the plastic cushions of the booth with a sigh.

"Feels *gut* to get off my feet," she said when she saw he was looking at her.

There was a candle on the table stuck in the neck

of an empty bottle of wine. Different colors of wax dripped down it. The candle flame cast a golden glow on Lavinia's face.

Abe reached for her hand and rubbed at the palm of it with his thumb. Public displays of affection were discouraged by their church, which was one reason why they liked the privacy of the booth at the rear of the restaurant. "You look so pretty tonight."

She shook her head. "I'm *schur* I look tired. It was a busy day, like I said. *Mamm* and I barely got to eat, and we didn't get to sit down but for a few minutes." Then she smiled. "I don't mean to complain. I like to stay busy. We sold two of my rugs today. It's nice to have people like them."

He was a man. He didn't know quite what to say about the decorative rugs. "Why wouldn't they? They're attractive and make a room look better. My *mudder* loves the one you gave her for the *dawdi haus*."

Lavinia shrugged as she picked up her drink to take a sip. "I just take scraps of fabric and make them into a rug."

"It takes creativity. And there's something nice about not wasting things, don't you think?"

"I guess."

An *Englisch familye* with several *kinner* took the table near them. He saw Lavinia's gaze go to them.

"A little girl came in today and wanted to know if I was a Pilgrim," she told him as she looked back at him. "You know, like from the *Mayflower*. Such a sweet *kind*. She was wearing a Disney princess dress."

"Disney?" He smiled at the server as she set the pizza on the table, made sure they had plenty of napkins, and left them.

"You know. Disney like in cartoons and movies," Lavinia said as she placed a slice of pizza on her plate. "I know neither of us was much interested in a *rumschpringe*, but you went to some movies, didn't you?"

"I don't remember seeing any Disney movies with princesses."

She laughed. "I guess you wouldn't have gone to one. Disney makes cartoons about *Englisch* fairy tales. Made me think how differently the idea of love and marriage are in those stories."

Abe paused with his slice halfway to his mouth. "How's that?"

"In their fairy tales, they talk about how someday a prince will come and the couple will live happily ever after."

"A prince, huh?"

"*Ya*, you know what a prince is, right?"

"Of course I know what a prince is." He bit into his pizza and thought about that. He was hardly what any woman would consider a prince, but then, Amish *maedels* didn't expect them.

But was she hinting about marriage? He chewed and swallowed and waited for her to say more.

Instead, she finished her first slice and reached for a second.

The server returned to see if they needed anything else and brought a box so they could take home leftovers.

When she left the check on the table, Lavinia reached for it. Abe grabbed the slip of paper away from her.

"What are you doing?" he asked.

"You shouldn't pick up the check every time we go out," she told him.

"That's what a man does."

She raised her eyebrows. "That's ridiculous. Let me pay for it this time. You've had so many expenses lately."

"I can afford to take you out for a pizza."

"And I can do the same." And yet she let him pull out his wallet and count out bills.

"You're being old-fashioned." She picked up her purse and stood. "That's another thing that's different between the *Englisch* and us Old Order Amish. I've heard that the *Englisch* men let the women pay for a date sometimes."

"Well, you're with an Amish man right now. And even if he's not a prince, he's getting the check."

They walked out to his buggy and got in.

"So this buggy won't change back into a pumpkin at the stroke of midnight?" she asked with a grin, and then had to explain what she meant as they began the drive home.

Chapter Twenty

Abe hadn't let her pay for their pizza date, so she suggested they go for a picnic on Saturday, and she'd make fried chicken and potato salad.

Summer was the worst time to be standing in a kitchen frying chicken on a hot stove, but it wouldn't be a picnic without it. Not to her, anyway, she thought as she turned the pieces in the cast-iron skillet.

"Smells *wunderbaar*," her *dat* said as he walked into the kitchen and got a glass from the cupboard.

"I'm making enough for your supper as well as the picnic," she told him. "And I just made fresh lemonade and put it in the refrigerator. Have some."

"I do believe I will. Where's your *mudder*?"

"Went to deliver some casseroles to a friend. Should be back soon."

She used tongs to lift chicken onto a plate lined with a paper towel to drain it. When she added more chicken to the skillet, the bubbling oil popped and hit her hand. "Ouch!"

"You *allrecht*?" her *dat* asked.

"I'm fine."

Amos set his glass down and walked over to her. He took her hand in his and examined it. "Go run some cold water on it and I'll get the burn ointment."

"It's fine." But she did as he said as he rummaged in a cabinet for the first aid kit.

She kept a careful eye on the chicken frying as she turned off the tap and dried her hand on a dish towel. Her *dat* dabbed burn ointment on the spot, then kissed her cheek.

"I remember the first time I did this," he said as he capped the tube. "Your *mudder* was teaching you to fry chicken."

"Guess I haven't learned much, have I?"

He shrugged. "Accidents happen. Feel any better?"

She nodded. "The ointment helped. Bacon's the worst. It pops a lot more unexpectedly than frying chicken does. Seems to hurt a lot more, too."

After she finished with the chicken, she turned off the flame under the skillet and poured her own glass of lemonade. The battery-operated fan on the nearby counter didn't do much to cool things off. She took the glass and rolled it across her forehead and felt a little cooler.

"Here, you can snack on this so you don't get into the chicken I put in the refrigerator for supper for you and

Mamm," she told him. She set a plate with a chicken leg and some potato salad she'd made the night before in front of him.

"You're a *gut dochder*," he said, grinning at her.

"I know how you are with fried chicken," she told him fondly.

When she climbed into Abe's buggy a few minutes later and he sniffed appreciatively at the basket she set on the seat between them, she wondered if all men felt the same way about it.

"A picnic with your fried chicken is the best date ever."

She smiled. "Better than pizza?"

"You bet. It's going to rain in a few hours, though."

They went to a favorite park and enjoyed their food, but before they got to the cookies she'd packed, they heard the rumble of thunder overhead.

Summer and late afternoon showers just seemed to go together. They ran for the buggy and laughed as they piled inside, damp but cooler. Rain pattered down and enclosed them in their own private shelter as *eldres* scrambled to get their picnic things and *kinner* inside their vehicles.

Lavinia sat there watching and felt mixed emotions. *Ya*, she and Abe were closer than ever, but she wondered if he was going to ask her to marry him this wedding season. She knew he was very traditional, like many Amish men, but was she going to sit passively and then be sorry if they just drifted along and it became too late to marry until next year?

Impulse had her turning to look at him, and she caught him peeking into the picnic basket. "Abe?"

He jumped, and the lid slammed on his fingers. "Ouch!"

"We need to talk about our relationship."

"*Allrecht.*" He looked at her warily.

"I think we should get married," she blurted out.

"You—" he began, then cleared his throat. "You do?"

She nodded. "I love you, and if you don't know it, then there, I've said it." Emboldened, she went on. "I don't think you realize how soon harvest will be over—"

"I know when harvest is," he interrupted her.

"Well, you seemed surprised at what time of year it was when you picked me up in town to have pizza."

"I just haven't been in town to notice how busy it is now," he said defensively.

She shook her head. "We're getting off track. If you don't love me—if I'm completely wrong about the way you feel—then say so."

Looking chastened, he reached for her hand. "I do love you. When you were walking out of the shop yesterday, it hit me. I didn't say anything because I didn't know if you felt the same way."

She stared at him. "Would I have spent so much time with you in the hospital if I didn't love you? Worried about you? Visited you at home since you were released?"

"We've always been friends, but...I guess not. Still, I don't think I realized it until yesterday." He shook his head. "Guess I'm slow."

"*Ya.*" She waited. "So?"

Abe frowned. "I worry that I can't offer you much, Lavinia. All I have is a dairy farm that's hanging on by a thread."

"Do you think I care about that? I know how traditional you are, Abe, but don't you think that's really being old-fashioned?"

"*Nee*, I think it's being realistic."

"I'm *schur* your *eldres* would tell you that every farm goes through its ups and downs. My own *familye*'s certainly has. But having a partner to work with you helps, don't you think?"

"That's what my *dat* has told me," he admitted. "But if we wait until things are more stable—"

"We might be old and gray," she snapped.

His eyes widened. "I wasn't thinking of waiting that long."

Maybe she shouldn't have been so blunt. But it needed to be said. "I don't want to just sit and hope things will get better," she said. "Why can't we be together while we're working to make the farm profitable? Why do we have to be apart?"

Abe studied their clasped hands. "We don't," he said after a long moment. "Lavinia, will you marry me?"

She smiled and nodded and felt like laughing with joy. "I thought you'd never ask."

They kissed and sat for a long time, listening to the rain and making plans for the future.

* * *

Abe was driving them home and meant to only wave at his *eldres*, but Lavinia tugged at his sleeve.

"Stop! I want some ice cream. I love your *mudder*'s ice cream."

"You want to tell them?" he asked.

"Do you want to?"

"It's up to you," he said as he pulled the buggy over in front of the house.

She shook her head. "It feels a little new. Does that make any sense?"

"I guess." He sat there studying her. If she wanted to wait, that was fine with him. It still felt a little strange to be engaged—in a *gut* way—to him.

They got out and walked over to the farm stand. Abe tried to hold back his grin when the clackety-clack of the machine grew louder as they approached it. It was such an outlandish contraption, but his *dat* got such a kick out of it, and it was proving to attract people to stop and sample the ice cream. Two cars pulled up behind his buggy as they walked to the stand.

Lavinia reached into her purse for money, but Abe stopped her. "You are *not* paying for it."

"Absolutely not!" Waneta agreed. "We have vanilla, chocolate, and strawberry."

"Strawberry for me."

"Cone or cup?"

"Cone."

"Strawberry for me, too," Abe said.

"As if I didn't know," his *mudder* said with a smile. "He's asked for strawberry since he was a *bu*. When I'd send him out to pick them, he'd come back with strawberry juice smeared all over his face and a half-full pail in his hands."

"Funny, I don't remember it that way," Abe said, looking embarrassed.

Waneta scooped up ice cream and handed Lavinia a cone with two big scoops.

"Wow. That's a lot," Lavinia told her. "Maybe make me one with one scoop and I'll give this one to Abe."

Waneta grinned and shook her head. "*Nee.* Cones come with two scoops." She made a cone for Abe and then turned to her other customers.

Abe ate his cone while she served up ice cream and Faron collected money.

When the customers had walked away with their treats, Waneta turned to Faron. "I think I'm going in to get a glass of water. Feeling pretty warm out here."

Faron looked up from squirting oil on the chain of his machine. "Bring me out one when you come back?"

"*Schur.*" She looked at Lavinia. "Want to come with me?"

"*Allrecht.*" Lavinia licked her cone as she walked with the older woman into the house.

Abe finished his cone and watched his *dat* fussing over his beloved contraption. Well, he guessed the man deserved to have a hobby after all his years of working hard.

* * *

Lavinia sat at the table eating her cone as Waneta got a pitcher of ice water from the refrigerator and poured two glasses.

Waneta fanned her face with her hand as she drank thirstily. "Are you staying for supper? We're just having some leftovers. I have baked chicken from last night, some macaroni salad and such. It's so warm today."

Then she set the glass on the table so suddenly water sloshed in it, and she fell to the floor.

Shocked, Lavinia dropped her cone and rushed to her side. She knelt beside Waneta and called her name but the woman lay still and silent, her eyes closed, her face so pale.

Pushing to her feet, Lavinia ran to the front door and yelled for Abe and Faron, then rushed back to Waneta. She wet a dish towel with the ice water from one of the glasses and knelt to press it to Waneta's forehead.

The men came into the kitchen as fast as they could, both limping a little and leaning on canes.

"She was complaining about being warm and then just collapsed!" Lavinia cried as they approached.

As Faron joined her at his *fraa*'s side, Waneta stirred and opened her eyes. "What happened?" she asked, looking confused.

"You just fell," Lavinia told her as she stroked the wet cloth over her forehead. She looked at Abe. "Call nine-one-one."

"Don't be silly." Waneta struggled to sit up. "The heat just got to me. Could happen to anyone."

Abe looked at his *dat*. "*Daed?*"

Faron frowned. "Let's get your *mudder* up off the floor and see how she does."

"Let us," Lavinia insisted, worried that with his MS

Faron could lose his balance and end up on the floor along with his *fraa*.

Waneta fussed at them as Lavinia and Abe grasped her elbows and helped her to stand, then lowered her into a chair at the table. As she reached for a glass of water, her hand shook, but she drank the contents. "I'm feeling better," she declared. "No one is calling nine-one-one."

"Always was stubborn," Faron said as he took a seat.

Waneta pushed one of the glasses toward him. "There's the water I was going to bring you."

"You're looking awful pale."

"Faron, I'm *allrecht*."

"*Mamm*, I think we should have you checked out," Abe said.

She glanced at the clock on the wall. "I'm going to cool off, then I'm going to go out and get everything inside."

"*Nee*," Abe said firmly. "You're going to sit here and rest. I'll go out and take care of it." He turned on the battery-operated fan on a nearby counter and directed it to blow on her. "*Daed*, keep an eye on her and yell if you need me."

"Will do."

Abe walked back out to the farm stand with Lavinia. "It's all my fault," he said as he began piling the insulated chest with the ice cream and cartons of cones into a wooden wagon his *mudder* used to transport them from house to stand.

"How do you figure it's your fault?" she asked as

she gathered up the metal ice-cream scoops and basket of paper napkins and put them in the wagon.

"She's been doing too much to help around here since my accident. They both have. They're too old to be doing all they do."

"They love every minute of it," she told him.

He shook his head. "It's too much. I need to find a way to get them both to stop overdoing."

She put her hand on his arm. "They will as soon as you're better."

A car pulled up, and *kinner* began tumbling out of the back doors as their frazzled-looking *mudder* called after them to wait for her.

"Ice cream!" the oldest, looking about seven or eight, cried.

Abe hesitated. He had almost everything packed up. But one look at the *mudder* and he couldn't send her away with disappointed *kinner*. So he pulled the ice chest out of the wagon and began taking orders for cones. The *kinner* wanted double chocolate cones, but their *mudder* shook her head and said to give them single scoops. After an apparent battle with herself, the *mudder* asked for a single strawberry cone. Lavinia handed out plenty of napkins.

"Thank you so much," the woman said. "It looked like you were shutting down just as we pulled up. I don't know what I'd have done with the kids if you hadn't served us."

"It's our pleasure." He scooped up the last of the strawberry, piled it into a cone, and handed it to her.

She took a taste and sighed. "Oh my, this is delicious. We'll be back."

He shook his head when she handed him money. "It's on me. Call it a mom special." He didn't want to tell her she might not get to stop by again if he had his way.

The woman tucked her money back in the pocket of her shorts. "Thank you. That's very kind. Kids, say thank you to the nice couple."

"Thank you!" they chorused.

She shooed them back into the car, and they waved as they left.

Abe went back to packing everything up again. "If *Mamm* doesn't look better, we have to find a way to make her get checked out."

Lavinia took a deep breath, then let it out. "This should be interesting. Like your *dat* said, she's one stubborn woman."

Chapter Twenty-One

They were halfway up the walk to the front porch when Lavinia had an idea.

She stopped and turned to Abe. "We should call Rebecca."

"Rebecca? The midwife?"

Lavinia nodded vigorously.

"Who's having a *boppli*?"

She punched him lightly on the arm. "Rebecca won't mind taking a look at your *mudder*, checking her out. She can make *schur* Waneta isn't having a problem with her blood pressure. Make *schur* it's just the heat that got to her today."

"That's a *gut* idea." He handed her his cell phone. "Call her."

"You can call her."

He held up his hands. "*Nee, danki.* You do it."

Lavinia took the phone from him and dialed the number. "You'd think you're afraid of catching something from a phone call," she muttered. "Rebecca? Hi, it's Lavinia." She briefly explained the situation and then smiled. "*Danki.* See you soon."

She disconnected the call, then handed the phone to Abe with a satisfied smile. "There. Problem solved."

He nodded. "Now all you have to do is go inside and tell *Mamm* that Rebecca is coming to see her."

Her smile faded. "Why can't you do it?"

"Because it was your idea." He picked up the handle of the wagon and began walking up the ramp to the porch.

"I heard that!" she called as she hurried after him.

"What?"

"You snickered. You think it's funny? I'm not afraid to tell your *mudder* Rebecca's coming to make *schur* she's *allrecht*. I love your *mudder* and just want her to be well. I think she's going to be happy I thought to ask Rebecca here."

She didn't feel so certain when Abe chuckled. "*Schur.*"

They went up the ramp and into the house with the wagon. Abe's *eldres* were still sitting at the table. Lavinia was glad to see that Waneta looked a little better, but Abe had managed to make her doubt what she'd done.

"How are you feeling?" she asked the older woman.

"Much better. *Danki.*"

"I know you didn't want us to call nine-one-one, so I came up with another way to make *schur* you're really *allrecht*."

"Oh?" Waneta frowned. "How?"

"I called Rebecca to ask her to drop by and take a look at you."

Waneta stared at her for a long moment, and Lavinia held her breath. And then Waneta began laughing. She laughed and laughed until tears rolled down her cheeks. When she finally stopped, she lifted a corner of her apron and wiped her streaming eyes.

"*Kind*, I'm not having a *boppli*."

"Well, of course you're not. But Rebecca said she wouldn't mind checking your blood pressure and such."

"Blood pressure's just fine," Waneta said. "I went in for a checkup last week, and it was fine."

"It can't hurt to have Rebecca check you over," Faron said, taking her hand in his. "It was smart of Lavinia to think to call her."

"I suppose so." She looked at Lavinia. "I know you meant well."

Lavinia glanced over at Abe as he leaned against a kitchen counter watching them. He lifted the glass of water in his hand, acknowledging her success.

Waneta glanced at the clock on the wall. "I should be starting supper."

"Please let me do that," Lavinia said.

Before she could ask what she should cook, there was a knock on the door and Rebecca poked her head in.

"So, Waneta, I hear you're feeling a little under the weather," Rebecca said as she walked into the room carrying her medical bag. She moved slowly, one hand resting protectively on her belly.

Lavinia couldn't help staring at it. It seemed to her that the woman's baby bump had grown a lot since the last time she'd seen her.

Rebecca caught her gaze and grinned. "I still have months. I'm not going to have the baby here." She turned to Waneta. "Would you like to go into the other room so I can take your blood pressure?"

Waneta shook her head. "Here's fine." She patted the chair beside her. "Sit and take a load off."

"I will in a minute." Rebecca took out her stethoscope and a blood pressure cuff from her bag, wrapped the cuff around Waneta's arm, and proceeded to measure her pressure.

"A little high," she noted as she removed the cuff and replaced it and the stethoscope in her bag. She took Waneta's pulse and nodded. "A bit fast. How did you feel before you fainted?" she asked as she sat in a chair.

"Too warm. A little lightheaded. I came in for a drink of water. Like I said, I'm feeling fine now."

Rebecca pursed her lips and stared at the older woman for a long moment. "Well, I think you probably overdid today and didn't hydrate. You've got heat exhaustion. We usually see it earlier in the summer, but you were away. You're not used to the heat yet. I prescribe some rest this evening, and if you should feel any symptoms, you call your doctor right away. Promise me you'll put your feet up and relax the rest of the day?"

Waneta sighed. "Promise."

Nodding, Rebecca levered herself up out of the chair and picked up her bag.

"Abe, carry that bag out to Rebecca's buggy for her," Waneta told him.

She laughed. "Don't be silly. I'm fine." She patted Waneta's shoulder. "You take care."

"I will. *Danki* for coming."

Relieved, Lavinia saw her to the door, then turned back to Waneta. "What shall I fix for supper?"

* * *

Abe scooped up the last of his strawberry shortcake and sighed with satisfaction.

"Great supper," he told Lavinia.

She shrugged. "Thank your *mudder*. I just tossed together the leftovers from the refrigerator."

"You did a *gut* job," Waneta told her. "I have to say, I like your recipe for chicken salad better than mine. I wouldn't have thought to put a little lemon juice in it. Brightens it up just fine."

"My *mudder* always adds it," Lavinia told her. "I'm glad you liked it." She looked at Abe. "Now your *sohn* and I are going to do the dishes so you can go relax like you promised Rebecca you would."

Faron wiped his mouth on his napkin and stood. "*Danki* for supper, Lavinia."

"You're *wilkumm*."

He turned to his *fraa*. "*Kumm*, we're going to go sit on the porch and relax. A promise is a promise, Waneta."

"I know." Waneta drained her glass of iced tea and got to her feet. "*Danki* for supper. And for thinking to call Rebecca," she told Lavinia. She bent to kiss Lavinia's cheek.

Lavinia blushed and nodded.

Abe watched his *eldres* walk out of the room and then stood. He began clearing the table.

"Something wrong?" Lavinia asked.

"Hmm?" He set the dishes in the sink and turned back to her.

"You were quiet all through supper."

"*Mamm* always said not to talk with your mouth full."

She smiled and shook her head. "That's not why you were quiet. You're still worried about your *mudder*, aren't you?"

He glanced at the doorway to make *schur* they were alone. "I guess I always thought *Mamm* was indestructible. It was *Daed* we both worried about after his diagnosis."

"Your *mudder* isn't going anywhere anytime soon," she told him as she filled one side of the double sink with warm water and squirted in dishwashing liquid. "I do think it was just overwork and the heat that bothered her today."

"Well, she's going to stop overdoing," he said firmly.

She smiled. "How are you going to do that?"

"I won't have her working herself into the ground for the farm." He stared out the kitchen window.

"The farm's important to her."

He turned back to look at her. "*Familye*'s more important."

"Your *familye* is strong. You'll all survive the tough times."

Turning, he leaned against the counter and studied her. "You always know the right thing to say."

"I wish that was true," she said as she handed him a clean dish towel. She plunged her hands into the sudsy water and scrubbed a dish. After rinsing it in the clean water in the other side of the sink, she handed it to him. "I just feel things are going to work out. There isn't a farm in this area—maybe anywhere—that hasn't gone through some big challenges."

"*Daed* said much the same thing."

She looked at him. "So remember his words, Abe. Remember his words."

He sighed and nodded. She handed him a plate to dry, and he thought about how right she looked here in his home. Imagined what it would be like when they were married and living here, just the two of them. Oh, *schur*, his *eldres* would be in the *dawdi haus*, and there would be times the four of them would share a meal, but they'd all give each other time to be alone with their spouses. His gaze drifted to the stairs leading up to the bedrooms, before realizing he shouldn't be thinking about the time they'd have there together one day. He forced himself to return his attention to the chore of drying a dish.

"There you go again," she said mildly.

"Hmm?"

"You went someplace else while I was talking. What were you thinking about?" Her eyes widened. "Why, Abe! You're blushing!"

"I am not. Men don't blush."

She laughed. "You are!" She rinsed another dish, handed it to him, met his gaze, and her expression became serious. "I've known you too long not to know what you're thinking."

"Is that so?" He leaned closer. "Tell me what I'm thinking."

He watched her face turn a rosy pink.

They heard the thump of a cane and jumped apart.

"Any more of that iced tea left?" Faron asked as he came into the room.

"I'll get it for you," Lavinia said quickly. She took the empty glass from him and filled it from the pitcher in the refrigerator. "Does Waneta want some?"

"The glass is for her." He moved closer to Abe. "Sorry to interrupt," he murmured.

"Didn't."

His *dat* just chuckled. "Your *mudder* and I have washed a dish or two together, you know."

Abe rolled his eyes. Lavinia shut the refrigerator door and handed Faron the glass. Abe couldn't help noticing that his *dat* left the room in a quieter fashion.

Chapter Twenty-Two

On Monday, the minute there was a lull in customers, Lavinia took a break from working at the shop and hurried over to Hannah's. She didn't need quilting supplies or scraps left from a class to make her rugs. Today was the day she finally got to buy the material to make The Dress.

Her heart beat faster as she opened the door to the shop. Hannah *had* to still have the fabric Lavinia had yearned to buy weeks ago but had been too afraid to. She just *had* to have it.

Hannah glanced over from helping a customer at the cutting table and smiled a greeting as Lavinia walked to the table where the special fabrics were displayed. She looked over the bolts, moving each one aside as she looked for the one she wanted. But she didn't find it.

Her heart sank. She'd so hoped for the rich, summery violet-blue—her favorite color. She looked at other colors and told herself that she could use the periwinkle or the robin's-egg blue. But she'd so wanted the violet....

"Looking for something?" Hannah asked.

Lavinia turned. "*Ya.* I guess you sold out of it." She couldn't help sounding disappointed.

"You mean this one?" Hannah brought out a bolt of violet-blue fabric from behind her back. "I put it aside for you."

"You did?"

Hannah nodded. "I knew you'd be wanting it, the way you looked at it." She moved to the cutting table.

Neither of them talked about what the dress was for, because such things were private. But there was an air of suppressed excitement as Hannah cut the yardage and they matched spools of thread to the fabric.

"*Danki* for saving it for me."

"What are friends for?" Hannah impulsively hugged her. "I'm happy for you."

"*Danki.*"

They walked to the counter and Hannah rang up the sale. Then she carefully wrapped the fine fabric in tissue before folding it, placing it in a shopping bag, and handing it to Lavinia.

The bell over the door rang. Several ladies walked in and began browsing.

"Well, I'd better get back to the shop," Lavinia said.

She felt guilty when she returned to the shop and

found her *mudder* busily ringing up sales as several customers waited in line. She went behind the counter and tucked away the shopping bag under it, then walked over to help customers.

When the shop finally cleared, her *mudder* turned to her. Her eyes sparkled. "So did you get something special from Hannah's?"

Lavinia pulled the bag out from under the counter. She drew the fabric from its tissue, held it up to her, and felt gratified when her *mudder* sighed.

"It's lovely." Rachel touched it. "Feels lovely, too. It's perfect for a wedding dress. I knew that's why you wanted to go to Hannah's. I can't wait to see you in it."

"How did you know that's why I wanted to go to Hannah's?" she asked as she wrapped the fabric in the tissue and put it back into the bag.

"You've never looked so excited to go to her shop." She stroked Lavinia's cheek. "But I knew something was up before you went over there. Even your *dat* noticed there was something different about you this morning at breakfast."

"He did? He didn't say anything to me." She tilted her head and studied her *mudder*. "When did he say something to you? We were in the same room until we left for work."

Rachel smiled. "Couples married as long as your *dat* and me don't always need to talk to communicate."

Lavinia thought about that. She knew her *eldres* were very close, but she guessed she'd have to watch them more to see what her *mudder* was talking about. Maybe she could learn how to communicate better with Abe.

"You think *Daed* will be happy when I tell him?"

"If you're happy, your *dat* will be happy. Besides, he likes Abe. Anyone who sees the two of you together can tell you love each other."

"I *am* happy," she said and hugged her *mudder*. "Actually, Abe didn't propose."

"I don't understand."

Lavinia laughed. "Well, he didn't propose first. I got impatient, *Mamm*. It didn't feel like he was ever going to propose. I know he's been through a lot, and he's traditional. He wanted to wait until things were more stable on his farm. But I don't want to wait until everything's perfect to get married. If we don't get married after this harvest, we'd have to wait a whole year. So I did it. I proposed, and then he did." She sat down on the stool behind the counter. "I shocked him. But he said *ya*."

Rachel patted her cheek. "Who could resist you?"

"Well, thankfully, he didn't." She frowned. "We didn't tell his *eldres* yet. It felt too soon somehow, seeing them right afterward."

But it felt right to tell her *mudder*. After all, Rachel wasn't just her *mudder*. She was her best friend.

"We stopped by Abe's house on the way home, and while we were there getting some ice cream, Waneta got sick. Rebecca came over and checked her out," she hurried to say when Rachel looked alarmed. "Waneta felt the heat got to her and Rebecca pretty much agreed. Abe's worried about his *mudder* doing too much, but I told him she's not going to stop."

"I'm afraid you're right."

"Anyway, I hope that things get better for Abe's farm, because it's *schur* causing him a lot of worry."

"Things will work out. Farms have their ups and downs, just like so many things in life." She glanced at the shop window as several people stopped to look at the display. "Shop business isn't always steady either, as you've noticed."

They didn't get to talk more, as the shop got busy and stayed that way until closing. But a busy shop was a profitable shop, and that's what every shopkeeper wanted. They rode home tired but happy they'd had a successful day.

And the best part was the hug Lavinia got when she told her *dat* her good news when the *familye* sat down to eat supper.

"Abe's a *gut* man," he said, and her *mudder* smiled as their gazes met.

* * *

Abe was sitting at the kitchen table going over farm paperwork after lunch the next day when Wayne came to the door.

"Can you come take a look at Bessie?"

"*Schur.* What's wrong?"

"I want you to take a look, see what you think."

"*Allrecht.*" He got up and used his cane to follow Wayne out to the pasture. There, he saw that Bessie's eyes were dull and her breathing a bit labored.

"Came on quick," Wayne said. "She was fine this morning."

"Call the vet," Abe said without hesitating. "I don't want you trying to take her temp without assistance, and I can't help you with that with my arm in a cast. And I don't want to risk *Daed* getting hurt."

"I could call someone—" Wayne began.

Abe shook his head. "Call the doc."

Wayne got out his cell phone and did as he asked. Abe sat beside the cow. He knew Bessie was old and a low producer, and she was a bit cranky these days. But she had produced a *gut* number of calves and milk in her time, and he felt a bond with her. It wasn't true that a dairy farmer didn't feel anything for his stock.

It didn't take long for the vet to show up.

"Was in the neighborhood looking at one of Samuel Miller's horses," he said as he knelt to examine Bessie. "Your oldest, isn't she?"

Abe nodded.

Bessie wasn't happy having her temperature taken, but the vet and Wayne managed it together. *Schur* enough, the cow had a fever.

"Nothing's going around," the vet announced after using his stethoscope to listen to her lungs. "I'm thinking it's pneumonia."

He drew a blood sample, then administered a shot of antibiotics and told Abe to call if she wasn't improved in the morning. "I'll call you as soon as I get back to the office and take a look at the sample. In the meantime, keep her isolated from the other cows."

"Thanks for coming so quickly. Give me a minute and I'll write you a check."

"I'll bill you," the vet said. "You know I'm not worried about you paying." His cell phone rang. "Busy day," he said after he checked the display. "Gotta take this. Call if you need me."

He got in his truck, took the call, and then waved goodbye as he drove away.

"Nick hasn't picked up this morning's milk, has he?" Abe asked. Nick was an *Englisch* driver who picked up milk from the dairy farms and drove it to a plant for pasteurizing.

Wayne shook his head.

"We have to dump it until we hear back from the vet."

Wayne nodded. "Tough break." He pulled out his cell phone. "I'll tell him we'll let him know when we need a pickup again." After he completed the call, he turned to the cow. "C'mon, Bessie, let's go put you in a stall away from the others."

Abe followed him into the barn and made *schur* she had plenty of water and was comfortable. He sighed. Bessie was getting old, but he hoped she'd pull through this.

He went back in the house and tried to concentrate on his paperwork. It was hard not to wince at the feed bill. A dairy cow ate as much as a hundred pounds a day. They ate pasture grass in spring and summer, and silage—

chopped grass—in the other seasons. Like many other dairy farmers, Abe grew as much of their food as possible but supplemented with grain and soybean meal. Add in the supplements and the bill was hefty.

"Saw Doc Smith was here," his *mudder* said as she walked into the kitchen.

"Bessie's not doing well."

"Oh dear, that's not *gut*."

Abe told her what the doctor had said and shook his head. "I'm hoping the antibiotics get her through this." He put stamps on the envelopes and walked out to the mailbox. He stood there for a moment watching the late-afternoon traffic on the road and wondered what kind of day Lavinia had had at the shop. The last time he'd been in town, he'd been surprised at how the tourist season had sneaked up on him with all that had been happening in his life. Each year it seemed more people came to Lancaster County to get a glimpse of life here. He didn't see the attraction the *Englisch* had for seeing rural life and the Amish, but then again it was his life.

With a shrug, he walked back to the house. His *dat* sat in a rocking chair on the front porch reading *The Budget*.

"Wayne told me about Bessie," he said, setting the newspaper down as Abe sat in the chair beside him. "She's pulled through such before," he reminded Abe.

Abe nodded. "But she was younger then. She's getting older."

"Aren't we all," his *dat* said as his faded blue eyes studied his *sohn*.

Abe glanced at the front door. "I want to talk about *Mamm*."

Now it was Faron's turn to make *schur* they were alone. "I wouldn't be using the word 'old' around your *mudder*. Not if *you* want to stay well."

"How can we keep her from overdoing and getting sick like yesterday?"

Faron sighed and shook his head. "Woman's always worked too hard."

"She really scared me," Abe blurted out.

His *dat* patted his hand. "Me too." He frowned. "The thing is, she really enjoys making cheese and ice cream and helping the farm prosper. Always has. She's a *gut* farm *fraa*. Loves the land as much as we do. Always has." He used his foot to make the chair rock in a gentle motion. "Seems to me that you found a *maedel* just as loyal, just as hardworking."

Abe nodded.

"She'll be a *gut* helpmate to you, a *gut* partner to you."

Abe debated telling his *dat* that he and Lavinia had gotten engaged the day before, but felt it was something they should do together.

"It's *gut* land, a *gut* place to live and raise a *familye*," his *dat* mused. "It'll go on a long time after all of us."

Abe had always assumed that the farm would go on after him. But his fall and all the problems since had made him wonder if it would stay in the *familye*. He sat in the rocking chair and stared out at the fields on the other side of the road and thought about what his *dat* had said.

Chapter Twenty-Three

"It's time we had the talk."

Lavinia stopped stamping the store logo on a pile of shopping bags. "Because I'm engaged? *Mamm*, I know what married couples do."

Rachel stared at her and then burst out laughing. "The talk we haven't had about hiring part-time help for the season."

"Oh." Now it was her turn to laugh and shake her head.

"We need the help at the shop, and I'd like to take a day now and then to do some canning. It's too much for your *schweschder* to do our kitchen-garden upkeep and canning as well as her own, what with her pregnancy. I remember being pregnant during the summer and having to do the canning."

She glanced over as several women stopped to look in their display window.

"I thought about asking Emma, but she's busy helping out part-time at both Hannah's quilt shop and Gideon's toy shop."

Lavinia nodded. "She might have as many hours as she feels she can manage, with John being a toddler now." She resumed stamping the bags while they had a few minutes without customers. "Still, I think you should ask her. She's *gut* with customers, and she's already coming into town several days a week."

"I think I will. She's at Hannah's this morning. Do you need anything from Hannah's while I go over and talk to Emma?"

Lavinia shook her head. She'd indulged in the fine fabric she'd bought for her wedding dress and would be watching her pennies for a while.

"Say hi to Hannah and Emma for me. And John, if he's spending the morning at the shop with Emma."

"I will."

When the lull continued without customers, Lavinia decided to use the landline to call Abe.

When he answered the phone, his voice sounded huskier than usual.

"Are you *allrecht*?" she asked quickly.

"*Ya*," he said. But she heard a sniff.

"You're not. Bessie's not doing better?" He'd told her about the cow being sick the night before when they talked on the phone.

"*Nee*," he admitted.

"I'm sorry." She knew the cow was more than just livestock for him.

They talked for a few minutes, but she had to go when customers walked in. The first chance she got to be alone again, she prayed for Abe and Bessie and decided she'd ask Liz to drop her at his house on her way home.

Rachel returned with *gut* news. Emma would be able to give them a few hours three days a week.

A little while later, Emma popped in for a quick visit with John in his stroller. They were on their way to Gideon's for the afternoon. John had been in the shop before, but his big blue eyes were alive with curiosity as he looked around.

"Out?" he asked his *mudder*, and he held up his arms.

She shook her head. "We're going to *Onkel* Gideon's. Remember?"

"Toys!" he cried, and bounced in his seat.

She laughed. "*Ya*. Just give me a minute to talk to Rachel and Lavinia." She glanced around the shop. "I haven't been in here in a while. Looks like you have some new vendors with some interesting crafts. Oh, and Lavinia, I love the rug you're working on," she said as she walked over to the worktable near the front window. "So colorful."

Lavinia picked up a strand of fabric and dangled it in front of John. He giggled and grabbed at it, and they played tug-of-war.

"My *mudder*'s been wanting to have him visit, so I think I might let her do that the first day I work for you."

"Oh, but it's such fun to have a *kind* in the shop," Rachel protested. "My *kinner* grew up spending time here. Lavinia liked it more than her *schweschder* and ended up working with me after she graduated from *schul*."

"He'll come with me sometimes if you don't mind. Hannah has a folding playpen we can bring with us." She turned to John. "Well, shall we go visit *Onkel* Gideon?"

"Toys!"

She laughed. "John loves going there best."

"What *kind* wouldn't?" Lavinia said. The scrap of fabric they'd played with would soon be forgotten when he got to the toy shop.

The shop seemed less bright when Emma wheeled John out. Lavinia agreed with her *mudder* that it was going to be fun to have him coming with Emma, and she found herself daydreaming for a moment about bringing her own *kinner* to the shop when she had them.

Together, she and her *mudder* spent the rest of the day so busy they had little time to talk.

Liz's passengers who worked in shops had been just as busy, so it was quiet in the van as they relaxed and got off their feet for the first time that day. Some dozed.

Lavinia decided to get out at her house with her *mudder* and then walk the short distance to Abe's house. She liked her privacy and didn't want others speculating on why she was stopping at Abe's house.

She went directly to the barn and saw Abe sitting on a bale of hay in the stall with Bessie. The cow lay on her side sleeping, her breathing sounding labored. Her heart sank. Bessie wasn't doing well at all.

Abe looked up in surprise when he heard footsteps.

"Hi," Lavinia said, quietly so she wouldn't wake Bessie. But the cow opened her eyes and stared at her for a long moment before closing them again.

"I didn't think you were stopping by today," Abe said.

"*Allrecht* if I come in?" she asked, and slipped inside when he nodded. "You sounded upset when we talked earlier."

He shrugged. "I should be used to this, growing up on a dairy farm. But there's always been something about Bessie." He stroked her black-and-white-spotted flank. "The *gut* news is it's pneumonia and not something worse. And none of the rest of the herd has come down with it. The bad news was that we had to dump milk until we found out."

"But Bessie's going to get better?"

Abe gazed up at her, and he looked sad. "*Daed* reminded me that she's pulled through bad times before. But I don't think that's going to happen this time."

"I'm sorry."

"*Danki.*" He sighed. "When's all the bad news going to end? Sometimes I think it would be easier to have a crop farm than a dairy farm. I get attached to the cows."

Lavinia knelt and touched his face. "I know. It's life, *lieb*. We weren't promised an easy one. But we *were* promised He'd be with us during it. We aren't alone."

They heard the clanging of a bell. "That's *Mamm* calling me in for supper. Will you join us?"

"*Schur.*"

"I'll be back soon," he told Bessie. "You get some rest, old girl."

They left the stall and walked to the farmhouse.

"Did you have a *gut* day?" he asked her.

"I did. A busy one. Emma and John came by. *Mamm* decided we needed some part-time help, and Emma's going to give us some hours. She's already helping Hannah and Gideon."

Waneta and Faron greeted her as they entered the kitchen.

"Any change?" Faron asked quietly, and Abe shook his head.

"I hope you're joining us for supper?" Waneta asked as she set a big bowl of buttered corn on the cob on the table. "We've got plenty."

"*Danki*, I will. Anything I can do?"

"Everything's ready. Grab yourself a plate and fork."

With the ease of someone who'd been in the kitchen often, Lavinia went to the cupboard for a plate, then got a fork from the silverware drawer. Abe watched her as he washed his hands, picturing her in the room in the future. It cheered him up a little. When he sat, the scent of the fried pork chops on a platter in the center of the table made him realize he was *hungerich*. His *mudder* had brought a sandwich out to the barn at lunchtime while he watched over Bessie, but he hadn't felt like eating.

"How are you feeling today?" Lavinia asked his *mudder*.

"Just fine. You're a sweet *maedel* to ask."

His *dat* said the blessing and then began passing the platter of pork chops and the bowls of corn on the cob and sweet-and-sour green beans around the table. Abe added more butter to an ear of corn and decided maybe the day was looking up as he took a bite. He loved corn on the cob and could eat it every day of the week.

His *mudder* refused Lavinia's offer to wash the supper dishes when they finished their meal. "You've been working all day."

"So have you," Lavinia said, gesturing at the mason jars of vegetables from her kitchen garden Waneta had obviously canned that day. She knew from experience how exhausting it was to can in summer heat.

"Go, have a visit with Abe. Faron will help me. Cleaning up won't take long."

Abe looked at Lavinia. "Might as well give up."

Shaking her head, Lavinia thanked her for supper and walked out to the front porch with Abe.

Once outside, they sat in the rocking chairs.

"Feels so peaceful after a day in town," Lavinia murmured. "Abe, your *mudder*'s overdoing again. I saw how much she canned today. It's hard, hot work."

"I know. *Daed* and I helped some. He washed vegetables and I chopped for a little while when Wayne gave me a break."

"*Mamm*'s talking about taking a day off now and then when Emma can help us. My *schweschder*'s been doing some of the canning for us, but it's a lot for her when she's got her own work and she's expecting."

"What will you do when your *mudder* decides she doesn't want to run the shop anymore?"

She stopped rocking and stared at him in surprise. "I can't see that day happening."

"Our *eldres* are getting older," he told her. "I've come to realize that recently."

"True. But it's more likely that I'd stop working there for a while."

"You?" Now he stopped rocking and stared at her.

"For a little while. After we have a *boppli*." She grinned. "You do want *kinner* after we're married, right?"

"Oh. *Ya*. Of course."

"I'll take our *kinner* to the shop," she said. "I spent a lot of time there before I started *schul* and then during holiday and summer breaks. I loved it."

They chatted a little longer, and then she reluctantly stood. "I need to get home, and you need to check on Bessie again."

"I'm walking you home. I'm doing so well the physical therapist wants me to take some short walks and get more exercise." He stood and grabbed his cane.

The walk took a little more out of him than he thought it would, but he got a chance to kiss her as darkness fell before he left her, so he figured it was worth the effort.

His legs were shaking by the time he got to sit on the bale of hay beside Bessie. And he was still there half-dozing as dawn light filtered in through the barn doors and she drew her last breath and left him.

Chapter Twenty-Four

Lavinia was tired from her day, but when she got back to the house she went to her bedroom and got out the fabric she'd bought from Hannah's. She was glad she'd spent a little extra on it. The fabric had a soft sheen that made it drape beautifully when she held the length up to her and studied it in the mirror over her dresser.

She took it and her sewing basket down to the kitchen, and after making sure that the table was clean and dry, she spread the fabric out and placed her pattern pieces on it. It didn't take long to pin the pieces and cut it out.

Her excitement increased as she worked. She was making her wedding dress. What *maedel* didn't look forward to making the dress she'd wear to her wedding?

Her *dat* walked in to pour himself a cup of coffee. He looked at her curiously as he turned from the pot on the stove. "Making yourself a new dress?"

She looked up and smiled. "A special one, *Daed*. My wedding dress."

"It can't be time for that already, can it?" he asked, looking a little sad as he glanced at the calendar on the wall.

"I can't wait until the last minute."

Her *mudder* walked into the room. When she saw what Lavinia was doing, she reached into a drawer and pulled out a pad of paper and a pencil.

"I should start planning," she said as she sat at the table. "She's right, Amos. These things can't be put off until the last minute."

He set his cup on the counter. "I guess I'll go take a last trip out to the barn, make *schur* everything's *allrecht*."

"Leave it to a man to disappear," Rachel said.

He patted her shoulder. "You'll find plenty for me to do as we get closer to the date. And there'll be all that setting up of benches and tables I do so much better than planning and cooking."

Rachel sighed. "You're right."

He grinned. "Lavinia, you're my witness to your *mudder* saying I'm right."

She tucked her tongue firmly in her cheek. "I'm so glad I'm here for that historic event."

Her *dat*'s jaw dropped and he stared at her. Then he laughed and shook his head. "Got a smart mouth on you there. Wonder who you got that from?" he mused as he stared at his *fraa*.

Rachel just smiled. "Very funny."

Her *dat*'s cell phone rang. He answered it, then quickly handed it to Rachel. "It's Sadie."

Lavinia's heart beat faster as her *mudder* took the phone from her *dat*.

"Sadie?"

Her *schweschder*'s voice was so loud Lavinia could hear it. "*Mamm!* The *boppli*'s coming!"

"I'll be right there," Rachel said quickly. "Amos, go hitch up the buggy. Sadie's in labor." She turned her attention back to her *dochder*. "Have you called Rebecca?"

"*Ya*," said Sadie. "But please come!"

"We'll be right there. Now you sit down and stay calm." She disconnected the call and turned to Lavinia. "Sadie's in labor."

"I heard," she said with a grin. "I thought she'd be calmer with her second."

"We'll see if you are with yours." Her *mudder* grabbed her purse. "Are you coming with?"

"I wouldn't miss it for the world." She grabbed her own purse and locked the door on the way out.

When they arrived at Sadie's, Lavinia saw Rebecca's buggy was already parked in the drive.

Naiman, Sadie's *mann*, welcomed them inside and didn't look much calmer than Sadie had sounded.

"She's in the front bedroom," he told them.

Lavinia and her *mudder* rushed there and found Sadie

propped up in bed, breathing through a contraction while Rebecca monitored her pulse.

"*Mamm!* You're here!" Sadie cried when the contraction eased.

Rebecca released her wrist and stood back as Rachel rushed over to her side. "She's doing well," she reassured them.

It felt a little crowded in the small room with the three of them, and Lavinia knew Sadie wanted their *mudder* more than her, so after a quick hug she returned to the kitchen. There she found her *dat* and Naiman drinking coffee.

"Want some coffee?" Naiman asked her.

Lavinia shook her head. "*Nee, danki.* Where's Anna Mae?"

"In bed. We were just about to go to bed, too, when Sadie said she was having contractions."

When she heard the faint rustle on the stairs leading up to the bedrooms, Lavinia saw her two-year-old niece peering down.

"Somebody's still awake," she whispered to Naiman.

He sighed and started to get up, but she gestured at him to stay seated. "Let me."

She climbed the stairs and held out her arms. "Hi, Anna Mae. Let's go back to bed."

"Want *Mamm*," she said, her lips trembling. She clutched a stuffed bear under her arm.

Lavinia stroked her wispy blond hair back from her face. "She's busy, *lieb*. *Kumm*, *Aenti* Lavinia will read you a story."

She got the *kind* back in bed and stretched out beside her, the bear tucked under the sheet between them. Anna Mae smelled of soap and baby powder. Lavinia read one of Anna Mae's well-worn books, and before she reached the end, she saw the *kind* was asleep.

Lavinia lingered. While she wasn't looking forward to going through what her *schweschder* was experiencing right now, it was so sweet to lie here and cuddle with a *kind* and think about having one of her own. Reluctantly, she climbed out of bed and went downstairs to join her *eldres*.

"Rebecca said it won't be long now," her *mudder* said. "Naiman's in with her." She yawned and glanced at the clock on the wall.

"Why don't you stay home tomorrow, and you can come over and help Sadie?" Lavinia said.

"The shop's been so busy."

"I can manage. And you know you want to be here."

Rachel smiled and reached to hold Amos's hand. "It's not every day you get to be with a new *kinskind*." She glanced at the stairs. "Your *dat* said you went up to put Anna Mae back in bed."

She nodded. "Read her a story and she was asleep before I finished. It was nice. I haven't had enough time to spend with her lately. Maybe I can come over after work tomorrow and give her some attention while you're with Sadie."

"Sounds *gut*."

They fell silent and listened to the clock ticking away the minutes.

Then, as one, they turned in the direction of the front of the house as they heard the indignant wail of a newborn.

A few minutes later, Naiman rushed into the room. "It's a *bu*! Sadie and I have a *bu*!"

It was late by the time Lavinia and her *eldres* got to meet the new *boppli* and congratulate Sadie. Lavinia had to wait until her *mudder* and *dat* held him and fussed over him, and then it was her turn.

She held the squirming bundle and studied the tiny face and agreed with Naiman that *ya*, his *sohn* had his nose. And she couldn't help wondering if this time next year she might be married and holding a *boppli* of her own.

* * *

Abe felt a hand touch his shoulder.

"Sorry you lost her," Wayne said. "I really hoped when I came to work this morning that she'd pulled through it. She always has in the past."

He glanced up at Wayne. He'd been so miserable sitting here on the bale of hay in Bessie's stall he hadn't heard the man approach.

"I know. I'm sorry I couldn't be of more help with Bessie after—afterward." He stared down at the cast on his arm. "Can't wait to get this off."

"No problem. Your *dat* and I managed. He's an old hand at it. I'm heading home for supper unless there's something else you need."

Abe shook his head. "Been a long day."

"Get some sleep. You look half-dead on your feet."

"I dozed some here watching Bessie last night."

They walked out of the barn and headed for their houses.

As Abe washed his hands at the sink, he couldn't help glancing at the meal his *mudder* was putting on the table. He didn't think he could handle it if it was beef.

"Tuna salad plate," she said as she caught the direction of his gaze. "Wanted something simple and cold after canning again today."

He nodded. "Sounds *gut*."

"*Sohn*, I remember how you felt when you were a *kind* and you found out the chicken and dumplings you were eating came from one of the chickens you fed every day."

He grunted. "I'm older. I should be used to it. Cycle of life and all that."

"Sometimes we form an attachment to an animal," Faron said quietly. "It's not a sign of weakness."

"I know." Abe sighed. But he was glad he was eating tuna for supper tonight and not beef.

"Made your favorite pie," she told him. "Strawberry rhubarb."

"You did?" He'd been so lost in thought when he walked into the room he hadn't noticed the pie cooling on the counter. "*Danki*."

He bent his head for the blessing of the meal, then watched his *dat* slide two fat slices of tomato onto his plate.

"I think these are the biggest tomatoes you've grown yet," Faron told Waneta.

"I do, too. And the yield was better. I made a lot of spaghetti sauce today." She sighed. "We'll enjoy that when cold weather comes for *schur*."

"Feels like it'll never get cold," Abe said.

She nodded. "Summer feels forever in Lancaster County. Faron, turn that fan a little more in my direction, would you, please?"

Abe glanced at her sharply. "Are you *allrecht*?"

She patted his hand. "Just fine."

They'd just finished with supper and Abe was helping clear the table—he thought his *dat* looked a little tuckered out from helping Wayne with Bessie—when his cell phone rang. It was Lavinia calling to tell him she was stopping by Sadie's to see the new *boppli*.

"I figured you'd do that," he told her, and tried not to sound disappointed. "See you tomorrow."

"Lavinia won't be coming by," he told his *eldres*. "Her *schweschder* Sadie had her *boppli* last night. A *bu*."

"How nice. Now Sadie and Naiman have one of each. Rachel must be thrilled at having another *kinskind*." She filled the sink with warm water and squirted in dishwashing liquid. "Nothing better than a *kinskind*. Or so I hear."

Abe stared at her. "Is that a hint?"

She just looked at him and smiled.

For a moment, he thought about telling them he and Lavinia were engaged. But he wanted to do that with Lavinia.

"You falling asleep?" she teased.

He shook his head. "Just thinking about something."

"Clean dish towels in the drawer there," she told him.

"I know where they're kept," he growled, but with a small smile for his *mudder*.

When he glanced over at his *dat*, he saw he was helping himself to another slice of pie. He thought about tattling on him, but his *mudder* suddenly said, "Faron!"

"Woman's got eyes in the back of her head," Faron complained, but he was grinning.

"I just know my *mann*," she retorted, without turning to look at him. "That's your third piece!"

"Now Waneta, a man's got to have more than some fish and salad after a hard day's work," he said. "'Sides, it's fruit, so it's *gut* for me."

She sighed and shook her head as she rinsed a dish and handed it to Abe to dry.

After they finished, Abe wondered what to do with himself. He was so used to spending time most evenings with Lavinia.

"Let's take a walk out to the barn," his *dat* suggested.

"Didn't you spend enough time working today?" he asked him. "Thought you'd want to sit in your recliner with *The Budget*."

"You saying I'm old, *bu*?"

"*Nee.* But you and *Mamm* worked hard today, and it was hot."

"Got something to show you. Might cheer you up a little."

As they walked out to the barn, Abe and his *dat* took their time navigating the uneven gravel of the drive with their canes. Abe pushed the barn door open so they could walk inside, wondering what his *dat* wanted to show him.

Faron stopped in front of a stall and gestured for Abe to look inside. He did so and felt himself tear up when he saw the calf.

"Forgot about her, didn't you?"

Abe nodded as he leaned over the top of the gate to the stall. Inside was the last calf Bessie had borne. She had the same big brown eyes and black-and-white-spotted hide.

"It's like having part of her here, don't you think?" Faron said, patting Abe on the shoulder.

"*Ya. Danki* for reminding me."

"Well, I'm going to head back in and sit in that recliner like you said. Coming?"

"I think I'll stay out here for a while."

Faron nodded and headed back out of the barn.

Abe just stood there, elbows resting on the gate of the stall, looking down at Bessie's calf.

Chapter Twenty-Five

I don't think we're going to see any more customers," Lavinia told her *mudder* as she looked out the front window of the shop.

The bad storm that had been predicted had arrived. A few customers had come in early in the day, but when thunder boomed and the rain grew heavier, the sidewalks and streets emptied of locals and tourists.

Lavinia walked back to her table and returned to stocking shelves.

And then she heard the strangest sound—a pinging at the front display window. She hurried to it and her eyes widened.

"*Mamm!* Come look! There's hail!"

Rachel hurried over, and they watched as balls of

ice as big as walnuts rained down and bounced off the sidewalk and street.

"Haven't seen hail that big in years," she told Lavinia. She frowned and grasped Lavinia's hand. "We need to pray. This isn't *gut* for the crops."

They prayed, and Lavinia felt some relief when the hail stopped a few minutes later. But the rain continued to pound down. They walked away from the window. Lavinia returned to stocking shelves, and her *mudder* sat down at her loom.

Lavinia always loved watching her *mudder* weave at the loom set up in a corner of the shop. She looked so peaceful, almost as if she was in another world as she worked the shuttle in a rhythmic motion through the strands of yarn. Layers of color and pattern formed and lengthened. It was an old craft, one Rachel had learned how to do from her own *mudder* as a *maedel* and soon discovered she had a talent for.

After selling the place mats and throws she made at farmer's markets and such, she took a risk, with the support of Lavinia's *dat*, and opened the shop in town, inviting other Amish who made arts and crafts to sell their work alongside hers. Her hard work—at her own craft and in promoting the arts and crafts of other Amish—had made her shop successful.

Lavinia was proud of her *dat* for encouraging her *mudder* to have her own work and not just be there as a farm *fraa*. It might have been easier for him to have her home every day sometimes, but they had the kind of partnership she hoped to have with a *mann* someday.

She knew she'd want to continue the craft she loved and work in the shop like her *mudder*, to be a *gut* businesswoman as well as a *gut fraa* and *mudder*.

Thunder boomed again, and she cast a wary eye toward the display window. But her *mudder* continued to work, looking like a center of calm in spite of it. That's what she was for her *familye*. Lavinia told herself not to worry about the storm and to concentrate on what she could control.

Time always passed slowly when there were no customers, but after she'd done everything she could think of, Lavinia sat down to work on another rag rug and found some peace while the storm raged. The rug she worked on was all bright, bold colors she'd decided to make into a large oval for a living or dining room. She got a lot accomplished by the time they took a break.

Lavinia caught her *mudder* up on what was happening with her old schoolteacher, Phoebe, and they decided they'd stop by the next day after work to give Ruth, Phoebe's *dochder*, a break. Rachel called them and left a message on their answering machine. After she finished, she put the phone down and sighed. "When we get home, we'll call the other women in the church and set up a schedule to help Ruth."

Closing time finally came. They ran for Liz's van when she parked at the curb. Even with umbrellas, they still jumped into their seats damp and a little chilled. The temperature had dropped with the hailstorm. The drive home was quiet, as passengers stayed silent so Liz could concentrate on the slick roads. Lavinia could see others looking worried as they peered out the windows. Whether you owned a farm or not, you were concerned with weather affecting crops this time of year.

Thankfully, the rain lessened by the time Liz pulled in front of their house. They skipped the umbrellas and ran for the house, standing on the front porch and shaking raindrops off before they went inside.

Her *dat* came out of the kitchen and greeted them with a relieved smile. "I'm glad you got home safely. That was some storm."

"You weren't out in the fields when it started, were you?"

Lavinia knew her *mudder* worried because years ago a storm had blown up quickly and lightning had struck a tree on the edge of the field where a group of men, including Amos, had been working. One of the men had nearly been trampled by the plow horses frightened by the noise.

He shook his head. "I got the horses in safely before it started." He kissed his *fraa* on the cheek. "I just put the casserole you left in the refrigerator in the oven. Why don't the two of you change out of those wet clothes while I go out and check on things?"

They headed upstairs. Lavinia took off her dress and pulled on another, then hung the damp dress up to dry. As she went downstairs, she heard someone knock at the kitchen door. She hesitated, remembering the time Ben had stopped by. *Nee*, he wouldn't be back. She continued on down the stairs and opened the door.

To her relief, it was Luke, a friend of her *dat*'s. She invited him in, but the man shook his head and said he wanted to see how Amos's crops had fared. He went out to the barn when told that was where Amos was.

Supper was ready when her *dat* returned with a relieved expression. "The storm did less damage than I feared. Luke told me that his was the same. Let's hope other farmers in the area weren't affected too badly."

After supper, both her *eldres* got on phones—her *mudder* to line up other women to help Ruth, and her *dat* to check with other farmers.

Lavinia took care of doing the dishes and then cleaning up the kitchen. Afterward she felt restless. Unsettled. Abe wasn't returning her calls. She'd called him twice today and each time had gotten his voicemail. She didn't want to take a walk or work on a rug or read a book. She didn't know what she wanted to do. With a sigh, she went up to her room, but it was too early to go to bed.

She walked over to stare out the window. Lonely. She wasn't just feeling restless and unsettled. She was feeling lonely and concerned. Why was Abe not calling her back?

Unbidden, the memory of what had happened last year to her friend Lovina Zook came to mind. Lovina had been planning to marry Daniel Lapp after harvest, but he'd suddenly stopped calling and seeing her, and then not only did he leave her at the altar—he left town. Lovina had been so shaken she still wasn't seeing anyone. One day, when they'd talked after church, Lovina had actually voiced the fear that she'd become *en alt maedel*. Lavinia had reassured her that it was unlikely, reminding her friend she was only twenty-two and it was way too early to be thinking that way.

And it was very silly for Lavinia to be thinking something was wrong just because Abe hadn't called her for one day. Abe would never treat her the way Daniel had Lovina. He wasn't like Daniel at all. She was letting her imagination run wild, and she never did that. But while one unreturned call meant Abe was busy, two, then three couldn't be ignored. She needed to know why he wasn't calling. Surely if something had happened to him she'd have heard about it. If his farm had sustained damage from the storm, they would get through it together after they were married.

If she truly believed that God had set aside a man for her and that man was Abe, she needed to have some faith and some patience and not stress over the fact that he hadn't called her since the big storm. *Ya*, usually they talked by phone several times a day and often saw each other daily. But one day without either a call or seeing each other was nothing to worry about. She laughed and shook her head again. Just how much faith and patience did she have to have?

Grabbing the work tote that she'd tossed on her bed, she pulled out the rug she'd started at the shop and began working on it. Being busy helped keep her from worrying. She reminded herself of what Phoebe had always said about worry being arrogant—that God knew what he was doing. Soon the repetitive motions of her hands soothed her restlessness. She had a good portion done by the time her *eldres* stopped by her door to say *gut nacht*.

Lavinia smiled after they left her. It was worth the

wait to have a marriage like theirs, wasn't it? A love that began with God first and then with each other, a partnership and support through all the joys and tears of life, a foundation to build a happy *familye* on.

She gazed off into the distance and daydreamed for a moment, imagining, as she didn't often allow herself to, how it would feel when she and Abe married after the harvest. How she would feel when they had *kinner* like her *schweschder*.

* * *

Abe found he was clenching his jaw as he waited for Wayne to get back from walking the fields to check for storm damage. He felt so helpless sitting here in the kitchen.

His *dat* must have noticed his tension. He patted his shoulder as he walked past him. "Coffee?"

Abe shook his head. "*Nee. Danki*," he added when he realized he'd been abrupt in his refusal.

With his MS, his *dat* couldn't go out to the muddy fields either. The only sound in the kitchen was the rustle of papers as his *dat* turned the pages of *The Budget* as he sipped his coffee. How could he stay so calm?

Faron glanced up as if he heard Abe's thoughts. "Everything will work out. Stop worrying."

"I didn't need anything else to go wrong."

"God knows what we can bear."

Abe stared down at the cast on his arm and shook his head. "He's giving me credit for a lot more than I think I can bear."

Waneta walked in. "Bear? Somebody hungry as a bear?"

Faron chuckled. "Our *bu* is sitting here worrying. Thinks God's giving him more than he can bear. Tell him he's wrong, Waneta."

"Listen to your *dat*," she told Abe. "He's right." She glanced at the kitchen clock. "Time to start supper."

She bustled about, getting a big bowl of ham salad and another of pasta salad from the refrigerator and setting them on the table. "I'm glad I got the lettuce in before the storm." She washed a head of it off at the sink, pulled it apart and patted the leaves dry, then arranged it on a plate with some sliced cucumbers and tomatoes. "It's nice to have a cold supper on a warm afternoon," she said.

"Hmm," Faron murmured in agreement.

Wayne walked in, and Abe's heart sank when he saw his expression. He took a seat next to Abe and pulled out his cell phone. Faron joined them. "Took some photos so you could see."

He scrolled down on the screen, and Abe sighed at the sight of hay, corn, and soybeans that looked like a giant foot had trampled them into the mud.

"We'll salvage what we can, but I reckon we're going to end up having to buy some feed," Wayne said as he finished showing the photos.

"A lot of feed," Abe said, feeling sick to his stomach.

Faron took his seat again. "It happens some years. We'll manage."

We, thought Abe. He felt guilty that because he'd had his accident, his *dat* and *mudder* were helping him, when they'd turned the farm over to him and should be doing some relaxing in their later years.

"Well, let's eat," Waneta said cheerfully. "Everything looks a little better after a *gut* meal."

Abe worried the price of hay and corn and soybeans would rise if they were in short supply. And he hoped that the other farms that raised these crops hadn't been dealt the same crushing blow this was to him.

"Wayne? Joining us?"

"That'd be great," he said as he walked over to wash his hands at the kitchen sink. "My *eldres* are at my *bruder*'s tonight."

After the prayer, the bowls and serving plates were passed around, and everyone began eating. Everyone but Abe. He pushed a spoonful of the pasta salad around on his plate. Food was the last thing on his mind—at least food for himself. Waneta passed him the basket of bread so he could make a sandwich of the ham salad. He made half a sandwich and tried to eat a few bites. He knew she'd fuss if he left the table without eating anything.

When the meal was finished, Waneta brought out a lemon icebox pie. Faron perked up as she set it on the table. "Where'd you hide that?"

She smiled. "I'm not telling."

The dessert was one of his *mudder*'s best pies, but even that couldn't tempt him out of his depression. He shook his head when his *mudder* offered him a slice.

"*Danki.* Maybe later." He pushed away from the table and left the room.

He walked out to the front porch and stared moodily at

the rain-soaked grass and fields. The bishop passed in his buggy and raised a hand in greeting. He was undoubtedly out checking on his flock, seeing how they'd been affected by the storm. That meant he might stop by here. Abe sighed. He knew Lester meant well, but he didn't think he could take being told about God's plan and how all would work out and such, like his *dat* had done. But he had no escape.

He retreated to his room, and if the man stopped by, no one came to his room to tell him they had a visitor. He ignored another call from Lavinia on his cell phone and felt even worse.

* * *

Sunday came, and Abe's *mudder* wasn't having any excuses about him not attending church. "I heard all of them when you were a *bu*, and they didn't work then," she said sternly.

"But I'm having a lot of pain in my back," he repeated. "The bad weather we had didn't help my injury. Maybe I'm getting arthritis like *Grossdaadi* had."

"Then maybe we need to see the doctor tomorrow."

He didn't want that, either.

"Might as well hear some healing words from God while you hurt," Waneta said practically. "Now do you need help dressing?"

He pulled his sheets up to his chin. "*Nee, Mamm.* I'm not a *boppli*."

She shrugged. "I'll send your *dat* in. Hurry it up if you want breakfast."

He knew he wouldn't make it through the three-hour service if he didn't eat, especially after having had so little supper the night before. So he was already at the door of his bedroom when his *dat* appeared.

Faron grinned. "I knew you wouldn't need my help."

"If we were dead, she'd still insist we had to attend church," he muttered.

"*Ya.*" His *dat* chuckled.

A half hour later, Abe was in an even worse mood about attending church services. He hadn't known that they were being held at Lavinia's house this Sunday. He cast his eyes heavenward and wondered what God was planning. Since church services were at Lavinia's house, he'd be seeing her, and he was feeling depressed about the crop damage. He grimaced.

"Somebody's in a *gut* mood this morning," Wayne remarked, misunderstanding his grimace.

"Can't be Abe," Waneta said as she climbed out of the buggy and proceeded up the walk to the house. "He's been brooding since you showed him the crop damage."

"I don't brood," Abe muttered.

"Hah!" she retorted.

"Woman can hear everything," Abe said, shaking his head.

"I heard that!"

Wayne grinned as they climbed the steps and went into the house. Then Abe saw Lavinia standing in the living room, greeting church members. They moved on, and then she saw him.

"Abe." She looked startled, as if she hadn't expected to see him.

"*Guder mariye*," he said.

"You haven't been returning my calls. I thought something was wrong."

"Sorry." He couldn't look at her. "Been busy." He shifted uncomfortably, and his hand began to sweat on his cane.

"Rebecca! *Guder mariye*," Lavinia said as the midwife walked up. "Save me a seat, will you?"

He realized he was holding things up, so he started to walk past her.

"Abe?"

He stopped but didn't look at her. "*Ya?*"

"We need to talk after church."

"I came with my *eldres*." It was a pitiful excuse but the only one he could think of.

"I'm *schur* they won't mind waiting a few minutes for you," she said crisply.

He found a seat in the men's section and brooded. She'd find a way to make him talk to her. How was he going to tell her he just didn't see a way for them to get married with his farm going down the drain? She had to see that they needed to put off marrying until next year.

You're going to lose her, his conscience told him.

His shoulders slumped and he stared at his hands clasped in his lap.

Chapter Twenty-Six

Lavinia kept a sharp eye out for Abe when the church service ended. She didn't think he'd try to leave without talking to her, but his behavior hadn't been typical the last day either.

Since her *familye* was hosting service today, she couldn't go rushing over to talk to him. But it didn't appear that Waneta and Faron, or anyone else for that matter, was leaving right away. Sunday service wasn't just a time to seek religious comfort and inspiration but also a time for fellowship, especially in such a busy season as harvest.

So she went into the kitchen to see if there was anything special her *mudder* wanted her to do before she found Abe and made him talk to her.

She didn't even have to ask. Rachel looked up from

filling a carafe of coffee and smiled. "Take this out and start filling cups, will you?"

Lavinia nodded and took the carafe. It was the perfect way to approach Abe without looking like she was singling him out.

Abe's *mudder* was sitting at a table the men of the church had set up after moving the benches that had been placed in the home. "Haven't seen you since before the storm," Waneta said. "How did your farm fare?"

"We had little damage compared to other farms. How did yours?"

Waneta looked surprised. "Abe didn't tell you?"

She shook her head.

"Interesting." Waneta shot a glance over at Abe, who was talking with a man on the other side of the room. She looked back at Lavinia. "It was bad. Really bad. We didn't have any damage to the house, but a lot of the crop we grow to feed the cows was ruined. Abe is upset, because it means a lot more expense he wasn't expecting."

Lavinia had always felt that the expression about someone's heart skipping a beat didn't make sense. How could a heart skip a beat? It just kept beating or it stopped, didn't it? Until now. "Oh no."

Waneta nodded. "He's been through so much lately. I know he'll bounce back, but it'll take a few days. And your loving support."

She shook her head. "He obviously didn't want my support, or he'd have called me."

"Sounds like the two of you need to talk."

"We will," Lavinia said firmly. "We will."

"My money's on you," Waneta told her. "You're going to be *gut* for Abe. You *have* been *gut* for him."

Lavinia felt tears rush into her eyes. "*Danki*, Waneta. That means a lot to me." Now she felt mixed emotions that she and Abe hadn't shared with Waneta and Faron that they were engaged. Well, who knew what her relationship with Abe was now?

She walked around and served coffee and bided her time. Finally, church members began saying their goodbyes.

When she saw Abe get up and stroll to the front door, she followed him. When he went outside, she followed him and found him standing on the front porch, staring out at the line of buggies leaving the property.

"I heard about the storm damage," she said quietly. "I'm so sorry."

"*Danki*." He didn't turn.

"Why didn't you call me and tell me about it?"

"Didn't want to dump more bad news on your shoulders," he said as he shrugged. "You've had enough with me."

He turned and started to say something but stopped when the front door opened. Several church members came out and walked down the steps.

"It's not dumping, Abe. I love you, and I want to be there for you with the *gut* and the bad."

Looking frustrated, he ran a hand through his hair, disordering it. "You have to see we can't get married now. We have to wait and get married next year."

"We've already talked about that. I don't want to do that."

"I could lose the farm," he blurted out.

"Then we'll find someplace else to live. I don't care if it's a one-room apartment, Abe."

"I do. A man should provide for his *fraa*."

"We might be Old Order, Abe, but that's just outdated, and we've discussed it before." She spun on her heel and turned away from him. She took a deep breath and then faced him. "I earn a salary from the shop and will contribute to the family expenses, just like my *mudder* does."

But he stood there staring at her, looking stubborn.

"And you've forgotten something, Abraham Stoltzfus. *God* provides, not man!" Then, drained from the emotion he'd stirred up in her, she shook her head. "But have it your way, Abe. Feel sorry for yourself. Don't marry me. But don't expect me to sit around and wait until you think it's a *gut* time to get married."

She stormed off, going into the house and letting the door slam behind her—and nearly ran into Waneta and Faron. "Oh, sorry!" she said.

"I'm guessing your talk didn't go so well," Waneta said, taking her arm and drawing her aside.

"The man has such a hard head," she fumed.

Waneta nodded. "Got it from his *dat*."

"Hey!" Faron said, looking aggrieved.

She merely glanced at him. "You know you have a hard head. But I love you anyway."

He looked a little mollified.

"I'm really sorry, my dear," Waneta told her. "Give Abe a little time and he'll come around."

"That's what he wants. Time," Lavinia muttered. "Well, I'm not waiting another year to get married."

"Married? You were going to marry after harvest?"

Lavinia sighed. "*Ya.* I'm sorry. We decided to wait a bit before telling you and Faron."

Waneta's eyes shone. "I'm so happy! Faron, did you hear what she said?"

He grinned. "*Ya.* That's *gut* news, Lavinia. You know Waneta and I love you like a *dochder*."

"*Danki*, Faron. But he wants to wait until next year."

"What he wants and what he gets are two different things," Waneta said with a smile, and she hugged Lavinia.

"I'll have a talk with the *bu*," Faron told them.

"Two hard heads," Waneta commented as she watched him walk out the door. "We're going to go home now. I think you'll be hearing from Abe soon, dear."

She walked out the door, leaving Lavinia staring after her.

* * *

Abe heard the door open and turned to see his *dat* walk out.

"Just saw Lavinia," he began. "What's this nonsense about putting off getting married?"

"It's not nonsense. How can we marry when things are such a mess?"

Faron shook his head. "If I'd thought that way, we wouldn't be talking now. You wouldn't be here."

"I know you said the farm's had its ups and downs—"

"They weren't all after your *mudder* and I got married," Faron interrupted. "The farm wasn't doing all that well when the two of us got hitched. But we didn't let that stop us."

The door opened again and his *mudder* stepped out. She took one look at Abe, shook her head, and made a tsking sound.

"I'll go get the buggy," Faron said, and headed down the porch steps. "We'll talk on the way home."

Abe watched his *dat* move faster than he'd seen him move in a long time. He looked at his *mudder* and saw what his *dat* had: there was a lecture coming.

"I'm walking home," he told her.

She folded her arms across her chest. "I'll see you there."

He sighed. Was there no escape? He started down the walkway and headed down the road, taking his time. A few minutes later, a buggy pulled up beside him.

"*Sohn*, want a lift?" Faron called out.

Abe heard the laughter in his *dat*'s voice and frowned. "*Nee, danki.*"

"Faron, let him walk off some of that stubbornness," he heard his *mudder* say, and then the buggy began rolling on down the road.

Great. So his *eldres* were on Lavinia's side.

He'd walked another couple blocks when he heard another buggy approaching. He looked over and saw Wayne and Katie Ann.

"I thought you were riding home with your *eldres*," Wayne said.

"So did I," he muttered. "I decided I'd get some exercise."

"We can give you a ride if you've changed your mind," Katie Ann told him. "It's awfully warm today to be walking."

"Feels *gut*," he lied.

The last thing he wanted was to be riding in a buggy with two lovebirds. Then he chided himself for such an ungenerous thought.

"You two have a *gut* afternoon," he said, and summoned a smile.

"You too," Katie Ann said.

The buggy rolled away.

Abe wasn't as tired as he was the last time he walked over to Lavinia's, but he was pulling out a handkerchief and wiping sweat from his face by the time he climbed the stairs to his house. When he walked inside, he could hear his *eldres* talking in the kitchen. He stopped and thought about going into his bedroom, but he smelled something delicious wafting from the kitchen. His stomach chose that moment to growl and remind him he was *hungerich*.

Still, he hesitated. He could go into his room and wait until his *eldres* ate their meal and then forage for leftovers when they'd gone into the *dawdi haus* for their usual Sunday afternoon nap.

His stomach growled again. Knowing his *mudder*, he was just putting off the inevitable. And he was a grown man. He could tell her it was his business what he did or didn't do with his life. Politely, of course. Otherwise he'd get his ear cuffed like when he'd been a teenager and smarted off to her.

With a sigh, he walked into the kitchen and greeted them. He hung his hat on a peg near the door, washed his hands, and sat at the table.

"Took you long enough to get here," his *mudder* said tartly. "Your *dat* was ready to eat your share."

Abe didn't doubt that for a minute. For a skinny guy, he *schur* could pack away food the way he'd always claimed Abe could do as a teenager.

"About Lavinia," his *mudder* began.

"Waneta, let the *bu* eat," his *dat* said. "Remember, you're the one who's always saying no arguing at the table."

"I'm not arguing. I'm discussing."

"Don't want to upset the digestion," Faron said calmly.

Waneta subsided.

Abe ate as quickly as he could and escaped into his room. Sundays were supposed to be a day of rest, but cows still had to be milked and fed and watered. But he had some time before Wayne would be back to do most of the work. Seemed to be a *gut* time for a nap. But he tossed and turned, and his dreams were filled with happier times with Lavinia. He woke restless and confused. The fan barely stirred the warm air in the room.

Giving up, he left the room and went into the kitchen for something cold to drink. Then he walked outside.

Wayne was walking to the cow barn, so he joined him. They moved the cows into position and hooked up milking equipment. But Wayne still had to do more of the work, with Abe's arm being in a cast.

It took only a few minutes to realize that Wayne was in an unusually *gut* mood.

"You're whistling," said Abe.

Wayne looked at him and grinned. "*Ya.* Had a *gut* time having lunch and a drive with Katie Ann. How about you?"

"How about me what?"

"Did you spend time with Lavinia?"

"A little," he said, not elaborating.

Wayne nodded as he worked. "We've got us two *wunderbaar maedels*."

Abe grunted and Wayne resumed whistling. Then he stopped and looked at Abe. "I'm thinking of asking Katie Ann to marry me."

Abe stared at him. "Really?"

"*Ya.* I don't have enough saved up for our own place yet, so we'll be living with her *eldres* for a while." He shrugged. "But that's fine with me."

"Have you talked about that with her?"

"*Schur.* She's fine with it, too. Why wouldn't she be? Lots of couples do it. Not everyone inherits, and land's expensive in Lancaster County these days." Wayne spoke to one of the cows and then turned to him. "Katie Ann's bakery is doing well, so she'll be able to help contribute to buying our own place when we're married."

Abe remembered what Lavinia had said about how she didn't want to wait. How she called him old-fashioned and said she had a job and would be contributing to household expenses.

Wayne began disconnecting the milking equipment, and Abe led the cows back out to pasture. Shadows lengthened on the property as Wayne returned.

"Gonna head home unless you need something else."

"*Nee. Danki* for the help. And listen, I'm glad to hear about you and Katie Ann."

Wayne grinned and nodded. "Just gotta figure out the right time and place to ask her."

As Wayne walked away whistling, Abe found himself thinking about how Lavinia had asked him to marry her. And what she'd said about how she wanted to be with him whether things were *gut* or bad. Was he being old-fashioned and stubborn to want things to be *gut* when they got married?

He sighed and shook his head. He didn't know what to do.

Chapter Twenty-Seven

Lavinia had the shop to herself as her *mudder* took the day off to help with the new *boppli* in the *familye*. She loved her job and loved the shop, but today she wanted to be anywhere but here, having to pretend all was well when she just wanted to hide in her bedroom and avoid people.

Well, it wasn't like her to have a pity party. So she let herself into the shop, started a pot of coffee, and put her things in the back room. Soon it was time to open, and she had her hands full with so many customers she didn't have a moment to think about her argument with Abe.

Emma came after lunch and found Lavinia busy ringing up sales while several customers stood in line. She pushed John's stroller behind the counter where Lavinia stood and jumped into action immediately.

John reached out and tugged at the hem of Lavinia's

dress, and she bent down to say hello. "I am so glad to see you and your *mamm*, John."

"Where's your *mudder*?" Emma asked.

"At Sadie's house, helping with the new *boppli*."

Lavinia folded a set of woven place mats into a shopping bag and handed it to her customer. "Thank you for shopping with us today. I hope you'll come again."

"I will. You have some lovely things."

The next customer stepped up with one of Lavinia's rugs. "Do you have another in this same color and size? I'd really like to have two in my family room."

"I'd be happy to make it for you," she said.

"That would be wonderful. I'd need it mailed, since we're here on vacation."

"That's no problem. I'll make it for you right away and put it in the mail to you."

"So you made it?"

Lavinia nodded and smiled. "I'm glad you like it. Let me ring this up, and then I can fill out an order form for you."

Emma took over the register while Lavinia got out an order form and took down the information.

"That worked out well, selling one rug and getting an order for another," Emma remarked when the woman left and they had a brief lull.

Lavinia picked John up. "I didn't get to say much of a hello to you, big guy."

He grinned and patted her cheeks.

"Tell me about Sadie's new *boppli*," Emma said. "I heard she had a *bu*."

"She did. He's so cute. Looks like his *dat*. We were there the night he was born." She bounced John on her hip, and he chuckled.

Emma glanced at the clock. "Have you had lunch?"

Lavinia shook her head. "I was too busy."

"Why don't you go in the back and eat before we get busy again? John and I ate at Hannah's before we came over here."

"I think I'll take you up on that. C'mon, John, keep me company."

"You don't have to take him."

She looked at Emma. "I like *buwe*. They haven't grown up to be irritating men yet."

"Oh my. There's a story there. I want details."

Lavinia just laughed and walked to the back room with John. There, she and her *mudder* had set up a playpen for the days Emma brought John to the shop. After she put him in it, she showed him the pile of toys in one corner, then got out her lunch. She ate her sandwich and apple quickly in case the shop got busy again, and when she finished and looked out into the shop, she saw that customers were streaming in. After draining her glass of iced tea, she put her lunch tote away.

Meanwhile, John had tired of the toys and lain down in the playpen. Soon his eyes were drifting shut and he was sound asleep. She slipped out of the room quietly and went back out into the shop.

"John got bored with me and fell asleep," she told Emma.

His *mudder* laughed. "You're not boring. It was time

for his nap." She put her elbows on the shop counter. "Now, I want the details. Tell me about the *bu* who grew up and got irritating."

Lavinia sighed. "I shouldn't have said that. It's unkind to complain about someone."

"But sometimes we need to. My friends were so *gut* to me when I had my unexpected blessing and left town because his *dat* didn't want to marry me. My friend in Ohio listened and helped support me when I couldn't work. I don't know what I would have done without her." Emma sighed. "Then when John and I moved back here, Hannah and Gideon and Rebecca were such *gut* friends to listen and help me work things out. And my *schwemudder* treated me like a *dochder*." She paused. "Listen, I can tell you love Abe, and I'm sorry if he's done something to upset you. You don't have to talk about it if you don't want to."

She saw understanding in Emma's eyes. "He's just so old-fashioned. Thinks we shouldn't get married while his farm is struggling. Says he wants to take care of his *fraa*."

Emma nodded. "Some of the Old Order men are still thinking that way. But they forget their *fraas* have always been their partners with farmwork." She was silent for a moment. "You know, Hannah went through that with Gideon. He and Eli inherited the farm after their *dat* died, and they agreed the first to marry would live in the farmhouse. So that meant when I came back with John, and Eli and I got married, suddenly Gideon didn't have the house he thought he would have, and he felt he couldn't marry Hannah."

Lavinia sank down on the stool behind the counter. She hadn't heard the story because neither had talked with her about it. In a small community, many felt it was best to keep some matters private to reduce gossip.

"But it all turned out so well in the end," Emma said. "Eli found a way to help them build their own house on part of the farmland, and now we're one big happy *familye* with my *schwemudder* living in the *dawdi haus*. And one day our *kinner* will play together and work the farm together."

"Sounds like such a happy ending."

"It was. It felt so *gut* to stand there in the field with Eli and hear him tell them about his plans for the land and their house. Lavinia, what the four of us—Gideon and Hannah and Eli and I—learned is that when we try to figure out everything and control our lives, it just doesn't work."

"Abe said he wanted to provide for me. I told him I had a job and could provide for myself, and besides, it's God who provides."

"You're right. What did he say?"

"I didn't give him a chance to answer. I walked away and let him think about that."

Emma smiled. "And I bet he's doing a lot of thinking right now."

* * *

Days passed, and Abe didn't see or hear from Lavinia. He kept busy and told himself it was for the best. When she thought it over, he was *schur* she would see he was right. They could still see each other, spend time together. They just wouldn't be married, which meant they wouldn't be struggling, maybe even fighting over how to pay the bills. The last thing a man wanted was to have the woman he loved hurt by his failure to protect her, support her. Support himself. That wasn't pride. It was looking out for her. Wanting the best for her. She'd see that soon, wouldn't she?

He could still remember going with his *dat* to the auction of a dairy farm, even though it was years ago. The owner hadn't been able to keep the farm going, and so it had been put on the auction block.

He frowned and rubbed at his temple. He was getting a headache from the din of his *dat*'s machine, which clacked noisily as it churned the ice-cream mixture his *mudder* made. She was inside taking a break from the heat after the two of them had insisted.

"What are you fretting about?" his *dat* asked him as they sat in front of the house tending the farm stand.

They'd just scooped up ice cream for a flurry of customers, and there was a welcome lull to catch their breath.

"I was remembering the auction the two of us went to when I was younger. Joseph Miller's dairy farm."

His *dat* nodded. "I remember that. It happens. If he was alive now, he'd be the first to tell you that he never had the heart for dairy farming. He took over the farm when his *dat* died and there was no one to inherit. Joseph always wanted to work in construction, and he got to do that after he sold the farm." He looked at Abe. "He didn't lose it because of problems, Abe. He simply decided he wanted another path."

Abe hadn't remembered it that way. He'd thought Joseph lost it.

"Besides, that's not you. I remember one day you went missing when you were a *kind*. Do you remember that?"

When Abe shook his head, Faron grinned. "You were four. We found you out in the pasture lying on the grass watching the cows. Couldn't keep you away from them. All you wanted was to help me milk them and take care of them." He paused. "Now if you feel differently, if you don't want to continue to be a dairy farmer, then we'll talk about what to do."

"*Nee*," Abe blurted out, so quickly he surprised himself.

"Then stop thinking about what you might lose and think about how you can keep what you value. Don't look at how big the problems are. Look at how big your God is." Faron got up, reached for his cane, and, leaning on it, looked at Abe. "And think about what you could lose if you hold onto your pride and don't marry Lavinia." He straightened. "Going to go inside, get something cold to drink. Holler if you need me."

Abe thought about what his *dat* said. His *mudder* was still letting him know she was upset that he hadn't made up with Lavinia. He wondered if Lavinia's *eldres* knew what happened and if they said anything to her about it.

A buggy pulled up, and Gideon Troyer climbed out and walked up to him. "Thought I'd pick up a pint of ice cream on my way home. Hannah's fond of your *mudder*'s strawberry."

Abe set about filling a pint container with the fresh strawberry. "And what about you?"

"I'm a fan of the chocolate."

"Don't usually see you around this time of day." Abe put a lid on the container, then rinsed the scoop in a bowl of water and started filling another container with chocolate.

"Eli's covering the shop for me. He gives me a break now and then to take care of some errands. Just like I help him with the farm when I can." He took a seat on the wooden stool Faron had vacated.

"The two of you work together well."

"We've been doing it since before we were born," Gideon joked. "Being *zwillingbopplin*."

Abe put the containers in a small bag and accepted money from Gideon.

"How's the house coming?"

"Almost finished the inside. You know how women are. Hannah's still carrying around paint chips and trying to decide what color to paint the last couple rooms."

Gideon gazed out at the field in front of them. "This time last year, I didn't know what I was going to do. I wanted to marry Hannah, but Eli and I had made a deal that the first of us to marry would take over the farmhouse. We always thought it would be me. But then along came John and everything changed. Eli and Emma and John were the ones who moved into the farmhouse." He turned his gaze to Abe. "And then Eli got this idea that we could build a house for Hannah and me on part of the farmland." He took the bag from Abe. "I don't think it was Eli's idea."

"Whose idea was it?"

Gideon stood. "I think he got it from God." He stared off for a long moment, then looked at Abe. "Eli's smart, but I'm not *schur* he could come up with such a *gut* idea on his own." He stood. "Well, I guess I should get this home before it melts."

"*Danki* for stopping by. Say hello to Hannah for me."

"I will."

He'd no sooner left than Faron came out in time to help with the next carload of *Englisch* customers that stopped. Abe helped them mechanically and thought about what Gideon had said.

"You've got that thinking look going again," Faron said as the customers left licking their cones. He took a seat on the wooden stool.

He shrugged. "Gideon Troyer stopped by, and we were talking. He made me think about something I need to do."

"Now?"

Abe shook his head. "I need to do some thinking about it first."

His *dat* slapped a hand on his shoulder. "Careful, don't strain your brain," he joked, and laughed uproariously.

"I need some aspirin," Abe told him. "Sorry, but that contraption of yours has given me a bit of a headache."

"Hey, it's working for you to bring in some dollars," Faron told him as another car stopped and people walked over to look curiously at the machine. "Money in the bank, *bu*, money in the bank."

The cashbox did indeed benefit from all the cones they sold to the occupants of the car. His *dat* offered to go get him some aspirin and Abe let him, figuring it was *gut* to get him out of the heat that didn't seem to be letting up even though it was approaching five o'clock.

A car stopped, and a young man got out and walked up to him.

"Well, glad to see you're doing well," the man said. "Jason Halliday. I happened to drive up just after you fell off the roof. Your wife scared me to death that day running in front of my car, waving her arms at me and shouting at me to stop and call nine-one-one."

Abe stood and shook his hand. "Lavinia told me about you calling for help and then waiting with her until it arrived. Thank you so much." He didn't explain that Lavinia wasn't his wife.

"I've stopped here before and bought some great cheese from an older woman."

"My mother." He waved a hand at the basket of cheeses on the table. "Here, I want you to have this," he said, picking up the basket and handing the whole thing to the man.

"I can't take all that," he said, stepping back and holding up his hands.

"Trust me, she would want you to have it, and if you don't believe me, I can call her out here."

Jason laughed. "No, that's not necessary. Thanks. My girlfriend and I will certainly enjoy this. Listen, I left my card with your wife that day and said if you needed any help to call me."

"I appreciate that. My parents live with me, so I've been pretty well taken care of."

"Well, I design websites. I'd be happy to set up a website for you so you can sell your products online."

"We've had a lot of unexpected expenses lately with the storm and dairy prices down, so I doubt I could afford it. But thanks."

"I saw that in the news. It made me think I should stop next time I was driving by, see if I could be of assistance. I could set up the site for free for you."

He pulled out a business card and handed it to Abe. "Think about it. My company encourages us to do pro bono work—free consults and work—for the community where we see a need. At some point, if things are better and the site is doing well for you, then we can discuss a reasonable payment for helping you run the site in the future."

Abe fingered the card. He knew of an Amish church member who sold the handmade baskets his *familye* made online, using the services of an *Englischer*. The arrangement worked for both sides.

"I'll do that," he said slowly. "Thank you."

Waneta came out with a bottle of aspirin and a glass of water. Abe introduced her to Jason. She shook the man's hand enthusiastically and thanked him.

"I told Jason you'd want him to have the basket as a way of thanking him."

"Absolutely. And Abe, give him some pints of ice cream as well. What's your favorite, Jason?"

As the man drove off with the gifts, Abe turned to his *mudder*. "The last customer of the day turned out to be the best one. He wants to help us sell our cheese online."

"How *wunderbaar*!"

When Faron walked up to turn off his machine, she told him the news.

Faron gave him a thoughtful look. "Well, isn't that something?" he said.

Abe put the bottle of aspirin in his pocket. His headache had miraculously disappeared.

Chapter Twenty-Eight

Lavinia glanced out the van window as Liz drove past Abe's farm. A young *Englisch* man was talking to Abe as he sat behind the farm stand where Waneta enjoyed selling her homemade cheese and ice cream. Something about the man looked familiar, but she couldn't think why.

She was getting out of the van when she remembered. He was the man who'd stopped his car when she'd run out into the road in front of Abe's house when he fell off the roof. She'd been so upset that day seeing Abe fall off the roof in front of her, then lie there unconscious, his body twisted on the ground. She wasn't *schur* she'd thanked the man properly before she climbed into the ambulance and rode to the hospital with Abe. For a moment, she thought about walking back and thanking him now, but she talked herself out of it. That would mean seeing Abe, and she didn't want that.

She went inside her house, and as she put away her things, she wondered what the man was doing talking to Abe. When she tried to remember details about the stranger, she recalled him giving her a business card and urging her to call if he could help in any way. She couldn't remember if she'd given the card to Abe.

The house was quiet. Her *mudder* must still be over at Sadie's. Had her *dat* gone there as well? She glanced out the kitchen window and saw that the barn door was open. That meant he was home and doing evening chores.

She decided she should start supper. Her *mudder* would undoubtedly be making *schur* that Sadie was taking care of her new *boppli* and not on her feet cooking. A search of the refrigerator freezer revealed a big empty space where her *mudder* usually kept a number of frozen casseroles prepared ahead of time that her *dat* could put in the oven for supper while Lavinia and her *mudder* were traveling home after work. She had a feeling that those casseroles were probably residing in her *schweschder*'s refrigerator freezer now, as worry-free meals for the coming week.

After she got out a pound of ground chicken and set it on a plate on the counter, she checked the pantry and saw the items she needed for tacos. Grabbing a basket, she went out to the kitchen garden and walked around gathering a head of lettuce, some ripe red tomatoes, and a few peppers and onions.

She stared at the patch of celery in the corner of the garden for a long moment and felt a pang of regret. It was a Lancaster County custom to serve celery at Amish weddings, either raw or creamed or both. Sometimes it was possible to guess that a *familye* was planning a wedding by the amount of celery they were growing in their kitchen garden. With a sigh, she pulled a stalk from the ground, put it in her basket, and went back inside.

She washed the vegetables and set them in a big colander to drain, then got out a skillet and began browning the chicken. After it was cooked, she drained it on a paper-towel-lined plate, used another paper towel to wipe out the skillet, then returned the meat to it and stirred in a jar of tomato sauce her *schweschder* had canned. She felt herself relaxing as she worked. The simple chores of gathering vegetables from the garden and cooking were ones she enjoyed, even after a long day at the shop. The scents made her realize she was *hungerich*.

While the chicken and sauce simmered, she put a can of refried beans on to warm, then chopped the vegetables and set them in bowls. Planting and caring for the kitchen garden was a lot of work for her *mudder* and herself on top of their shop work, but the bounty of fresh produce in summer and the cans they used in the winter were such a blessing.

The kitchen door opened, and her *dat* walked in. He sniffed as he went to the sink to wash his hands. "Smells *gut*. What are we having?"

"I thought chicken tacos would be nice."

He nodded, turned off the faucet, and dried his hands on a dish towel. "Your *mudder* called me earlier and said not to wait for her. She's going to eat at Sadie's."

"*Allrecht*. It'll be ready in a few minutes."

He poured glasses of iced tea for them and settled

at the table as she finished putting bowls of chopped vegetables and refried beans on it.

Her *dat* wasn't the only one who liked tacos. They were a favorite of hers as well. Her *mudder* kept boxes of tacos and cans of refried beans in the pantry for use in quick meals. They were fun to assemble, and she'd always enjoyed putting the amount of each ingredient that suited her in a taco. First came the chicken, followed by lots of grated cheddar cheese, then lettuce and juicy tomatoes, and finally, salsa they'd canned on top. It was a hearty meal that satisfied. And there was plenty left over for her *dat* to have for lunch the next day.

He helped himself to a handful of chocolate chip cookies from the jar for dessert and pronounced himself full.

Lavinia cleaned up the kitchen and washed the dishes while he went back out to finish the evening chores in the barn, taking a couple of carrots with him as treats for their horses.

She settled down at the table and worked on a rug. The shop was too busy to do them there, and they were running low.

Her *mudder* returned as dark fell and was full of stories of what the new *boppli* had done that day.

"You're not going to tell me he smiled at you, are you?" Lavinia asked indulgently.

"*Nee*, not yet. But he looks at me so seriously, as if he's trying to figure me out," she said, fixing herself a glass of tea and settling down for a chat.

They talked about how the day had gone at the

shop, although Lavinia left out how she and Emma had talked about Abe.

When she couldn't stop yawning, Lavinia tucked the rug in her work tote, packed lunches for herself and her *mudder*, and went on up to bed.

After she'd changed into a nightgown, unpinned her *kapp*, and brushed out her hair, she climbed into bed. She lay there waiting for sleep to come and tried not to look at the calendar hanging on her wall. The days were passing so quickly. Wedding season was coming too soon. She sighed and lay there awake too long into the night.

* * *

Abe thought long and hard about what to do about Lavinia. Chocolates weren't going to help this time. So he spent all that evening and most of the next morning working up a plan. The last time he'd seen her had been in her house after the church service. When she'd said her piece and walked away and there had been nothing he could do about it.

This time, he needed a time and place where she'd have to listen to him. He might even have to grovel. He wasn't looking forward to that. But apologizing to her—getting her to forgive him and say she'd still marry him—was too important. He'd gotten so worried about what he thought he was supposed to do for her as her *mann* that he'd forgotten what she'd done for him before they'd even married.

That website guy—a stranger to him—had told him how she'd run out into the road to get him help. What the man didn't know was Lavinia had broken a rule of their faith and lied about being his *fraa* so that she could go with him to the hospital and make *schur* that he got the care he needed until she could contact his *eldres* for him. And then she'd sat at the hospital for hours with him until they came. And even after they'd arrived safely, she'd spent a lot of time away from her job and her *familye* visiting him, and he *schur* hadn't always been in the best of moods.

Before all this had happened, he'd felt she was the woman God had set aside for him. Her actions since then had shown him what kind of *fraa* she would be. He was lucky that she'd felt he was the man she wanted to be with the rest of her life, in spite of the way he'd let the accident affect him. The way he'd let fear of the future keep him from living for each day he had *now*.

She'd told him that she'd had enough that fateful Sunday. Could he convince her to change her mind?

He was determined to try.

He woke before dawn like usual and worked with Wayne to get the milking done. Then he went into the house to eat breakfast. As he sat at the table drinking his coffee, he happened to notice how threadbare the rug that lay in front of the kitchen sink was.

Rug.

Lavinia made rugs. Pretty rugs woven from colorful scraps of fabric. An idea began to form. *Schur*, there were more romantic places to propose, but first you had to figure out how to get the woman to talk to you. If he went into town and saw Lavinia in her shop, she'd have to talk to him. Be polite. Right?

It was a start.

"Abe?"

"Hmm?" He dragged his attention back to see his *mudder* standing before him holding a plate. "You off visiting some planet?" she asked as she set the plate down in front of him.

"*Bu*'s been doing a lot of thinking lately," his *dat* said as he used a piece of golden-brown biscuit to sop up the yolks of his *dippy* eggs.

Abe took the plate from his *mudder* and thanked her. Then he looked at his *dat*. "I need to run into town. *Allrecht* if I take the buggy?"

"*Schur.* Not going anyplace today, are we, Waneta?"

She shook her head. "Only out to the front of the house to sell ice cream and cheese."

"I'll be back in time to sit out there during the worst of the heat," Abe told her. "Promise me you two won't get overheated."

"I'll make *schur* she doesn't," his *dat* told him, reaching over to pat his *fraa*'s hand as she sat to drink a cup of coffee.

She snorted. "*I* have to keep an eye on you like a hawk. Take your medicine, Faron. Get some rest, Faron. Don't eat so many sweets, Faron."

He chuckled. "Don't overdo, Waneta. Don't—"

"Oh, shush," she said, chuckling.

They were a pair, Abe thought as he ate quickly. He hoped he and Lavinia would have as loving—and as long—a union.

He finished eating, drained his cup of coffee, then rose and put his plate and cup in the sink.

"*Danki* for breakfast."

His *mudder* started to say something and then stopped.

"I wasn't going to ask him," he heard her mutter to his *dat* as he walked away.

"You know you were," his *dat* said.

Abe grinned as he heard her sigh. She'd stopped finding ways to let him know she was disappointed about not seeing Lavinia. He figured that she knew that he had no doctor appointments in town, and he seldom went in without some purpose. But he couldn't tell her the reason he was going into town was to see Lavinia when he had no idea if his mission would be successful.

Traffic was heavier in town than the last time he'd driven there. Tourists thronged the sidewalks in order to get as much shopping and sightseeing in as possible before it got hot. He parked behind Lavinia's shop and took a deep breath before walking inside.

Rachel saw him first and looked surprised as she stood at the shop counter and tucked a customer's purchase into a shopping bag. She nodded at Abe and then glanced at Lavinia, who stood in an aisle looking as pretty as ever as she spoke to another customer.

Abe waited until Lavinia finished talking with the woman and then stepped up to her. "*Guder mariye*, Lavinia," he said quietly.

She turned and stared at him, looking startled. "Abe, what are you doing here?"

"I came in to see you."

"I'm sorry, but I'm working. I haven't got time to talk to you."

He was prepared for this. "I'd like you to show me some of your rugs."

She stared at him blankly. "My rugs."

"*Ya.* You still carry them here, right? I'm in the market for one."

"You don't need a rug."

"I do. For my kitchen. What do you think would go well in front of the sink? *Mamm* always keeps one there because she says it's hard on the back standing on the wood floor when she washes dishes. Well, that rug's looking pretty worn."

Lavinia sighed. "*Allrecht*, I'll show you a rug."

She walked quickly to the next aisle and gestured at several of them displayed on a shelf, then started to leave.

"Which one would you choose?" he asked her. "You know the colors in the room. Which one would you buy?"

"Abe—"

"I remember how we stood at that sink and washed dishes together," he said, moving closer. "I always pictured you there one day in the future, the two of us talking after supper was over, the day winding down. Thinking about how soon we could go upstairs."

"Don't do this to me." She closed her eyes and then opened them. "It's not fair."

"My *mudder* calls the kitchen the heart of the home," he told her as he looked deep into her eyes. "You have such a big heart, Lavinia. Marry me. Make a home with me."

She opened her eyes, and he hurt when he saw there were tears in them.

"I was wrong to tell you we should wait to get married,

Lavinia. You were right. We belong together now. I need you in my life, however it's going. Somehow we'll make things work." He reached for her hand. "Look, I'm sorry if I've been old-fashioned and stubborn. I'm a farmer. Always have been. Always will be. It's my nature to tend, to take care of what I love, whether it's the land or the animals in my care or the people I love. But you're right that we're supposed to be partners, that we're supposed to trust God to provide. Lavinia, you proposed to me and I said yes. Will you do the same?"

"This year?" she asked him.

"This year."

A tear spilled from one eye, and she nodded. "*Ya.* I'll marry you, Abraham Stoltzfus."

He sealed the promise with a quick kiss, vowing to do better when they weren't in the shop.

When a customer approached, he stood back while Lavinia answered her question.

"I don't suppose you can go to lunch with me before I head home?" he asked when she joined him again.

She laughed and shook her head. "*Nee*, we're too busy."

"*Allrecht*, then I'll pick you up and take you to supper after the shop closes."

"That would be *wunderbaar*."

He started to walk away, but she touched his arm. "I thought you wanted a rug."

"I do." Inspiration hit. "I want you to make one in the colors you love and give it to me as a wedding gift."

"I can do that," she said, and her smile was so bright. "I can do that."

Epilogue

Lavinia and Abe stood at the back of the rows of benches that had been set up in her home. They could hear the murmur of conversation as people waited for them to enter the room.

He held out his arm and she took it. "We're doing it."

She nodded and smiled brilliantly. "We are." She felt the thin cast that he still wore on his left arm beneath the sleeve of his black Sunday-best suit.

"You look beautiful," he told her, his gaze intent.

She *felt* beautiful in her dress of fine fabric the color of summer violets. "*Danki.* And you look so handsome today." She took a deep breath. "Ready?"

"So ready."

They walked slowly toward the front of the room to meet Elmer and be married. Abe limped a little, but he had worked hard on his therapy and had been able to retire his cane.

All four of their *eldres*—Rachel and Amos and Waneta and Faron—and members of their *familye* were there to support them with their presence today. Levi, Abe's *bruder*, had brought his *fraa* and *kinner* from out of state, and Sadie was here with Naiman and their two *kinner*. And so many friends, like Rebecca and Samuel and Emma and Eli and Hannah and Gideon and Wayne and Arnita, were smiling at them as they passed. Everyone turned out for such an occasion to give the bridal couple all their prayers and *gut* wishes.

There were the traditional songs and prayers and then the timeless vows: "Do you promise . . . this if either of you should be afflicted with bodily weakness, sickness, or some other circumstance, that you will care for each other as is fitting for a Christian *mann* and *fraa*? Do you solemnly promise to one another that you will love and bear and be patient with each other and shall not separate from each other until dear God shall part you from each other through death?"

And then Abe and Lavinia were *mann* and *fraa*.

The service lasted three hours, so everyone was ready for the meal that followed. Lavinia and Abe sat at the *eck*, the corner of the table, and accepted the congratulations of their *familye*, friends, and church members.

Lavinia saw a box wrapped in festive paper and ribbons next to her plate.

"Open it," Abe told her. "It's from me."

When she unwrapped it, she found a box of the same type of chocolates he'd given her when he apologized after their argument.

"Sweets for the sweetest," he said with a grin. "I promise you won't get them just for an apology."

She just laughed. No couple agreed all the time, and she told him so.

The day passed in happy celebration. The adults enjoyed talking and relaxing after long hours harvesting all the crops. The *kinner* raced in and out of the house playing games. Lavinia and Abe enjoyed their midday meal of baked chicken and *roasht* and so many vegetables from heavily laden tables.

Katie Ann had provided the wedding cake, and it was a many-layered confection that was decorated with violets made of fondant.

"It's given me an idea for my own cake," she told Lavinia. "Daisies are my favorite flower, so my cake will have fondant daisies on it." She sighed. "I've been so busy baking cakes for the weddings of other *brauts* I haven't had time to think what I want—and Wayne and I are getting married next week!" She glanced around and nodded with satisfaction as she watched attendees enjoying the rich yellow cake. "Next year, I'm hiring some part-time help during wedding season. Things have been a little hectic."

The hours passed in a happy blur for Lavinia. Guests were served another meal at suppertime, and then they began gathering their *kinner* and saying goodbye and heading home.

Phoebe and Ruth stopped at their table to say goodbye.

"Stopped running, have you?" Phoebe asked Abe.

"*Ya*," he said with a chuckle.

"*Gut*," Phoebe said with a nod, and she walked off with her *dochder*.

"Finally, we get to go home," Abe whispered in her ear, and she blushed.

Usually the *braut* and *breidicham* stayed at her home on the wedding night to help clean up the next day, but her *mudder* had insisted that Lavinia and Abe start their new life together at his farmhouse. They'd wake to a new day together as *mann* and *fraa* in *their* farmhouse. So instead of walking upstairs to her room, she and Abe walked to his buggy parked outside.

When she climbed into the passenger side, Lavinia found he'd picked a bouquet of violets and left it on the seat for her. Touched, she lifted it and buried her face in the petals, inhaling their sweet, delicate scent. "*Danki.*"

"You're *wilkumm*." He climbed into the driver's seat and called, "Giddyap" to his horse.

When Abe checked for traffic and made a U-turn to go in the opposite direction, she glanced at him curiously. "You're going the wrong way."

He shook his head. "Taking the long way home. I want to enjoy this beautiful sunset with my new *fraa*."

She smiled and took his hand and squeezed it. The drive was leisurely with the horse clip-clopping along and the late summer breeze carrying the scent of honeysuckle that twined along fences.

They didn't know what lay ahead, but they would be together, and that was all that mattered. God would provide.

Dusk fell and a full moon came out to light their way home.

Glossary

aenti—aunt
allrecht—all right
boppli—baby
bopplin—babies
braut—bride
breidicham—bridegroom
bruder—brother
bu—boy
buwe—boys
Daedi—Daddy
danki—thank you
dat—father
dawdi haus—a small home added to or near the main

house into which the farmer moves after passing the farm and main house to one of his children

Deitsch—Pennsylvania German

dippy eggs—over-easy eggs

dochder—daughter

en alt maedel—an old maid

Englisch, Englischer—what the Amish call a non-Amish person

familye—family

fraa—wife

grossdaadi—grandfather

guder mariye—good morning

gut—good

hungerich—hungry

kapp—prayer covering or cap worn by girls and women

kind—child

kinskind—grandchild

kinner—children

kumm—come

lieb—love, a term of endearment

maedel—young single woman

mamm—mom

mann—husband

mudder—mother

nacht—night

nee—no

onkel—uncle

Ordnung—The rules of the Amish, both written and unwritten. Certain behavior has been expected within the Amish community for many, many years.

These rules vary from community to community, but the most common are to have no electricity in the home, to not own or drive a car.

roasht—roast, a stuffing or dressing side dish made of cubes of bread, chopped celery, and onion

rumschpringe—time period when teenagers are allowed to experience the *Englisch* world while deciding if they should join the church

schul—school

schur—sure

schwardochder—daughter-in-law

schwemudder—mother-in-law

schweschder—sister

sohn—son

wilkumm—welcome

wittfraa—widow

wunderbaar—wonderful

ya—yes

zwillingboppli—twin

zwillingbopplin—twins

Note: While there are many similarities between Amish communities around the country, each community makes its own rules. The Lancaster County, Pennsylvania, Amish community allows cell phones, while some other Amish communities limit or ban them.

Recipes

Haystacks

Ingredients

- 2 pounds ground beef
- 1-ounce package taco seasoning mix
- 1 24-ounce jar spaghetti sauce
- 2 cups crushed soda crackers or saltines
- 1 bag tortilla chips
- 2 cups hot cooked rice
- 1 head iceberg lettuce
- 2 cups diced tomatoes
- 1 cup chopped carrots
- 1 cup chopped onion
- 1 cup sliced, pitted ripe olives
- 1 cup diced green pepper
- 1 cup diced celery
- 1½ cups shredded Cheddar cheese
- 1 (8-ounce) jar salsa

Directions

In a 12-inch skillet, brown the ground beef over medium-high heat. Add the taco seasoning and spaghetti sauce and heat to boiling. Reduce heat to low; simmer, uncovered, until most of the liquid evaporates.

Mix the crushed crackers and tortilla chips in a bowl. Place the ground-beef mixture, rice, and remaining ingredients in individual bowls.

Layer the lettuce, crushed crackers/chips, meat mixture, rice, tomatoes, carrots, onions, olives, pepper, celery, cheese, and salsa—in the order you like. There is no wrong way to make a haystack! Serves six.

Sweet-and-Sour Green Beans

This slightly sweet, slightly sour green bean recipe takes just a few minutes to make and is great served at room temperature. Make it ahead and let the green beans marinate in the dressing, soaking up flavor.

Ingredients

- 2 pounds green beans, trimmed
- ¼ cup apple cider vinegar
- ¼ cup sugar
- 1 ice cube
- 1 cup thinly sliced shallots or onions
- 2 tablespoons canola oil
- ½ teaspoon salt

Directions

Fit a large pot with a steamer basket; add 1 to 2 inches water, and bring to a boil. Add the green beans and cover and steam until tender-crisp, 5 to 8 minutes. Drain.

Meanwhile, heat the vinegar and sugar in a small saucepan over medium heat, stirring occasionally, until the sugar dissolves, 1 to 2 minutes. Remove from the heat. Stir in the ice cube until it dissolves. Whisk in the shallots or onions, oil, and salt.

Transfer the green beans to a large bowl, pour the dressing over them, and toss to coat. Serves four.

Strawberry Rhubarb Pie

Ingredients for filling

- 1½ cups sugar
- ⅓ cup cornstarch
- 2 cups whole strawberries
- 2 cups rhubarb, cut up
- 1½ tablespoons butter

Directions

Preheat oven to 425°F. Mix the sugar and cornstarch, then lightly stir together the strawberries and rhubarb. Set aside while you make the pie crust (unless you're using purchased pie crusts).

Ingredients for crust

- 4 cups all-purpose flour
- 1 tablespoon granulated sugar
- 1½ teaspoons salt
- 1½ cups vegetable shortening, cubed
- 1 egg, beaten
- 1 tablespoon vinegar
- ½ cup water

Directions

Mix together the flour, sugar, and salt. Add the shortening and work with a fork until it forms pea-sized crumbs. Transfer the dough to a large bowl and let sit. In a small bowl, whisk together the egg, vinegar, and water. Pour over the dough and mix until combined (dough will be sticky). Cover with plastic wrap and chill in the refrigerator for at least 1 hour before rolling.

Divide the chilled dough in half on a generously floured work surface. Roll half of the dough to ¼-inch thickness and transfer to a 9-inch pie dish. Pour in strawberry-rhubarb filling. Dot with butter. Top with crust. Flute edges and cut slits in top. Bake 40 to 50 minutes, or until the crust is nicely browned and juice begins to bubble through slits in pie crust. Best if served slightly warm. Serves eight.

Book Discussion Questions

Spoiler alert! Please don't read before completing the book, as the questions contain spoilers!

1. Abe is doing maintenance on the roof of his two-story farmhouse when he suddenly slips and falls off in front of a horrified Lavinia. Has your life ever been disrupted by such a horrific accident? What happened? How did it affect your life? Your relationship with other people? Your faith?

2. Abe is worried about keeping the family farm running in a time when dairy farming is experiencing some problems. Have you ever had a financial struggle that made you wonder about your future? What did you do?

3. Lavinia makes handmade rugs from scraps of fabric. Sometimes she doesn't think it's particularly creative. Do you do something creative for your work or for a leisure-time hobby? What do you do? Why do you enjoy doing it?

4. Lavinia works with her mother at a shop that features Amish arts and crafts in town. Have you ever worked with a family member? How did that go?

5. Some people are interested in the Amish lifestyle because it looks simpler and more faith-based than *Englisch* life. It's also more rural and based on farms—definitely not urban. Have you ever thought about living in an Amish community? What do you think would be the hardest part of adapting to life in one?

6. Abe experiences the loss of a farm animal that he has come to feel an affection for. Have you ever experienced this or lost a pet that meant a lot to you? How did you deal with your grief?

7. The Amish community is a close-knit one, with people who help each other out. Are you a member of some type of group at work or at church that provides support when needed?

8. When it seems like Abe is taking forever to propose to her, Lavinia decides she's tired of waiting and proposes. Have you ever done something similar?

9. The Amish know their marriage partners for a long time—often they grew up together. If you're married, how long did you know your spouse before you got married?

10. Amish parents move into a *dawdi haus*—a sort of mother-in-law apartment. Would you want your

parents or in-laws to live with you in such an arrangement? Why or why not?

11. The Amish believe God sets aside a partner for us. Do you believe this?

12. Have you ever visited an Amish community? Which one?

About the Author

Barbara Cameron enjoys writing about the spiritual values and simple joys of the Amish. She is the best-selling author of more than forty fiction and nonfiction books and three nationally televised movies. She is the winner of the first Romance Writers of America Golden Heart Award, and her books have been nominated for Carol Awards and the Inspirational Reader's Choice Award from RWA's Faith, Hope, and Love chapter. Barbara lives in Jacksonville, Florida.

You can learn more at:
BarbaraCameron.com
Facebook.com/Barbara.Cameron1

Can't get enough of that small-town charm? Forever has you covered with these heartwarming contemporary romances!

THE INN ON MIRROR LAKE
by Debbie Mason

Elliana MacLeod has come home to whip the Mirror Lake Inn into tip-top shape so her mother won't sell the beloved family business. And now that Highland Falls is vying to be named the Most Romantic Small Town in America, she can't refuse any offer of help—even if it's from the gorgeous law enforcement officer next door. But Nathan Black has made it abundantly clear they're friends, and nothing more. Little do they know the town matchmakers are out to prove them wrong.

FALLING FOR YOU
by Barb Curtis

Faith Rotolo is shocked to inherit a historic mansion in quaint Sapphire Springs. But her new home needs some major fixing up. Too bad the handsome local contractor, Rob Milan, is spoiling her daydreams with the harsh realities of the project...and his grouchy personality. But as they work together, their spirited clashes wind up sparking a powerful attraction. As work nears completion, will she and Rob realize that they deserve a fresh start too?

Find more great reads on Instagram with @ReadForeverPub

THE AMISH FARMER'S PROPOSAL
by Barbara Cameron

When Amish dairy farmer Abe Stoltzfus tumbles from his roof, he's lucky his longtime friend Lavinia Fisher is there to help. He secretly hoped to propose to her, but now, with his injuries, his dairy farm in danger, and his harvest at stake, Abe worries he'll only be a burden. But as he heals with Lavinia's gentle support and unflagging optimism, the two grow even closer. Will she be able to convince him that real love doesn't need perfect timing?

AUNT IVY'S COTTAGE
by Kristin Harper

When Zoey returns to Dune Island, she's shocked to find her elderly Aunt Ivy being pushed into a nursing home by a cousin. As the family clashes, Zoey meets Nick, the local lighthouse keeper with ocean-blue eyes and a warm laugh. With Nick as her ally, Zoey is determined to keep Aunt Ivy free. But when they discover a secret that threatens to upend Ivy's life, will they still be able to ensure her final years are filled with happiness…and maybe find love with each other along the way?

Connect with us at Facebook.com/ReadForeverPub

THE HOUSE ON SUNSHINE CORNER
by Phoebe Mills

Abby Engel has a great life. She's the owner of Sunshine Corner, the daycare she runs with her girlfriends; she has the most adoring grandmother (aka the Baby Whisperer); and she lives in a hidden gem of a town. All that's missing is love. Then her ex returns home to win back the one woman he's never been able to forget. But after breaking her heart years ago, can Carter convince Abby that he's her happy-ever-after?

TO ALL THE DOGS I'VE LOVED BEFORE
by Lizzie Shane

The last person librarian Elinor Rodriguez wants to see at her door is her first love, town sheriff Levi Jackson, but her mischievous rescue dog has other ideas. Without fail, Dory slips from the house whenever Elinor's back is turned—and it's up to Levi to bring her back. The quietly intense lawman broke Elinor's heart years ago, and she's determined to move on, no matter how much she misses him. But will this four-legged friend prove that a second chance is in store? Includes a bonus story by Hope Ramsay!

Discover bonus content and more on read-forever.com

COMING HOME TO SEASHELL HARBOR
by Miranda Liasson

After a *very* public breakup, Hadley Wells is returning home to get back on her feet. But Seashell Harbor has trouble of its own. An injury forced her ex-boyfriend Tony Cammareri into early retirement, and the former NFL pro is making waves with a splashy new restaurant. They're on opposing sides of a decision over the town's future, but as their rivalry intensifies, they must decide what's worth fighting for—and what it truly means to be happy. Includes a bonus story by Jeannie Chin!

SUMMER BY THE SEA
by Jenny Hale

Faith can never forget the summer she found her first love—or how her younger sister, Casey, stole the man of her dreams. They've been estranged ever since. But at the request of their grandmother, Faith agrees to spend the summer with Casey at the beach where their feud began. While Faith is ready to forget—if not forgive—old hurts, she's *not* ready for her unexpected chemistry with their neighbor, Jake Buchanan. But for a truly unforgettable summer, she'll need to open her heart.

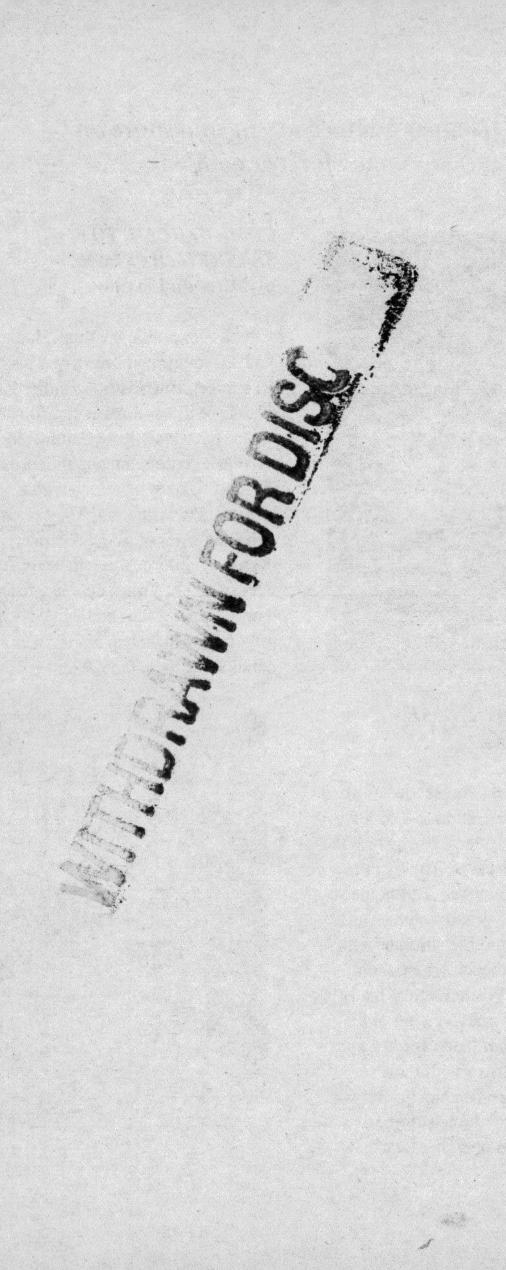